THE HEART OF THE WEST

Two Novels By

Kelly Dawson

Copyright © 2015 by Kelly Dawson

Published by Stormy Night Publications and Design, LLC.
www.StormyNightPublications.com

Cover design by Korey Mae Johnson
www.koreymaejohnson.com

Images by The Killion Group, 123RF/Anton Havelaar, and Bigstock/Leaf

All rights reserved.

1st Print Edition. November 2015

ISBN-13: 978-1519500830

ISBN-10: 1519500831

FOR AUDIENCES 18+ ONLY

This book is intended for adults only. Spanking and other sexual activities represented in this book are fantasies only, intended for adults.

The Ways of the West

CHAPTER ONE

"Noooooo!" The agonized cry echoed all across the frontier plains and Johnny's heart broke for the girl. He watched as Jessica, hitching up her skirts, ran as fast as she could toward the smoldering remains of the wagon train and crumpled in a desperate heap in the dust next to the bloodied body of her mother. She kept screaming, a heartbroken, forlorn keening wail that went on and on as she scrabbled across the ground first to her little brother and then her father. All were dead.

Johnny had stumbled across the wagon train only a fortnight ago and had his eye on Jessica since the first moment he saw her—she was truly beautiful, with a mass of dark red curls, a few wild tendrils always escaping the pins holding it up to frame her delicate face. Her slim, yet curvaceous figure was accentuated by the height-of-fashion gowns she wore on the trail; despite the fact that plain pinafores would have been more practical, and were what the other women all seemed to prefer, Jessica always took pains to keep up her appearance. He'd thought of her as 'his girl' since first laying eyes on her, even though they'd barely spoken, beyond introductions and a few short, polite conversations here and there. She clearly thought herself above a dusty cowboy such as him, but that didn't matter; she would be a challenge, and he liked challenges.

He wondered about her though; she was clearly so unhappy on the trail—what had she left behind? Why had she come out here, to the frontier, if she was so against it? And she was against it, that much was clear. Her general demeanor during their journey had indicated that, and the argument he'd overheard earlier that day had confirmed it.

As they'd circled the wagons and stopped for the midday meal, Johnny had edged closer to the Walshes' wagon, hoping for the opportunity to talk to Jessica. But he hadn't been able to; Jessica had complained to her mother of not feeling well—sick, sore, and exhausted—and she'd gone to rest in the wagon. Her father had followed her in, and he'd overheard him accusing her of idleness, of shaming him before the other men because she was the only woman who wasn't out there working. Did she think she was the only tired one? The only sick one? The only sore one? She wasn't; they all were—yet they all kept working. "Now you get out there and get to work, before I take a strap to you!" he'd ordered gruffly.

"Do you think I wanted to come out here? I didn't! I wanted to stay in Boston, where I was happy!" she'd yelled back, before she stormed out of the wagon angrily, stomping away from camp.

"We couldn't stay there, you know that!" her father had yelled, but she had ignored him, scurrying away from camp at as fast a walk as she could manage. It would have been the perfect opportunity for Johnny to go off after her, but then the wagon master had asked him if he would be willing to hunt for fresh meat—there were families to feed, and their fresh meat had run out. So he'd gone. As soon as he'd heard the shooting he'd turned his horse and galloped back, without any meat, but he'd gotten back too late to do anything. The Indians were driving the horses away triumphantly as he crested the hill above the trail, the wagons were all ablaze and bloodied bodies were littered all around. There was nothing he could do.

Johnny approached Jessica warily, not wanting to startle her. She was in shock enough as it was; he didn't want to add to her terror. And that she was terrified he had no doubt—he could hear it in her screams, see it in her eyes.

"Jessica." He spoke softly, crouching down on the ground near enough to touch her, but not reaching out for her. "Jessica," he tried again. She looked at him through her tears, but she didn't say anything; she was traumatized. Then she turned back to her family, pressing her face into their bodies, trying desperately to will them back to life. Johnny watched, helpless, as she screamed her outrage at the Indians, wailed her grief at losing her beloved, sweet mama, then turned her wrath on her father, collapsing on the ground beside him, screaming at his lifeless body the loudest of all.

"You killed them!" she hollered, beating at his brutalized body with her fists. "It was you who wanted to come west!" she yelled. "We were quite happy, me and mama! Now she's gone and it's all your fault! And Petey! He was just a baby, with his whole life ahead of him! Now he's gone too and it's all… your… fault." She ground the words out between sobs, gasping for breath. Her flailing fists stilled and she curled up against the dead man's chest, sobbing, her body shaking, a broken woman.

Placing a gentle hand on her shoulder, Johnny spoke softly in her ear in what he hoped was a comforting tone. "Jessica, look at me." She didn't. Gently, he took her hands in his own and disengaged her fingers from the death grip they had on the lapel of her father's coat, wrapping his arms around her securely and pulling her in close against his chest. "Shhhh," he crooned softly, trying to calm her as though she were a baby. It worked. She responded to him, her sobs easing. Her shuddering slowly stilled, she got her breathing under control and began to relax in his arms. And she clung to him tightly, so tightly, as though she would never let go. Then she looked up at him and began to speak.

"They came out of nowhere, they just rose up all around us, as though they came up out of the ground. The wagons were completely surrounded. I tried to tell papa of the risk of Indians before we left Boston but he didn't listen. And now look... look at them now." She burst into tears again, sobs wracking her body once more as she stuffed her fist into her mouth trying to stifle her cries. Johnny wrapped his arms around her tightly again, wishing he could shield her from the pain, wishing she hadn't seen her entire family, the entire wagon train, get massacred.

"Where were you?" she asked him sharply, the tone of her voice suggesting she was blaming him for the attack.

"Out hunting meat," he told her gently. "I wish I'd been here," he whispered regretfully.

"You couldn't have done anything," she conceded. "Not one man against all those Indians. There were dozens of them. It wasn't just one or two—it was dozens."

"I can shoot," he told her.

"Some of the men did. But it didn't help them. There were just too many." She shook her head sadly. "One more gun wouldn't have made a difference." Swiping the back of her hand across her face to wipe away her tears, she wriggled out of Johnny's embrace and looked around at what remained of the camp.

"Do you think they will come back?" she asked him, her voice trembling.

Johnny shrugged. "I don't know. But I don't think so. They've got what they wanted out of here and hopefully they won't know there were any survivors." He admired her bravery; she had just witnessed her entire family being killed, she was all alone in the wilderness, yet she was blinking back her tears. And while he was trying hard to be reassuring, he was frightened too. He looked at the trembling girl beside him and put his arms around her again. As scared as he was, he knew he wasn't as terrified as the shaking girl in his arms with the vacant, haunted look in her eyes. And he didn't know why, but he felt the urge to protect her. He was a loner, a drifter—he'd been forced into that lifestyle several years ago after his hand was forced in a gun battle after a rigged poker game—and there had been no room for females in the life that he had led. There had been no females he'd been interested in either, until Jessica. She evoked feelings in him that no one else had done. He wanted her. She was beautiful, she was vulnerable, and she was in dire need of a man to take care of her. She had nothing at all; the Indians had taken the horses, the food, the blankets... and what they'd left behind had been turned to cinders. He would willingly share the little he had with her; he would do whatever it took to prove to her that he was more than just a dusty cowboy.

"Come on." He helped her to her feet. "We should make the most of the daylight that's left, see if there's anything we can salvage and find a shovel to bury the dead."

A sob that turned into a strangled moan escaped her lips, but she grasped the hand that Johnny proffered and stood up on wobbly legs, a determined look on her face. Steeling themselves against the gruesome sight, they sifted through the charred remains of the wagons one by one, trying to find anything that might prove useful.

"Over there," Jessica pointed to a shovel partially hidden under the remains of a wagon axle—it looked to have escaped the fire. While Johnny took the shovel and went to dig the graves, she continued to sift through the remains of the wagon train, desperately trying to find something, anything, worth salvaging. Her search proved fruitless—the Indians had destroyed it all.

As Johnny dug, he found his thoughts drifting to Jessica. He was curious about her—for a girl who seemed to be such a brat, she was coping so well now. She wasn't falling to pieces as he'd been expecting her to do—she was keeping her emotions firmly in check, and aside from her initial display of shock and grief, she was very composed. She didn't look to be very old; he guessed her to be around nineteen or twenty, just a few years younger than him.

It was nearly dark by the time they had dug enough graves to bury the dead, marking them with the names as best they could. Then they stood there in silence, side by side, lost in their thoughts. Needing to honor the lives that lay buried somehow, to show respect, to give a decent burial, Johnny left Jessica standing alone and retrieved his harmonica from his saddlebags, returning to stand next to her before he began playing. His mother had loved his music, and he was hesitant to play it now, for fear of the memories it would dredge up; he missed her. Watching Jessica out of the corner of his eye, he raised the harmonica to his lips. He kept watching her, noticing the tears streaming down her face as she remained stoic, her hands clenched firmly at her sides, as the sweet refrains of *Amazing Grace* filled the air. Then he listened in astonishment as she began singing the words of the hymn in a trembling voice, quiet at first, shaking, but growing stronger and more confident as she continued.

He felt helpless. When the hymn was over, he didn't know what to do, so he reached out for her, stretching an arm across her shoulders. She was tense at first, but she soon relaxed and moved closer to him, taking comfort in his presence. For a long time they stood there like that, both of them lost in their thoughts, their memories; his arm around her shoulders, her tears dripping on the ground at her feet.

"I'm going to get a fire going," Johnny murmured quietly to her, and she nodded mutely. "We're going to need it—it's going to get cold real soon."

Forming a small ring out of stones, he made a pile of sticks in the center of it and got a small fire started. He didn't want to alert any nearby Indians to their presence, but without many blankets, they would need what little warmth the fire would provide. There was enough partially burnt wood from the destroyed wagons to keep their small fire stoked, a small mercy for which he was glad—he really didn't want to have to leave their camp in search of firewood. He hoped his presence was a small comfort for

Jessica, although it didn't seem like she was aware of him at all at the moment, as she sat by the graves of her family, looking completely lost.

Fishing some jerked beef out of his saddlebag, he offered it to her, but she shook her head, her face expressionless.

"You need to eat something, you haven't eaten all day," he cajoled her. But she just shook her head again, ignoring him.

Filling a small billy with water from his canteen, Johnny added some of the jerked beef to it, making a broth over the fire. Jessica had to eat, he knew that much. The poor girl was probably still in shock, but it wouldn't do to let her starve to death, or die of thirst, both of which were distinct possibilities if he didn't act. Carrying the tin cup over to where she sat, he held it to her lips, urging her to drink. She shook her head and the liquid spilled out to dribble down her chin unchecked.

"Drink it," he told her sternly, more sternly than he'd intended, and immediately he felt guilty. Yes, it was important that she drink. But it was more important that he not add to her anguish. But she took a deep breath, took the cup from him, and swallowed the contents down.

"Good girl," he praised her. "It will help." She didn't look at him though; she just dropped the cup on the ground at his feet and continued staring at the mound of dirt where they'd buried her family just hours ago.

Throwing more sticks on the fire and stoking it to a decent blaze, Johnny unraveled his bedroll that he carried with him, tied to the back of his saddle on his horse. It was comfortable enough but it would be small for the two of them; however, it would have to do—the Indians had taken the bedding they wanted from the wagons and burnt that which they didn't—Jessica would have a very cold, uncomfortable night out in the open if he didn't take care of her. And he wanted to take care of her—her vulnerability appealed to the protective, masculine side of his nature and he felt a yearning to wrap her in his arms and hold her safe.

"Come over to the fire," he invited her, his tone gentle, and was surprised when she looked up, grasped his extended hand, and struggled to her feet. Putting his arm around her shoulders protectively, he led her over to the fire and sat down on the ground beside her, wrapping his blanket around their shoulders. They sat there in silence for a while, both lost in their thoughts. The silence of the dark night was interrupted every now and then by Jessica's sniffles, and the howl of a lone coyote.

"Are you okay?" he whispered some time later, giving her shoulders a squeeze, but there was no reply. Looking down at her, he could see she was asleep, her head resting lightly on his shoulder. Gently, he lowered her down to the ground, laying her out on his padded bedroll, covering her with a blanket. Stretching out on the other side of the fire, his head resting on his saddle, his hat covering his face, he went to sleep himself.

.

CHAPTER TWO

Where am I? Jessica sat up in a panic, looking around her, trying to get her bearings. The sun was just coming up over the horizon, and she squinted, struggling to see. Memories of the day before flashed into her mind and she looked around in horror, stifling a scream when she saw that it was, in fact, true. There really had been an Indian attack; the entire wagon train, save herself and Johnny, really were all dead. From where she was sitting she could see the freshly dug graves, crudely marked with the crosses they'd fashioned out of bits of broken, burnt wagon. *Johnny!* Where was he? He hadn't abandoned her, had he? She relaxed slightly as she caught sight of his sleeping form on the other side of the fire, which had all but gone out. Reaching forward, she stirred the embers into life, adding a few sticks from the pile of broken wagon pieces Johnny had gathered the night before. Immediately flames engulfed the wood and a small cry escaped her lips.

She'd thought she'd accepted what had happened yesterday, but that small flame was all it took to bring back the absolute horror of it all—the massacre of all those people she had begun to class as friends, the theft of all their belongings; the beginning of the end of her life. That it was nearly the end of her life she was certain, for surely she would die out here—she had nothing. No horse, no clothing other than what she was wearing, no food, no money. And she couldn't rely on Johnny... Mr. Truman, she corrected herself quickly, to save her. He'd been kind to her last night, but she knew that wouldn't last. Men wanted only one thing, and she had no intention of providing that one thing she knew Johnny would want of her. She began to wish the Indians had killed her too, then she wouldn't be in this predicament. And, if she were honest with herself, if she hadn't been such a brat yesterday, storming off like that, she wouldn't be here now—she would be dead. But her father made her so furious! She hadn't wanted to come west in the first place—she was quite happy in their little house in Boston, but she wasn't given the choice. Papa had simply announced his plans one day to move west, and the next thing she knew, they were going. She had refused, she'd begged, she'd pleaded... but it was no use.

She'd just been starting to make her mark on the social circle; her life had just been beginning, and there was no way her father was going to let her, an unmarried young woman, stay in Boston alone. She'd been starting to attract the attention of several local men, sons of prominent families in the district, and she was hopeful that one day she would gain a good husband out of one of those men. But none of them had acted quickly enough to save her from her uncertain fate headed westward on the trail, and now here she was... alone in the wilderness.

Well, not alone exactly, she admitted, having a decent look at Johnny—Mr. Truman—for the first time. He'd talked to her several times on the trail but she hadn't been interested in the likes of him. A dusty, dirty cowboy, he wasn't the sort of man she went for. But looking at him now, she could see how ruggedly handsome he was—six foot two of solid muscle, broad-shouldered, lean and wiry, sandy blond hair flattened on top from his hat, a chiseled jaw that looked like it hadn't seen a razor in days and eyes bluer than she'd ever seen. Then she immediately felt guilty. Her entire family was dead—she shouldn't be attracted to men, she should be too involved in her grief to feel any sparks of attraction.

"Are you okay this morning?" he asked her gently, interrupting her reverie, smiling at her kindly. She hadn't even realized he was awake, and hearing his voice made her feel numb all over again. Did he know that the last words she'd exchanged with her family had been angry ones? Did he hear her father threatening to take a strap to her? So much for that… her bottom tingled involuntarily at the thought. If the Indians hadn't come she'd be sore this morning, but even the pain of a thrashing would be preferable to the predicament she now faced; bruises would fade, but the pain of losing her family never would.

She met his eyes and tried to return the smile, but she just couldn't. Immediately her eyes filled with tears and her gaze went again to the freshly dug graves.

"I will be," she choked out, fighting back sobs as he put a comforting hand on her shoulder. *Mmmmm, kind as well as handsome,* she thought, then felt guilty for her naughty thoughts. She'd been very much a lady in Boston, raised by a woman—no, a *lady*—who put great importance on manners and correct behavior, and thinking about handsome men the day after burying her family was certainly not correct behavior. Come to think of it, spending the night with said handsome man would most definitely be classed as inappropriate behavior too. It didn't matter that he had slept on the other side of the fire as far away from her as he could get, and had been nothing but a gentleman—it was still inappropriate. But Jessica had always rebelled; she hated the restrictions the term 'lady' put on her behavior, and while she liked the fashions being a lady afforded, she objected to having to behave a certain way because she was a lady. So it felt fitting, in a strange way, to have spent her first night alone in the world with a man she barely knew, a man who was certainly not marriage material.

The deep timbre of Johnny's voice rumbled through her

as he asked if she wanted coffee. "I've got a bit in my saddlebags, enough for this morning, anyway." He smiled at her again and she blinked back tears. Johnny—Mr. Truman—was her only hope of survival; she didn't want him thinking her a useless, feeble female that he would have to risk his life to protect. She wanted him to think of her as strong and capable, someone who wouldn't impede his progress on the trail to the next town. If he was willing to take her along with him, that is. If he wasn't... well, there wasn't anything she could do. If he left her behind, she would die out here alone, making a meal for the vultures and other predators that lived on the frontier, always lurking, waiting for death.

She nodded and tried to smile as she accepted the offer of coffee, but she failed. Her lower lip trembled instead of curling upwards, and when she bit it in an attempt to stop the flow of tears, a sob escaped her lips.

"Yes, please," she clarified, stammering her words. "I would like coffee, Mr. Truman, thank you."

"Johnny."

"Huh?"

"Johnny. None of this 'Mr. Truman' stuff. Call me Johnny." He smiled at her again as he heated the billy over the coals, emptying the last of his coffee into the steaming water. Jessica didn't reply, but her heart thumped erratically, happily, in her chest. None of her suitors back home had extended that invitation to her; everything had been so formal there. She nearly smiled at the way her sweet mama would have been scandalized if she had been so forward as to call one of those gentlemen by their first names.

There was only the one battered tin mug, so they had to share—they took turns in sipping the hot beverage, savoring every mouthful; they knew it would be the last one they would enjoy for some time.

"Have you got any family anywhere?" Johnny asked her when the coffee was nearly all gone. "Apart from..." He swept his arm around the ruined campsite, indicating the graves helplessly. "Sorry," he apologized softly.

Jessica bit her lip. "I've got a great-aunt in Boston. I'll have to go there. She's old, but I don't know of anyone else."

"We'd better get going then. I don't know how far away the nearest town is, but we're sure to meet up with someone sooner or later who can help us. When we get to town you can send a wire to your aunt, and get on the stagecoach from there."

Johnny bustled about efficiently, saddling his horse, rolling up the bedroll and securing it to the back of the saddle, putting his billy and mug back into the saddlebag, putting out their fire. All the while Jessica stood there in a daze, her eyes locked on the graves of her family.

"We should have stayed in Boston." Jessica was staring at the graves as she softly murmured the words, wringing her hands in front of her as though she didn't know what else to do with them. "I tried to tell you the trail was dangerous, I tried to tell you how frightened I was. Now my worst fears have been realized—you're all dead. And I'm here all alone." She put her hands up to her face as she dissolved in tears, her shoulders shaking with her sobs. "I wish I'd died in that Indian attack too!" she cried, stamping her foot and sending up a cloud of dust.

She felt a hand on her shoulder, then Johnny was in front of her, wrapping his arms around her, bringing her in close to his broad chest. She could feel the roughness of his vest brushing against her cheek and she pressed her face up against him, seeking what little comfort he offered. "I should be dead too!" she sobbed, her voice muffled by Johnny's shirt. "If I hadn't argued with father and walked out of camp, I would be dead!"

"Shhhh," Johnny whispered, rubbing her back gently.

"My last words to my father were angry ones," she cried. "We argued over some work he thought I should be doing; even though I was ill, he thought I should be working. I resented being forced into working so hard by being out on the trail. I reminded him that I'd never wanted to come out here, that I'd been happy in Boston, had suitors courting me... he threatened to take a strap to me." She choked on a sob. It had been years since her father had taken a strap to her, even since he'd threatened to do it—that's why she had ignored his threat and continued storming out of camp. The action that had ultimately saved her life.

"I know," Johnny said softly.

"You know?" she asked in horror, embarrassed. "You heard father threaten me and treat me like a child?"

Johnny nodded. "I did."

Jessica groaned, burying her face against Johnny's shirt again. "I want to die," she whispered, her words barely audible.

But Johnny heard them. "What an awful thing to say!" he scolded. "The good Lord spared you for a reason, you should be grateful!" He pulled her back off his chest so he could look into her eyes, shaking her gently. "I don't want to hear any more of that talk!"

"It's easy for you to say," Jessica sniffed. "You're not all alone in the wilderness with absolutely nothing."

"Neither are you," Johnny pointed out. "You're not alone, you've got me."

"And why would you be interested in letting me tag along with you? I've got nothing. No clothes, no money, no food, no water, not even a horse. I'll just be a hindrance to you. Just go. Go, and leave me here to die."

Johnny shook her again. "You listen here, little lady, or I'll take you across my knee and tan your britches like your daddy shoulda done," he growled. "I'm not leaving you here to die, you're coming with me. I'll take care of you. I'll protect you. My mama raised me better than to leave a beautiful lady alone in the wilderness."

"How dare you!" Jessica exclaimed, outraged, her grief forgotten for the moment.

"How dare I what?" Johnny chuckled. "Take care of you?"

Jessica wrestled out of his grasp and stood away from him, staring up at him, her hands on her hips. "No! Threaten to spank me!" she clarified angrily.

Johnny chuckled again. "You behave yourself and you won't have nothing to worry about. I'm a man of my word. As I said, I'll take care of you. But if I think you deserve it, I won't hesitate to tan your backside. That's the way I was raised, and just the kind of man I am."

"I'm sorry," Jessica whimpered. "I'm just upset; after all, my entire family has just been killed, right in front of my very eyes!" Jessica took a deep breath and choked back her tears. "But if you're serious about letting me tag along with you, I would be very grateful. Thank you."

"I was serious." Johnny smiled kindly at her and took her hand. "Come on," he invited, "we really should get going. Get as far as we can today in the daylight. Do you want some time alone first?" He indicated the graves, but Jessica shook her head.

"No. I've said my goodbyes. There's nothing else left to say." Her voice cracked, and she wiped away a tear, then swallowed forcefully. "Right, let's go!"

Johnny mounted first then pulled Jessica up behind him. They knew there was no town back the way they'd come from, so they headed in another direction.

They rode slowly—Johnny's horse was carrying double, as well as the bedroll and saddlebags. It was clear to Jessica that Johnny was fond of his horse; many cowboys weren't, but he was. She noticed how he spoke to the horse softly, and rode gently, never hauling on the reins, never rough with him. It was obvious that the two shared a tight bond and had been together a good while. She was grateful to the loyal animal that willingly carried them; she was happy to ride slowly.

As they rode, Jessica broke the silence by telling Johnny about her childhood in Boston. She'd enjoyed it, and she'd been happy. Her family hadn't been a wealthy one, but they'd been a happy one. Her home had a lot of love in it, and she wished with all her heart that they were all still back there. For some reason, it had always been her pa's dream to come west. For as long as she could remember, he'd talked about it, making plans that would be carried out 'one day.' When that day had come, she'd tried to stay behind. Her mama didn't really want to go west either—her whole life had been spent in Boston—but she would follow her husband to the ends of the earth. However, she understood why Jessica wanted to stay behind, and had been happy for her to do so, but pa had refused. There had been no offers of marriage for her, and he wasn't letting her stay behind. She'd begged and pleaded, but his mind had been made up. He was finally going to realize his dream, and he wanted all of his family with him.

She teared up at the end and she leaned her forehead against Johnny's broad back, biting her lip to fight off the tears that were threatening to fall. It had been harder than she'd thought it would be, remembering.

Taking a deep breath, she sat up straight and swallowed hard. "Your turn," she told Johnny. "What was your childhood like?"

It was a long moment before Johnny spoke, and at first she thought he was going to refuse to tell her. But he did, and he spoke in a quiet, wistful voice that made her even sadder than she already was. She listened intently, reassured by Johnny's quiet, deep voice, as he told her about growing up in Missouri. He'd left home at just sixteen to work on a cattle ranch, and he hadn't been back since. His childhood had been a happy one too—his ma and pa and three little sisters had laughed a lot, sang around ma's piano, and had fun, but there hadn't been much money. That's why he couldn't go back home empty-handed—he had to get a stake for himself. If he went back home, he had to take something with him that would make ma and pa proud of him.

The hot sun beat down on them, and although they rode all day, they didn't come across any other travelers. To

Jessica, it felt as though they were truly the only two people on earth. She wasn't used to the wilderness. In Boston, she could step outside and see her neighbors. She could walk down the street and stop and talk to people she knew. She was never lonely—there was always the hustle and bustle of town not very far away. But out here, the loneliness and the sheer expanse of the prairie were totally unlike anything she'd ever known.

They saw wagon tracks, but no people. She had no idea where they were, or where they were going, or even what she would do when they got there. The only family she had left was her father's aunt Thelma, who lived in Boston. Great-aunt Thelma had never been close to her father—Jessica could only ever remember meeting her once—but as far as she knew, there was no one else. Hopefully the elderly woman would be kind enough to send her enough money to get a stagecoach back to Boston, where, hopefully, one of her old suitors would ask for her hand in marriage. Or if not, she may be able to find a job as a housekeeper or teacher. Jessica had a good education, she'd even gone to finishing school; why her father had paid for all that, then forced her out here to the prairie, she would never understand. It wasn't like the airs and graces she'd learned at Miss Bishop's Ladies' Academy would help her much out here..

CHAPTER THREE

They nibbled on jerky throughout the day, and tried to ration the water. Johnny's canteen was getting lighter, and there was no way of filling it. Neither of them had any idea of which direction to go to find the river, and they didn't want to run out. Jessica watched, worried, as Johnny tipped water into his hat for his horse when they stopped for a rest under the shade of a big tree.

"That's nearly empty," he remarked, when he replaced the canteen in his saddlebag. She just nodded dumbly. She knew how light the canteen was. Her throat was parched and dry, but she didn't want to drink any more of the precious water.

That night they had no fire; they had no wood, and nothing to cook over it anyway. Jessica's stomach rumbled loudly, and she was embarrassed. Johnny had tried to shoot a rabbit earlier that evening, but he'd missed, and there had been no other game close enough. So they nibbled on jerked beef in silence, feeling so small and insignificant as they lay down on the bedroll and looked up at the stars. It was cold without a fire, so Johnny lay down close to Jessica to keep her warm, wrapping her tightly in a blanket. He had a wool coat, but she didn't—her coat, along with the rest of her belongings, had been taken in the Indian raid. As she snuggled up close to him, her head so close to his chest that she could hear the steady rhythm of his beating heart, she felt safe. She hadn't felt safe since leaving Boston—there had always been a niggling fear in the back of her mind. Now the worst had happened and her family was gone, but she could feel Johnny's strong, muscular body next to her, hear him breathing, and she felt protected.

As soon as the sun was up the next morning, they got back in the saddle. Jessica knew they had to find water today—they drank the last drops out of the canteen to wash down the beef jerky they had for breakfast. She didn't know how long a person could survive without water for, but she knew that it wouldn't be all that long under this hot sun. Conserving her energy, she rested her head against Johnny's broad back as they rode, lost in memories of happier times with her family.

· · · · · · ·

"Look!" Johnny's exclamation startled her so much that she nearly fell off the horse in surprise. She must have dozed off, as none of the terrain they were now traveling looked familiar. But she looked curiously in the direction Johnny was pointing. Dust, lots of dust, and it wasn't more than a mile in front of them.

"What's making that, do you think?" she asked, rubbing her eyes.

"Cattle drive, I think. There's too much dust for it to be anything else."

Now that Jessica was awake, her stomach rumbled loudly, and she realized just how hungry she was, and thirsty. She'd never had so much beef jerky in her life, and while she was grateful for the nourishment it provided, she was desperate for a decent meal to fill her belly. Johnny must have heard her stomach protest, because he fished around in one of his saddlebags and pulled out a piece of jerky.

"Here you go—last one. You better pray the trail boss is nice, and willing to share some chow with us. I've got a bit of money to buy supplies off them, if they'll sell."

"You don't need to spend money on me, Johnny, I can't repay you."

Johnny twisted in his saddle to fix her with a stern stare. "Do you want a spanking?"

"No. I just…" Jessica shook her head emphatically, searching for the right words to express the way she was feeling. "It's just… I'm grateful, truly I am; I just don't want to be indebted to you. As I said, I can't repay you."

"I'm not asking to be repaid," Johnny snarled. "Dammit, woman, why can't you just let me care for you?"

"Why do you want to? I've got nothing to offer you."

Johnny flexed his hands as he crossed his ankle over the saddle horn and twisted around to face her properly. "You really do want a spanking, don't you? I told you I would take care of you, and I intend to do so. It's just the way I am. Besides, it's been a long time since I've had a pretty lady by my side. A mighty long time." Johnny turned back the right way, put his foot back in the stirrup, and pushed his horse into a faster pace.

• • • • • • •

They'd been able to see the cattle drive camp for several minutes before they rode into it, and although neither of them spoke, Jessica knew the drovers were their only hope for a hot meal, water for their canteen, and some coffee.

Jessica watched as a man stood up from his spot beside the fire and walked toward them, his bearing proud; a tall, striking-looking man with jet black hair.

"You the boss of this here outfit?" Johnny asked the man, reining his horse to a halt.

The man nodded his hand. "Yep. Jordan's my name, Wes Jordan."

"Johnny Truman." Johnny stuck out his hand toward

Mr. Jordan, who stepped forward and shook it, tipping his hat to Jessica.

"And this here is Miss Jessica Walsh. We were with a wagon train a couple of days ride southeast of here that got attacked by Indians. Everyone was killed, the wagons burned. We'd be mighty obliged if you would sell us enough provisions to get us through to the next town; unless you have room for another hand?"

Jessica gasped. The last thing she wanted was for Johnny to sign on as a drover in a cattle drive! What was she going to do if he did that?

"Come into camp." Mr. Jordan reached for Jessica, wrapping his hands around her slender waist and lifting her effortlessly down to the ground, smiling at her kindly as he did so. Jessica was grateful. She was hungry and thirsty, and her legs were cramped from being on horseback for so long. As she stood beside him, she got a good look at the man standing between them and a slow death of starvation and dehydration. It was hard to guess his age—he was probably several years older than Johnny, and stood slightly taller, with more bulk on his frame than Johnny had. He looked to be a tough man, with callused hands, but his eyes were kind.

"Are you a cattle man, Johnny?"

"I've done a bit." Johnny was honest. "A couple of years ago I was a hand on a ranch down Texas way."

"We could use another man," Mr. Jordan said, scratching his chin. "We could use both of you actually. Can you ride, miss?" He looked at Jessica.

"Oh, no." Jessica shook her head, disgust dripping from her voice. "No way. I'm not staying with a bunch of filthy, stinking cattle men! Drovers smell! We're not staying here!" She stomped her foot, sending a cloud of dust swirling up around her, making her cough. "I didn't come all the way out here to play nursemaid to a herd of stupid cattle!" she declared between coughs. "I want to go home!"

Mr. Jordan frowned, then turned away. "I'm sorry you

feel that way, miss." He strode back toward the camp, his fists clenched tightly by his sides in anger.

Jessica could feel the men's eyes on her. Had they heard her? She hadn't spoken that loudly, had she? Gulping, she knew that she had. Her objections hadn't been spoken softly, purely for the benefit of Johnny's ears. No, she'd shrieked her outrage loudly at the very idea of making camp with these men; they would have to be deaf not to have heard her.

She felt Johnny's hand grip her arm, then she squealed as he hauled her roughly up in front of him on his horse, draping her belly-down across his saddle, her body balanced precariously on his legs and dangling down either side of the horse, the saddle horn pressing into her side.

"Put me down!" she shrieked, crying in outrage and pain as Johnny started whaling away on her backside with his huge, hard palm. He wasn't holding back any either, as he swatted her again and again, making sure she was fully aware of how much her rudeness and lack of respect displeased him. The horse side-stepped beneath them as each blow landed, the sound of the swats and Jessica's accompanying yelps echoing across the plains.

Jessica was mortified. Not only that, she was in pain; it felt like her entire rear end was on fire! "I'm sorry! I'm sorry!" she yelled, tears streaming down her face. She was kicking and struggling, but Johnny was holding her firmly; there was no escaping the wickedly hard blows he was landing with precision. The layers of dress and petticoats should have afforded her more protection from the pain than what they did, but Johnny simply made up for the layers of clothing by laying into her harder.

"Mr. Jordan just offered us a lifeline," Johnny scolded, punctuating his words with another stinging slap. "And you just threw it in his face."

"I know! I'm sorry!" Jessica wailed, sobbing.

"How long do you think we're going to last with no food or water?" Johnny growled, smacking her bottom again with another hearty swat. "We've got nothing, Jessica, nothing!" The next volley of smacks was even harder than before, and the horse beneath them shied. Jessica squealed at the sudden movement, afraid she was going to fall off, scrabbling at Johnny's pants-clad leg in a panic. Picking up the reins, Johnny soothed the horse, holding onto Jessica with one hand to prevent her from sliding down the side of their mount.

"I'm sorry! Please just put me down, I'll go and apologize to Mr. Jordan," she begged through her sobs, sniffling and choking on her tears. Johnny had done as good a job at warming her bottom using just his hand as her father did with his strap, and if she hadn't been clinging frantically to the legs of his pants with both hands to stop herself from falling into the dirt beneath them, she would be trying to rub the sting out of it.

"Go on then," Johnny ordered her as he slid her gently down off the horse. Turning around to face the camp, Jessica looked up—straight into the eyes of Mr. Jordan, who was standing there looking stern with his arms folded across his chest, a small smile of amused approval on his face. Wanting to die of embarrassment and shame, knowing Mr. Jordan and many of his men had just witnessed her spanking, she nevertheless swallowed hard and held her head high with the small amount of pride she could muster.

"Please accept my sincere apologies, Mr. Jordan," she said formally. "I was rude, and I was wrong. If your offer of employment still stands, I would be very much obliged to work for you."

Mr. Jordan gave her a hard stare for a long moment, not saying anything. Jessica held her breath. He wasn't going to turn them away now, was he?

"Welcome aboard. Usual pay—a dollar a day plus all you can eat. Go and talk to Monty—he's the cook—and he'll find you some pants. That pretty dress isn't suitable for the trail." He smiled warmly at her and indicated toward the chuck wagon.

"Thank you, sir." Jessica tried to make herself sound more enthusiastic than she felt, and she even tried to smile, but she couldn't quite manage it—she blinked back more tears instead. She was miserable. Still grieving for her slaughtered family, now her bottom was aching. Even worse, she was being forced to make camp with a bunch of dusty, smelly cowboys!

Rubbing her bottom, she started to walk toward the chuck wagon when she heard Mr. Jordan's voice again. "And take your hands away from your backside. You shouldn't be rubbing after a spanking." Her face colored as red as she was sure her bottom was, but she brought her hands together in front of her, not daring to look back at Mr. Jordan.

Jessica didn't want to wear pants. She liked her dress; it was the only reminder she had of home, of the life she'd left behind. And while she had quite liked the idea of rebelling at first, her rebellion didn't quite extend to borrowing man's pants and dressing like a cowboy for the trail. She'd just spent two long days on horseback in her dress, so the full skirt didn't hinder her riding ability any. But, having gotten off to such a bad start with Mr. Jordan already, she wasn't game enough to disobey him. Deciding on a compromise—she would wear her dress in the evenings, in camp, and put on the pants during the daytime while riding—she went in search of Monty, the cook.

Monty was easy to find. He was standing at a table in front of the chuck wagon preparing food, barking orders at the young man standing beside him. He looked up at her as she approached and she was mesmerized by the way his eyes crinkled up at the corners when he smiled at her, showing a mouth full of missing teeth, framed by a graying moustache.

"Mr. Monty?" she asked hesitantly, shy now. Had he witnessed Johnny spanking her too? Or had he been too far away to see? "I... I'm Jessica. Jessica Walsh. Mr. Jordan sent me to you to borrow some pants. Please," she added as an afterthought.

Monty looked her up and down, as though sizing her up. He scratched his chin with a stubby finger, smearing flour over his face, then he beckoned her to follow him. Parked slightly behind the chuck wagon was another one, identical except for the foldout table that had been built onto the front. Clambering into the back of the wagon, Monty emerged just moments later with a pair of men's canvas trousers like Johnny wore, and a shirt. He thrust them at her. "These should fit." He indicated the supply wagon with his thumb. "You can get changed in there."

"Oh, no, I'm not wearing these until the morning. I couldn't possibly put them on now, and wear them all night!" she exclaimed, as though the very thought horrified her.

Monty shrugged. "Suit yourself." Then he went back to whatever it was he was preparing at the rickety table. She stood there stupidly for a moment, waiting for him to talk to her, to introduce the young man assisting him, but he didn't. He just continued on with his work, ignoring her completely. She risked a glance at the young man, and although he'd clearly been watching her, he looked down quickly, his face coloring, when their eyes met.

Is he shy? Or is he judging me too? She wondered. Not that she blamed him—she was fairly certain now that both Mr. Monty and his quiet assistant, and possibly every other man in the place had heard her outburst at Johnny before. And she was even more certain that they'd all witnessed what had come after. So it was no wonder that none of the men were throwing a welcoming party for her. It was a wonder they were stifling their groans as well as they were, at the thought of making camp with her for goodness knew how long.

Holding the pants and shirt folded over one arm, she went back to the edge of the camp where Johnny was still talking to Mr. Jordan. She felt uncomfortable by the campfire near the men; she hadn't been lying when she'd voiced her opinion of drovers before—it truly was how she felt. The men *did* smell, and she could feel some of them, probably only one or two, leering at her. At least, she thought they were leering. She knew she was an attractive woman—she'd been told so countless times before. And the dress she was wearing was pretty, even if it was covered with trail dust. It was possible though, she had to admit, that the men weren't leering at all, but simply felt awkward around her, now that they knew what she thought of them; that she considered them all beneath her. At any rate, none of them seemed to be particularly friendly.

Johnny smiled at her when she reached out for him, craving his protection, needing to feel his touch. He didn't disappoint her—he laid his hand gently on her shoulder, squeezing it softly, reminding her that he would take care of her. Mr. Jordan called to a man standing by the remuda, and he came and took Johnny's horse, ignoring Jessica and Johnny completely.

Oh, no, Jessica thought. *I really have offended every single one of them.*

"Come on," Mr. Jordan invited. "Monty will get you both some food and some hot coffee. You look as though you need it." He led the way to the campfire, his long strides eating up the ground, forcing Jessica to nearly run to keep up with him.

Most of the drovers were sitting on the ground around the campfire, and they all looked up as the trio approached. Jessica could see a few men on the outskirts of the camp, and more with the herd, but most of them were eating, or just finished. She could feel their eyes on her, and if it hadn't been for Johnny's strong grip on her arm as she struggled to keep up with Mr. Jordan, she probably would have run away. Facing up to her mistakes wasn't one of the things she was especially good at, but if there was one thing she had in abundance, it was pride. So she summoned up her reserves of pride now and held her head up high as they strode into camp.

"This is Johnny Truman and Miss Jessica Walsh. You will all treat Miss Jessica like a lady—which she is!" Mr.

Jordan said pointedly, looking hard at each of his men.

"She didn't look like no lady when she was atop that horse getting that butt of hers tanned!" one of the men said loudly, punctuating his words with a guffaw. There were a few chuckles of agreement, but the smiles died on the men's lips as Mr. Jordan glared at them fiercely, one eyebrow raised in warning.

Jessica wanted the ground to open up and swallow her whole. Instead, she forced herself to remain still, and looked at the dust on her shoes.

"Don't mind them, miss, they's just foolin' with ya," a cheerful voice called out as a man around Johnny's age, maybe a bit older, rose to his feet.

"This is Woody Carlson, ramrod." Mr. Jordan made the introductions as Woody gave Jessica a wide smile, tipping his hat to her.

"What's a ramrod?" Jessica stretched up to whisper in Johnny's ear. Even though he'd just spanked her, even though she barely knew him, he was all she had, and without wanting to, or even intending to, she relied on him for guidance and protection.

"Next in charge," he whispered back. She nodded as Johnny shook Woody's proffered hand. "Johnny Truman. Good to meet you."

Woody may have smiled, but none of the other men did. They were glaring at her, and she knew it was only Mr. Jordan's presence that was keeping them quiet. *Maybe I should apologize… it's what mama would expect of me.* She edged closer to Johnny and took a deep breath, steeling her nerves for the apology she knew she had to give.

"I can assure you all," Jessica declared. "I was raised in Boston to be very much a lady. I apologize for my very bad manners earlier—I am still somewhat in shock over the events of the previous few days. I am very grateful for your hospitality. My family was traveling with a wagon train a few days ride from here and while I was out walking, the entire company was attacked by Indians. My family—my mama, pa, and little brother, were all killed."

She thought she heard a collective gasp from the men around the campfire as she paused to wipe the tears from her eyes, but she wasn't sure. Johnny squeezed her shoulder, giving her the strength she needed to continue on, even though her voice was breaking and wavering. "Mr. Truman was out hunting for meat at the time of the attack—we were the only survivors. Mr. Truman has been kind enough to let me travel with him until now; I am very grateful for his kindness. I fear I would have perished if left alone on the prairie."

Jessica knew how true those words were; and while death still felt like it would be a blessing, she knew there were worse things than being under Johnny's care and protection—she couldn't end up like one of those saloon girls her ma had always scorned… or worse. "Good!" Mr. Jordan approved heartily as he clapped Johnny on the shoulder and guided Jessica gently over to the chuck wagon where Monty and his assistant were ladling aromatic stew onto tin plates.

"Coffee?" The young assistant asked, hefting the pot off the fire and pouring the steaming, tar-like liquid into dented metal mugs.

"Please," Johnny answered for them both.

Mr. Monty jabbed his thumb at the coffee-pouring assistant. "Billy," he said by way of introduction. "My louse."

"Louse? What kind of name is that?" Jessica asked, horrified.

"Helper," Billy answered proudly. "I'm the helper to the best range cook in the country. You wait 'til you taste his stew—you'll see what I mean." It was plain that Billy held his boss in high regard, and when Jessica looked across at Monty, she could see how much it meant to the older man that Billy revered him so.

Billy was right—Monty was a fantastic cook. The stew was the most delicious Jessica could ever remember tasting, and when Johnny went back for seconds, she knew it wasn't just her.

• • • • • • •

Once dinner was over and Woody had read out the roster of night riders and nighthawks, the camp was quiet. Men were talking and laughing softly around the campfire and Jessica found she was so weary she could barely keep her eyes open. She leaned her head gently against Johnny's shoulder and sidled in closer to him.

"You okay?" he whispered softly, smiling down at her.

"Just tired." It was strange though—it wasn't a physical exhaustion she felt but a mental one; she was wrung out emotionally. She pressed herself harder up against Johnny; his presence was comforting, and she appreciated it. And she smiled in contentment when he wrapped an arm around her waist and pulled her in closer, dropping a tender kiss on her hair.

"You can bed down in the supply wagon, Miss Jessica," Mr. Jordan informed them, as he observed Jessica's eyes closing of their own accord.

"Mmm, thank you, sir," Jessica murmured, already half asleep snuggled up against Johnny's strong shoulder, his arm wrapped around her protectively, cocooning her in safety.

CHAPTER FOUR

"Head 'em up and move 'em out!" Mr. Jordan called early the next morning, as everyone bustled around camp and finished saddling up their horses. Jessica had been assigned to ride drag with Johnny, and while she wasn't looking forward to spending the entire day eating the dust of nearly three thousand steers, she was hopeful that a day on drag might redeem her to the rest of the drovers and prove to them that she was grateful for their hospitality. And she was; Monty's cooking was delicious, and the bed he'd made for her in the back of the supply wagon was far more comfortable than Johnny's bedroll spread on the ground had been. Of course, it couldn't compare to the bed she'd left behind in Boston, but with a bit of luck she'd be back in Boston soon enough and able to enjoy all the comforts of civilization once again.

Folding her dress up carefully and stowing it away in the back of the supply wagon where Monty had told her to, Jessica stretched, trying to make the scratchy pants and man's shirt feel more comfortable. Billy found a spare hat for her, and a canteen that he'd filled from the barrels on the side of the wagon, and when she was as ready as she knew she would ever be, she stepped out of the wagon and into the morning, where Old Joe, the gray-haired wrangler, had a horse saddled up and waiting for her.

• • • • • • •

"How are you doing?" Johnny asked her gently, smiling, when they'd been on the trail for more than an hour.

She leaned down and rubbed her horse's neck. "Dusty." She'd tied a bandanna over her mouth and nose to try and keep the dust out, but it didn't help much—her throat was still clogged with dust and she wondered if she'd ever feel clean again. But much to her surprise, she was enjoying it. She liked horse riding—it had been something she had excelled at back home in Boston—and while there were plenty of things she'd rather be spending her morning doing other than chasing stray beeves, Johnny's company was pleasant, and she was enjoying being with him.

They didn't get the opportunity to talk a lot, as there were a lot of steers to keep moving forward, but his quiet presence, his gentle manner, and his kind smile all reassured her and made her forget about the reason she was here, riding at the back of a dusty cattle drive, the farthest place she could think of being from the clean streets of Boston.

The sun was high in the sky before they stopped for chow, and Jessica was starving. Even when she'd been traveling with Johnny, when she'd eaten nothing but his beef jerky, she hadn't been as hungry as she was now.

She sat next to Johnny while they ate and she could see one of the drovers watching him. It was definitely Johnny that Frank was watching, not her. *Why?* she wondered. *Does he know Johnny from somewhere?* It occurred to her then, how little she knew of the man sitting next to her. She liked him, he was gentle and kind, but who was Johnny Truman? Who was he really?

The rest of the day passed in the same manner as the preceding hours—following along on the heels of the bellowing critters, rounding up the strays trying to go the wrong way, eating the dust raised by the thousands of hooves in front of them.

"Are you getting on alright?" A young cowboy rode up beside her, fingering his moustache nervously. Jessica didn't know who he was. She smiled timidly.

"Yes, fine, thanks," she told him politely. "What is your name?" There were so many drovers on the cattle drive she didn't know how she would ever get all their names straight, but she was determined to try.

"I'm Chuck, ma'am," he told her, letting go of his moustache to tip his hat to her.

"Thank you, Chuck." Jessica smiled. "We're all okay here."

"I'll leave you to it then." Whirling his horse, he cantered away. Jessica stared after his retreating back, wishing all the drovers were as kind to her as Chuck had been just then.

The afternoon dragged on, and Jessica was tiring, hot under the beating sun. But always Johnny was there riding close to her with a ready smile, encouraging her, reminding her that she wasn't alone. And as the day wore on, all she wanted was to be in his arms again, and feel his chapped lips on her head as he tenderly kissed her hair the way he'd done last night. Would he kiss her hair like that again? Even better, would he kiss her properly, on the lips?

• • • • • • •

Never before had Jessica been so pleased to put on her pretty gown as she was that evening. She wanted to feel pretty again; she wanted to make herself attractive for Johnny. She'd never felt so dirty in all her life! Her clothing was covered in dust; it was up her nose, in her ears, and through her hair. After washing up as best as she could, using the basin Monty had given her, she shed her pants and shirt, shaking them vigorously to get rid of the worst of the dust, put on her gown, then pinned up her hair. She'd worn it flowing down her back all day, held off her face with her hat, but right now, she wanted to feel like the fine Boston lady she'd once been, not some dusty old cowhand on the cattle trail that she currently was.

Once she was respectable, she joined the line for some of Monty's famous stew. Billy had been right when he'd described Monty as the best range cook in the country—the stew smelt delicious. Monty smiled, pleased with her appreciation of his fine cuisine, as he handed her a battered tin plate piled high with hot stew.

"This smells so good. Thanks," she said, as she went to join Johnny and the other men around the campfire. Again, she noticed Frank's gaze on Johnny, and it filled her with unease. But Johnny didn't seem to notice, so she tried to push the feeling of dread aside and concentrate on her meal. *Why is Frank staring at Johnny?* she wondered, but no matter how hard she tried, she couldn't come up with a reason.

She'd gone to the chuck wagon for coffee when Frank stood up. "I know you!" he declared, pointing at Johnny. "You shot my brother!"

Jessica gasped. What? Johnny was a killer? She turned to look at the men in horror, her feet frozen to the spot.

"It was a fair fight—he drew first, I drew faster. The poker game was rigged. What was I supposed to do? Just stand there and let him shoot me? Hell, I'd never shot a man before, but I sure as shootin' wasn't just going to stand there while he killed me."

"At least my brother would be alive," Frank snarled.

"But I'd be dead."

"You'll be dead anyway," Frank threatened, lowering his hand to the butt of his gun but leaving it in the holster. "I will avenge my brother's death." There was a very slight emphasis on the word 'will' and both Johnny and Jessica caught it.

"Johnny!" Jessica screamed, as Johnny stood up, his hand on his gun. "No!" She picked up her skirts and began to run toward him, completely panicked. Johnny was all she had left—she couldn't let Frank shoot him. And if she could stop Johnny from drawing, Frank wouldn't shoot. Even though she didn't know him, she hoped Frank wouldn't shoot Johnny in cold blood.

"You stay out of this, Jessie!" Johnny yelled back, but Jessica kept running. She bounced off a solid mass and nearly fell down, but Mr. Jordan reached out and steadied her, taking hold of her tightly.

"Stop them, Mr. Jordan!" she pleaded. "Please stop them!"

"Hold it!" Mr. Jordan's voice was strong and even, spoken in a very authoritative tone that made it clear he wouldn't be disobeyed. "There'll be no fighting in my camp. There's a lady present. Both of you back off."

Frank released the grip he had on his gun but remained standing there glaring at Johnny, who was glaring fiercely back. "You'll keep," he muttered, before turning away.

Releasing the grip he had on Jessica, Mr. Jordan stepped forward. "Am I going to have trouble with you?" he asked Johnny sternly.

"No, sir," Johnny answered.

The trail boss turned to Frank. "How about you?"

"No, sir." Frank sauntered off, but every nuance of him told Johnny he wasn't done—not by a long shot. He would obey orders for now, but Mr. Jordan wouldn't be around to protect Johnny forever.

"I need to ask for your gun, Johnny," Mr. Jordan ordered in his no-nonsense tone.

"And leave me unarmed? I need to be able to defend myself. You saw the look he gave me—as far as he's concerned, this isn't over."

Mr. Jordan sighed. "All right, keep your gun then. But stay out of Frank's way."

"I was minding my own business, sir; I did nothing to provoke him." Johnny spoke respectfully, but it was obvious he wasn't going to back down. Suddenly, Jessica understood the significance of the six-shooter that Johnny kept strapped to his hip. It wasn't just for decoration, and it wasn't just for hunting for food. It was a lethal weapon, and he wasn't afraid to use it.

Neither of the men seemed to notice how pale Jessica was, or how badly she was shaking. Her whole body was trembling, nearly as bad as it had been the day her family had been murdered. *Johnny killed someone! He's been so nice to me since my family was murdered, but he's a murderer himself!* She cupped her hands on her face as desperation overwhelmed her; she was sure she was going to faint. Johnny stepped up to her and put his hand on her shoulder, and she tensed up and shrank away at his touch.

"Is it true?" she whispered, horror and devastation clear in her eyes. "Did you shoot that man?"

Johnny nodded slowly, just once, his eyes downcast. Holding up her hands, close to hysterics, Jessica backed away.

"Let me explain."

"There's nothing to explain!" she exclaimed, her voice shrill. "You're a murderer!" She turned on her heel and ran, holding her skirts up high with both hands as she ran blindly.

"Stay away from me!" she screamed as she heard Johnny's footsteps behind her. She crashed smack-bang into Mr. Jordan again and he reached out to steady her, but she dodged around him, desperate to get away. She kept running.

"Hold it, son," Mr. Jordan ordered Johnny, holding both hands up to stop him. "Leave her be. Let her calm down. She's been through a lot; give her time to adjust. Let her do that, then talk to her." Mr. Jordan spoke quietly, but with so much authority that Johnny obeyed him. He had to admit the advice was good—Jessica had been through a lot, and she was young. She did have a bad habit of running away whenever she got upset, but that was nothing that couldn't be worked through. It would have to be worked through pretty fast though—running away out in the wilderness wasn't the same as throwing a tantrum and running away back in Boston. The streets of Boston were relatively safe—the wilderness wasn't. There was all manner of danger out on the trail, especially for a young woman as beautiful and innocent as Jessica. With a worried expression on his face, Johnny looked in the direction Jessica had ran—she was now out of sight behind the scrub, but her footsteps were easy to track. Mr. Jordan noticed the look. He put a restraining, comforting hand on Johnny's shoulder. "Give her time. If she doesn't come back, I'll go."

• • • • • • •

She had no idea where she was going; she didn't have a destination in mind at all. She guessed she would have to return to the camp eventually, unless she could find someone else who was willing to help her. But after walking for what seemed like hours, she still hadn't found anyone. This truly was the wilderness—there were no signs of life anywhere. She shuddered. She felt so alone, so helpless. She didn't want to go back to the cattle drive camp. How could she face Johnny again, now that she knew he was a murderer? Sure, she owed him her life—she would surely have perished out there on the plains if he hadn't taken her with him on his horse—but was being indebted to a murderer really any better than dying? How could she return to the camp knowing Johnny was still there? Her family was dead, her belongings were all gone. She had nothing. Her only companion was a murderer. Death, even a slow one under the scorching sun, from dehydration, would surely be a blessing.

• • • • • • •

An hour had passed and Jessica still hadn't returned to camp. The sun was going down and the herd was bedded down for the night. Frank was one of the night riders out watching over the herd, and the nighthawk was watching over the remuda. All the men in camp were sitting around the campfire talking quietly amongst themselves. Mr. Jordan was surprised to see Johnny had obeyed his orders and remained in camp instead of going out after Jessica—it was obvious he had wanted to follow after her, even though Jessica had made it clear she didn't want him to.

"Jessica still hasn't returned," he said, concern evident in his voice.

Mr. Jordan nodded. "Right," he said. "I'll go find her. Davey!" he called, "you're coming with me. You can track Miss Jessica. We need to find her before dark." Swinging up into the saddle, both men rode out in the direction Jessica had headed.

Davey tracked her easily—her footprints left a distinctive mark to the rocks, and there were enough broken branches and misplaced stones that he was able to see clearly where she'd climbed over the rocks and dodged around the scrub. After just a quarter hour of riding they saw her, sitting huddled on a rock, her cheek resting on her knees. She was the picture of misery, and both men felt sorry for her instantly.

"You head on back, Davey," Mr. Jordan ordered gruffly. "I'll take it from here."

Jessica looked up as Mr. Jordan approached and he extended his hand out to her, intending to help her up onto his horse, behind him. "Come on up," he invited, "and I'll take you back to camp."

She shook her head. "No. I'm not going back."

"Well, you can't stay out here," Mr. Jordan told her sternly.

"I'm not going back there. I don't care if I die out here, I can't go back there."

"Why not?" Mr. Jordan asked.

"Because Johnny's a killer!" she declared. "I watched my entire family be murdered, now you want me to go back to the presence of a murderer?"

"Johnny's not a murderer." Mr. Jordan spoke softly,

calmly, his deep baritone voice gruff, making him sound angry, even though he wasn't. "You need to give him a chance to explain."

"What is there to explain?" Jessica cried, close to tears again.

"It's a very different place out here, from where you grew up. It's every man for himself out here, shoot or be shot. What would you have done in his shoes? At least hear him out."

Stubbornly, Jessica shook her head again. She couldn't; she just couldn't. She was too afraid. After seeing her entire family killed, and knowing how that felt, how could she trust a man she knew had killed someone? A man who clearly thought little of the value of human life; a man who was responsible for making a family feel the same utter desolation she felt now? She couldn't go back. Not if Johnny was going to be there.

Mr. Jordan leaned down and grabbed hold of her arm, but she struggled furiously. "Let me go!" she shrieked.

"Calm down," Mr. Jordan crooned, but Jessica ignored him.

"I will not calm down!" she yelled. "I don't think I will be calm ever again! Don't you tell me to calm down! You don't know what this is like for me!" She backed away from the horse, stumbling over the rock she'd been sitting on, nearly falling down.

Mr. Jordan dismounted and walked toward her.

"Get away from me!" she shouted, near hysterical. She tried to back away but she was trapped—Mr. Jordan was on one side of her, and on the other side was the rock. If she'd had more time she could have clambered over it, but there was no time; Mr. Jordan was reaching out for her. Putting a strong arm across her back and around her waist, he bent her over under his arm, holding her in position against his hip before landing a hard swat to her backside.

"Ow!" she shrieked, struggling to get away. She kicked out at Mr. Jordan's shins and fought furiously, but she was no match for his strength. A big man, Mr. Jordan was used to wrestling cattle and fighting grown men—a small woman such as Jessica was effortless to hold. He swatted her twice more, slightly harder.

"Are you ready to listen, and go back to camp now?" he asked, letting her stand up but keeping a firm grip on her shoulders.

"No!" she yelled in outrage. Who did Mr. Jordan think he was? She'd already been spanked by a man once since her family had been killed; was men spanking women some kind of code of the west out here? If it was, she didn't like it. She'd known she hadn't wanted to leave Boston and come west, but getting her backside blistered by men she barely knew hadn't been one of the reasons why. It had never occurred to her that it could possibly happen. Would any of her Boston suitors have dared to take her in hand like that? She knew they wouldn't have—they were civilized gentlemen, not cattle-driving brutes.

Mr. Jordan sighed. "We'll do this the hard way then." He dragged her over to the rock that had been blocking her escape just seconds ago and sat down on it, hauling her across his dusty thigh. With one hand on her back holding her firmly in place he swatted her again, putting a lot more power into the swats this time, spanking her hard and fast through her skirts and reducing her to a quivering, blubbering mess in no time. Each smack felt like she was being branded with a hot iron, and the pain from one had barely registered when another hard swat was landing. The fire in her bottom was intensifying, building with every successive smack the big man laid down. Jessica wriggled and squirmed, fighting to get away, but it was futile. The hard leather of his chaps dug into her and rubbed against her roughly with every movement, and still the spanks kept falling. Mr. Jordan seemed to be even stronger than Johnny was. And like Johnny before him, he didn't need to use a strap to set her bottom on fire; the powerful muscles behind his huge, hard hand did the job just fine.

"Okay, I'll go with you, just let me go! Please let me go!" she begged, tears streaming down her cheeks, barely able to breathe she was sobbing so hard.

Mr. Jordan let her up and it was all she could do to stand on her feet without falling over. She didn't remember ever crying so much in her life as she'd done just in the past few days. It seemed like all she did was cry. And when she wasn't crying, she was consumed with grief and wanted to cry.

"Stop crying, I wasn't that hard on you," Mr. Jordan scolded, but there was a kindness in his eyes, despite the stern gruffness of his tone.

With great effort, she fought back any further tears and suppressed the sobs that were building in her throat. "You don't get it, do you?" she sniffled, struggling to win the battle against her emotions. "I don't want to go back there. I just want you to leave me alone out here to die!"

Mr. Jordan shook his head slowly. "That won't be happening, miss." She watched as Mr. Jordan untied the bandanna that he wore knotted loosely around his neck and used it to wipe away her tears. "Now you listen up, 'cause I'm only going to say this once. You're going to get up behind me on my horse, we're going to ride back to camp, and you're going to hear Johnny out. And no more talk about dying, you hear?" Then he patted her shoulder gently and gave her a kind smile before getting back on his horse and helping her up behind him. She grabbed a handful of his waistcoat and held on tight, conscious of the powerful muscles of his work-hardened body beneath her fingers.

"Have you ever shot a man, Mr. Jordan?" she asked, as they were riding back to camp. It wasn't comfortable sitting on the horse; her bottom was aching terribly, and every time her body was jolted from the movement of the horse she was reminded of being over Mr. Jordan's knee, all thoughts of dignity gone as she flailed around helplessly trying to escape the stinging swats he was administering. She was mortified; now not only had Mr. Jordan seen Johnny spank her, he'd spanked her himself. She would never be able to look him in the eye again! What had she done in Boston that had been so terrible that the fates had led her to this?

Without turning around, he answered her. "I was in the war."

"But other than that, have you?" Jessica knew what war was like. While her family had been exempt from much of the suffering the war had caused, one of her Boston suitors had a brother who'd been killed in it, and his mother had never been the same since.

Mr. Jordan twisted his body around in the saddle and turned to look at her. "Yep," he admitted. "Not many of us drovers, cowboys, whatever you want to call us, haven't; usually in self-defense, always a fair fight. There's a difference between shooting because you have to and shooting because you want to. We don't just go around killing innocent people; they had it coming to 'em."

Jessica was silent for the rest of the ride back. She was lost in her thoughts. Mr. Jordan was right—the way she was raised was very different to the way of life out here. She wasn't sure if she could get used to it; she wasn't sure that she *wanted* to get used to it. She'd been born and bred in civilization; what did the wilderness have to offer someone like her? She hoped they would soon be in a town so she could wire her great-aunt and make the necessary arrangements to return home to Boston, to a life she understood.

Johnny was waiting for her when they got back to camp and he reached up for her, lifting her gently down to the ground. She tensed up when he put a hand against the small of her back to lead her away from the horse, but Mr. Jordan looked at her sternly, leaving her in no doubt as to what would happen if she didn't follow Johnny. Subconsciously, her hand went to her bottom to rub away the still-lingering sting, but she quickly pulled it away when Mr. Jordan cleared his throat. They went over to the relative privacy behind the chuck wagon, away from the men, away from listening ears, where Johnny could tell her the full story.

"I had a job as a hand on a cattle ranch in Texas," he said in his soft voice. "I liked it, wish I'd stayed there. Anyway, went into town one night, joined a poker game in the saloon. I didn't know it, but the game was rigged. It had been set up so that one of the men at the table would lose everything, revenge for something, I don't know what. I won a lot of money that night, winning game after game, and I'm not a good poker player. I'm not a gambler. As I said, it was rigged. Frank's brother, his name was Ted, accused me of cheating. I didn't know Ted, never seen him before in my life, but when he pulled his gun on me I reacted. He drew first; I was quicker. It was a fair fight, Jessie, I promise you. But I killed him. After that, I didn't know what to do. I couldn't go back to the ranch—the sheriff would catch me for sure. So I ran. And I've been runnin' ever since. And if that makes me a bad man in your eyes, then I'm sorry. There's nothing I can do about that. But I was raised in a good family, and I'd like to go back to that good family again one day, when I got myself something I'm proud of to take back with me."

Jessica didn't know what to say. What was there to say? Was he expecting her to just forgive him, to pretend everything was all right? Well, it wasn't. Nothing had changed. She'd obeyed Mr. Jordan's orders and heard Johnny out, but that was all she was able to do. The memories of her family's brutal murders were still too fresh in her mind for her to be able to be friendly to a man she knew was guilty of taking another man's life. He went to put his arm around her.

"No." Jessica shook her head, taking a step backwards away from him. His face fell; he obviously cared more about her than she'd thought, and for just a moment, she felt mean. "I'm sorry." Needing to get away, knowing she had to leave now, she turned and walked away, back to the supply wagon, where she bedded down for the night without speaking to anybody.

As she lay in the makeshift bed in the back of the wagon,

listening to the sounds of camp—muffled singing, laughter, whispered words—her mind wandered, confused. She'd felt so safe with Johnny, so protected, and she'd truly believed he would never let any harm befall her. So what had happened? What had changed? The truth had come out, but Johnny hadn't changed, had he?

She remembered the tender way Johnny had cared for her. The way he'd willingly shared his food and water, even though it meant he would run out himself before they reached the next town. The way he'd given her his bedroll that first night when they'd camped at the wagon train site. The caring, compassionate way he'd buried their dead, and how he'd tried so hard to be there for her. She remembered the way it felt to be in his arms, so strong and so secure, holding her so tightly, possessively, protecting her. She remembered how he'd kissed her briefly last night, and how she'd been looking forward to it happening again. Now it wouldn't… and it was that thought that made her saddest of all.

Her emotions were all over the place. She wished she didn't know the truth—she liked Johnny. But could she trust him again? Could she bring herself to trust a man who had taken the life of another?

What would ma have done? Then she realized how irrelevant it was, asking herself that question. Ma had been born and bred in Boston—and that wouldn't have happened in Boston. In Boston they had the law to settle matters. Out here, matters were settled as best as they could be, by the men involved. Boston was a whole world away from the wilderness and the lack of law, the code of the West.

As the noise of the camp died down, Jessica found she could barely keep her eyes open, and even though confused thoughts were still swirling around in her head, she drifted off to a dreamless sleep.

CHAPTER FIVE

Sometime in the night, Jessica woke up. After tossing and turning for a while, she went to the edge of the wagon and sat down, leaning out, watching the stars. She'd done that a lot as a child back in Boston; lying on the grass with Petey, just watching the stars. But as she got older and ma had started teaching her everything she would need to know to run a household, there hadn't been time for such simple pleasures as stargazing. Even in Boston, in their small house, with their maid, there had been a lot of work to be done. Her ma had liked to host dinner parties, using the fancy china and fine linen that had been her mother's, and Jessica had always helped with the preparation—polishing the silverware and helping in the kitchen. *I wonder what happened to all those nice things?* she wondered, trying to recall where it had all gone. It hadn't come along with them on the trail; pa had been adamant that all frivolities—and ma's lovely dinner set had been a frivolity—had to be left behind. The only things they'd been able to take with them had been those things that would be essential for setting up their new life out on the prairie.

What's that? She sat up straighter, straining her eyes to see. *There! It moved again!* There was someone over by the remuda, and it wasn't the night hawk. *I wonder who that is?* Curious, her senses on high alert, Jessica cautiously clambered over the tailgate of the wagon, being careful not to make a sound, and dropped silently to the ground. As swiftly as she could, trying to stay out of sight, she hurried toward the remuda. There was more than one person over there, that much was obvious, but there were no signs of a struggle; no noise, no battles. *What's happened to the nighthawk? Why isn't he raising the alarm?* She considered running back to camp to alert the drovers, but she wanted to be sure of what she was seeing before she woke everyone up—after all, she'd caused enough problems for the men already without disturbing their sleep unnecessarily.

As she got closer to the group of horses all tied to the rope at the edge of the camp, she knew what it was she was seeing: Indians. She gasped in horror as the memory of the brutal massacre of her family came back to haunt her. Were these the same ones? She had no idea, no way of knowing. But either way, same group or not, they were definitely up to no good. She took a deep breath, trying to calm her racing heart, wiping her clammy hands down the front of her petticoat. She shivered against the cold. She'd removed her gown to sleep, and her thin petticoat didn't provide much protection against the elements. She'd been so eager to find out who was disrupting the remuda that she hadn't thought to bring a blanket to cover herself, or a coat to keep out the wind. Crouching down on the ground, she rubbed her temples, trying to still her shaking body. *Indians... blood... death.* The images went racing round and round in her mind, blurring together, getting tangled and flipped upside down, searing into her brain. *No! They can't be here!* Desperately, she tried to force herself to breathe calmly, to think.

She couldn't stay here, she had to get away. She needed to wake the drovers. But as she stood up she discovered her legs wouldn't hold her up; they had turned to jelly, and she cried out as she crumpled to the ground. Immediately, she stuffed her fist into her mouth to stifle any more noises, but it was too late—there was movement just to the side of her.

"Johnny!" she screamed, then a huge hand clamped down over her mouth, pulling her backwards, lifting her off her feet. Panic gripped her. She tried to bite the hand that was covering her mouth, she kicked, flailed, wriggled, punched... she fought desperately to get away, but it was futile. The Indian who had grabbed her was too strong and he held her fast. He half-carried, half-dragged her over to a pinto pony and stuffed a rag in her mouth, tying it securely behind her head, effectively gagging her. Then he bound her wrists with a thin strip of rawhide before draping her across the back of the pony. There was no saddle, not even a blanket on the pony to protect her, and the rough hair tickled her, irritating her. The Indian leapt onto the pony as well, holding her firmly to stop her falling off, but leaving her in that most undignified position, belly-down over the pinto.

She was terrified. Even watching her family get slaughtered hadn't been as frightening as this was; her heart was beating so loudly she was sure her captor would be able to hear it. Positioned as she was, she couldn't draw a proper breath, but she was still breathing far too fast, the short, shallow inhalations doing nothing to calm her.

Whirling the pony around, the Indian took off at a gallop after the other Indians, abandoning whatever plans they may have had for the remuda.

Jessica struggled violently. She knew she had to get away. She worked at the gag in her mouth with her teeth and tongue, trying desperately to spit it out so she could scream; at the same time her fingers worked at the knot restraining her wrists. She was rolling her body and kicking, doing everything she could to roll off the pony, but her captor held her fast. Her struggles didn't even seem to bother him—he just kept galloping his pony after the others, not even noticing her efforts at escape.

Finally, her tongue loosened her gag enough for her to spit it partially out of her mouth. She took as big a breath as she could and screamed at the top of her lungs, an ear-piercing screech that echoed over the plains and jolted the Indian into action. Raising his fist, he brought it down hard on the side of her face. Jessica felt a dull thudding pain momentarily, then everything went black.

• • • • • • •

Johnny sat up. Someone, far away, had called his name. Screamed it rather desperately, in fact. *Jessica!* He sat bolt upright in his bedroll, throwing the blanket aside, hurriedly pulling on his boots before scurrying over to the supply wagon. He pulled aside the canvas cover and looked in. Nothing. *Where the hell was she?* He cursed under his breath, looking around. There was nothing amiss that he could see. But he couldn't see Jessica, either. Hoping she'd just gone to relieve herself in the bushes, he decided to wait. There would be no point returning to his bed now; he wouldn't be able to sleep, not until he knew she was okay. The minutes passed. Jessica didn't return.

"Is she in there?" Mr. Jordan asked quietly. The scream had obviously woken him too, and he brushed past Johnny to look inside the wagon himself. She was gone. "The remuda!" Mr. Jordan took off at a run with Johnny on his heels.

Mr. Jordan breathed a sigh of relief when he saw that the remuda was safe, but that relief quickly turned to a gasp of horror when he looked closer. Lying face down on the dusty ground, an arrow in his back, was the young nighthawk, a drover whose name Johnny didn't know. Crouching down beside him, Mr. Jordan rolled him onto his side gently. "He's dead."

"Indians?" He'd meant it as a statement rather than a question; Johnny knew it was Indians who had killed the young man—but it came out sounding like a question anyway.

"Yep." Mr. Jordan had already stood up from the

ground and was looking around, but there wasn't much to see; it was too dark.

"They've got Jessica!" It was a definite statement this time, and panic gripped him. *I've let her down! I promised to take care of her and I've let her down!* He pulled a match out of his coat pocket and struck it, holding it out in front of him, shielding the small flame from the breeze with his hand. Crouching to the ground, he could make out clear footprints, and the signs of a struggle. The Indians definitely had Jessica. *I've got to find her.*

Mr. Jordan was already striding back to camp to rouse the men. "Davey!" Johnny heard him holler, and relief flooded through him. Mr. Jordan was obviously not going to waste any time in finding her; Davey was a good scout, a good tracker, but how much would he be able to do in the dark? Stooping over, using the small, flickering flame as his guide, he squinted at the dusty ground before him, trying to make sense of it, but he couldn't see what direction the tracks led; there were footprints everywhere.

Davey was carrying a lantern he'd borrowed out of the supply wagon when he came and stood next to Johnny, crouching down so he could examine the footprints.

"Indians?" Johnny asked.

"I'm not sure," Davey replied. "All the Indians in these parts are friendly. Might be an outlaw gang wanting us to think they're Indians." He took another look at the tracks. "Either that or the same band of renegade Indians that attacked your wagon train." He looked directly at Johnny. "They're known for their brutality. They're not normally this far north, but it could be them."

"So it's either outlaws or rebel Indians. Either way, she's in danger," Johnny stated.

"Yes, I think so," Davey agreed. "We're not going to find her tonight though."

"Keep looking." The aggression in Johnny's tone surprised even himself, and his shoulders slumped. "I'm sorry, Davey, but I need to find her. She'll be terrified."

"I know." Davey stood up. "But I can't track her now, it's too dark. Even with the lantern I can't see enough." He shook his head as Mr. Jordan approached. "It's no good, boss, it's just too dark."

"We'll look for her at first light then."

"No!" Johnny was horrified. They had to find her! "We have to keep looking! I promised her I'd take care of her, we can't leave her out there alone... with them! Give me your lantern, Davey, I'm going myself." He reached out for it, but Davey stepped back.

"Just wait until morning." Mr. Jordan was insistent, implacable.

"No. I'm going now."

"Look, Johnny, if you go now, all that's going to happen is you're going to wipe away the tracks that are there. It's too dark to see, you won't find her, and you'll destroy what chance we have of finding her come daylight." Davey sounded impatient, but his words were sound. Johnny knew he couldn't fault the truth in that argument, but he still didn't like it.

"She'll be safe enough until morning," Mr. Jordan reassured him. "They won't do anything to her yet. We'll set off at first light, as soon as we can see." Mr. Jordan put a reassuring, restraining hand on Johnny's shoulder, and Johnny knew he was right. He didn't want to wait, he wanted to go now, but he wanted Jessica to have the best chance of rescue, and that meant waiting. "Davey, you take over as nighthawk for the rest of first watch. Johnny, you help me bring the body back over to camp. We'll bury him in the morning."

• • • • • • •

Where am I? Blinking rapidly, trying to help her eyes adjust to the dim light, she looked around her, but nothing looked familiar. She was tied to a tree, with her wrists bound tightly behind her, laced to the other side of the thick tree trunk. Her feet were stretched out in front of her and there was a cord around her ankles as well. Even worse, a dirty rag was stuffed in her mouth so tightly that she couldn't even move her tongue. Her jaw was aching from where the Indian had hit her. Suddenly, realization dawned as she figured out where she was, and she gasped in horror at the reality of her nightmare coming true. She remembered the way they'd ridden in to the wagon train camp on their paint ponies, their war cries echoing over the plains. She shuddered at the remembered crack of the rifles and gasped at the accuracy and swiftness of the silent arrows as they hit their mark time after time; watching her friends fall, bleeding and dying, one after the other. Her father had fallen first, and had lain on the ground writhing in agony, moaning in pain. Petey, her little brother, had been next. The Indians had shown no compassion, no mercy; the children had been killed just as easily as their fathers. And the women... they had suffered the same fate. The heartbroken scream her mother had uttered when Petey went down still sounded inside her head, but before she had reached him, an Indian arrow had cut her down, too. Now they had her... what fate awaited her at their hands?

Her heart stilled momentarily, then started racing as her breathing quickened, and every fiber of her being shrieked in terror. She tried to open her mouth to scream, but she couldn't—the gag was too tight. She was so paralyzed by fear, she couldn't even think. But she knew she had to. If she was going to come out of this alive, she had to think, had to come up with a plan.

Would Johnny rescue her? She didn't know. She'd shunned him the last time she'd seen him, so maybe he wouldn't. Maybe he'd be glad to see the last of her. He'd shown her nothing but kindness and she'd thrown it back in his face. She would deserve it if he abandoned her. But when she thought about it, even in her fuzzy, aching, panicking state, she knew Johnny wouldn't abandon her. She didn't know how she knew it, she just did. And she knew it for certain. There was always the distinct possibility that Johnny wouldn't be able to rescue her, but she knew he would try. *Oh, papa,* she groaned to herself. *Why did you make us leave Boston?*

• • • • • • •

The camp was quiet. Even though all the drovers had woken up and knew what had happened, they all fell back asleep almost instantly. *Don't they care about Jessica?* Johnny thought bitterly. *Aren't they worried about her?* Without even thinking about it, he knew the answer. It would take more than just one day on drag for her to redeem herself; she'd made it pretty obvious what she thought of them all. And even though she'd apologized, he knew words were so often shallow, meaningless. The men may not have realized her apology had been genuine. And drovers had their pride.

Sick of tossing and turning, he got up. *May as well make myself useful,* he thought, as he went to the supply wagon and found a shovel. There was a grave to dig, a body to bury, before they'd be able to move out in the morning, and the light of the moon was enough to see by to start that job. As he dug, his mind wandered back to that fateful day not very long ago when he'd dug the graves for the massacred wagon train and helped Jessica bury her family. And now she'd been captured by the very people responsible for that massacre. If Davey was right, and it was the one brutal outlaw band doing the killing, terrorizing and kidnapping, Jessica was in trouble.

Throwing the shovel down in disgust, he put his head in his hands for a moment, overwhelmed by the utter hopelessness that surrounded him. Outlaw Indians had Jessica and there was nothing he could do. He would have to rely on the help of the other men to rescue her; men who didn't care for her, didn't know her, probably didn't even like her very much. Sighing, knowing he would just have to wait, he picked up the shovel again and began digging with a renewed vigor. If there was one thing he was good at, it was digging graves.

• • • • • • •

The Indian camp was starting to come alive. It wasn't yet fully daylight but there were signs of activity; fires were being kindled, braves were moving around in the shadows. She had a good view of the entire camp from her position against the tree; it looked small, far too small to be a regular Indian village. There were only a few small, hastily erected teepees and it didn't look as if they'd been in this spot for very long. What tribe were these Indians? The only woman she could see was a white woman, blond, dressed in pants and a shirt, and she was carting water under the watchful eye of one of the men. Was she a slave? The woman looked fearfully across at Jessica, but no one came near her, and for that, she was grateful. As long as she was ignored, maybe they'd forget about her, and she might have a slim chance of survival. Then the irony of that thought hit her. It had only been last night when she'd wanted to die, when she'd told Mr. Jordan to leave her alone out there in the wilderness, when she'd declared that she didn't want to live anymore. And maybe that was still true—maybe she did still feel that way. But if she was going to die, she didn't want it to be at the hands of the Indians. So she sat still, pressing her back hard against the tree, trying to make herself invisible. She shivered; it was cold. She could feel bruising coming up on her jaw where her captor had hit her last night and her head was fuzzy. There was a blanket half over her legs that someone had obviously thrown on her last night to keep her warm but it had long since come off and she couldn't put it back. She tried to ease her legs further under it, but all she succeeded in doing was sliding it off more. Taking a deep breath, she forced down the bile that was rising up in her throat. It wouldn't do to lose the plot and start choking now—her best chance of survival was being ignored, giving Johnny time to rescue her. *Come on, Johnny,* she silently pleaded.

CHAPTER SIX

The early morning air was rent with the haunting melody of a hymn being played on Johnny's harmonica as the drovers stood around the grave he'd dug the night before, their hats in their hands as a mark of respect, their faces drawn and somber. It was always hard to lose one of their own, even more so in circumstances like this. The young nighthawk wouldn't have had a chance—they all knew how silently Indians could move in the shadows and how accurate their arrows were, even in the dark. No one envied Mr. Jordan his job of riding into town later in the day to wire the tragic news to the boy's parents, but it was a job that had to be done. Just twenty-one years old, his life had barely begun, now it had been snuffed out so ruthlessly, so needlessly. And there would be more bloodshed before the day was over.

• • • • • • •

"If they were interested in trading Jessica for steers they would have turned up here by now," Davey told them. "Their intent last night wasn't to trade; it was to steal. To get her back, we're going to have to fight for her."

"I say we just leave her there," one of the drovers, whose name Johnny didn't know, piped up. "She only thinks we're a pack of dusty, smelly cowhands anyway!" There were murmurs of agreement all around, and Johnny's heart clenched. What would he do if the men wouldn't help him rescue her? He couldn't do it by himself…

"Yeah," Frank agreed. "I say just leave her to the Indians. They're welcome to her!"

It took all Johnny's self-control not to walk over there and take Frank down, and his breath caught when Mr. Jordan took a deep breath beside him, preparing to issue an order. Which way would Mr. Jordan go? Would he rescue Jessica, or would he side with his men?

"It doesn't matter what she thinks of us!" Woody exclaimed. "We can't just leave her to the Indians! That could be any one of our women out there, any one of our sisters! Why should it be any different just because it's Jessica?" Relieved at the unexpected ally in Woody, Johnny smiled across at him.

"I'm with Woody," Chuck declared loudly. "I say we rescue her."

"She saved the remuda, remember that." Mr. Jordan fixed them all with a hard stare before continuing. "If she hadn't screamed, you'd all be in for a long walk this morning."

"She could have come and woken us up instead of screaming," Frank pointed out.

"You know she watched Indians kill her family; Davey thinks these are the same ones. She would have been terrified seeing them in camp!" Johnny was quick to defend her.

"Any man who doesn't want to come can stay here with the herd. Hold them here until we get back. If we're not back by noon tomorrow, move on." Mr. Jordan gave his orders in a stern, no-nonsense tone. Then he turned to his ramrod. "Woody, you're in charge."

"I'd like to come along, sir," Woody argued.

"I need someone with some brains here to take charge if necessary. Davey, I need you with me, and three more men. The rest of you, stay with the herd." The order was abrupt, and Mr. Jordan turned and started walking toward his horse with Davey, Chuck, and Johnny on his heels. After only a momentary pause, two more men followed. Frank wasn't among them.

It didn't take long for them to saddle up their horses and move out, and it wasn't hard for Davey to track them in the dim light of the early morning. He had some idea of where the Indians would have made their temporary camp; he'd scouted this trail before, and he knew the area well.

As they rode, they hatched a plan. It sounded so simple... Johnny just hoped it would work. If it didn't... well, that just didn't bear thinking about.

• • • • • • •

Jessica was cold. She was so cold she couldn't stop trembling, and her teeth were chattering so hard she could hear them rattling. Her thin petticoat had torn in her struggles last night and the blanket that had been partially covering her had slipped off more. Her jaw was aching and she was dizzy; even if she somehow did manage to loosen the knots in the cord binding her, she wondered if she would be able to run to freedom, given the opportunity, considering the state she was in. Her legs were cramped from being stretched out in front of her for so long and her wrists and ankles were chafed from being bound so tightly. She tried to swallow, but her mouth was too dry. The foul-tasting rag stuffed in her mouth had soaked up all the saliva and she couldn't move her tongue around to make any more. She tried to groan, but couldn't even manage that. *Come on, Johnny!* she silently pleaded.

Blinking rapidly to clear her vision, she looked toward the ridge edging the makeshift camp again. She blinked and looked again, squinting into the distance. She wasn't seeing things—the guard she'd been watching since the sun had first started to come up, had disappeared. He hadn't just gone for a walk; she'd seen him fall, and when she looked again after blinking, he still wasn't there. Did that mean Johnny was coming? She hadn't heard a shot, but that didn't mean anything. There were other, silent methods of disposing of a guard. She twisted around as much as her bonds would allow and craned her neck to see. Someone—was it Johnny? No, someone else, it was too short for Johnny—rode furiously into the Indians' camp, yelling and shooting, and stampeded the Indian horses, chasing them away. She looked around, bewildered, as the sound of gunshots echoed around, and several running braves fell. Not many of them were armed, and they were being shot down as they ran. The attack from the drovers had obviously caught them completely unawares—usually the sentries they had posted would warn them of any impending danger, or take care of it before it became a threat.

Looking around at the chaos surrounding her, Jessica smiled. *He's come.*

"Jessica!" Johnny hissed from beside her and she jumped, startled. She hadn't heard his footsteps over the sound of the gunshots, and she hadn't seen him coming either; she'd been looking in the other direction. He was opening the blade of a pocket knife.

"Mmmmf!" she mumbled, trying to speak. Grabbing the rag stuffed in her mouth, he pulled it out, throwing it violently to the ground beside them. Then with one swift movement he cut the cord tying her wrists and pulled her to her feet. Desperately, she swirled her tongue around inside her mouth, moistening it.

"Johnny!" she cried, tears of relief streaming down her face. She wrapped her arms around him, ignoring the searing pain in her hands as the blood flowed back into her fingers.

After cutting the cord around her ankles, he grabbed her hand and started running, but she stumbled, her legs numb from being outstretched for so long, and from the cold.

"Dammit, Jessica, run!" he yelled, but it was no use. She tried to stand up, but she promptly fell down again.

"I can't," she moaned, desperate. She willed her legs to move, but they just wouldn't. Wrapping an arm around her waist, Johnny threw her roughly over his broad shoulder and started running, and she clung frantically to the back of his shirt as Johnny raced in a zigzag, dodging flying arrows, back to the horses. Lifting her head to look, she could see an Indian drawing his bow, the arrow aimed at the drovers. "Look out!" she screamed, but it was too late. Johnny reached the horses and passed her up to Davey just as Chuck crumpled to the ground beside them. He'd been shooting from behind a rock, covering Johnny as he'd rescued her, and had just been mounting his horse when the arrow struck him.

Davey kicked his horse into a gallop before Jessica was properly on, and she clung to him, terrified, as they raced back toward the herd. In the distance, she could see drovers all heading in the same direction; they'd obviously had the Indian camp surrounded.

"Chuck!" she gasped, then had to grab tightly to Davey's leg when the horse dodged around a bush.

"Johnny will bring him. Hang on tight; we've got to get you out of here!"

She did hang on. She was draped most un-elegantly across Davey's saddle, and her mind was taken back to the last time she found herself in that position, on Johnny's horse, getting her butt spanked. There was no spanking going on this time though, just frantic clutching at Davey's pants leg as he held her tightly with one hand while they galloped. She was too focused on survival to be worried about the view Davey would have of her; and if she were honest, she didn't even care. She'd been kidnapped by Indians and heroically rescued; the fact that she was wearing nothing but a filthy, torn petticoat that was flapping around as they rode was the least of her worries.

They'd been galloping hard for several miles before Davey reined up. Mr. Jordan and the two other drovers who had been involved in her rescue had all gathered under a tree, waiting for them.

"Johnny and Chuck?" Mr. Jordan asked, his voice deep and gruff, concerned.

"Chuck took an arrow, Johnny's bringing him. I didn't stick around to check, just brought Jessica out as fast as I could." Davey slid her gently to the ground and she steadied herself by leaning against the neck of the heavily blowing horse.

"Are you okay, miss?" one of the drovers asked.

"Yes. Thanks to all of you." She recognized the drover who'd spoken to her as the cowboy who'd stampeded the Indians' horses, and she was grateful. Stampeding the horses had not only caused chaos within the camp, enabling Johnny to rescue her, but it meant the Indians wouldn't be able to chase after them. At least, not until they'd rounded up their horses, and by then, they'd all be back with the herd. It had been dangerous though—the cowboy had taken a risk, and she was pleased to see he'd escaped unscathed. Then her heart wrenched in pain when she thought of Chuck. Was there any chance he would survive? How about Johnny? Would he get hurt bringing Chuck's body back? She hoped not.

It was only a few seconds later that they saw two more horses galloping toward them, one rider slumped forward clearly in pain—Chuck and Johnny. A thrill went through her. *He's safe! They're both safe!* Immediately, those first words she'd spoken upon arrival in the trail drive camp came back to her, and she was ashamed. It was true—the drovers did smell, and they were dusty. There was no denying that. But they were courageous men, capable men, men who did whatever it took to get the job done. And at that very moment, she had nothing but admiration for the lot of them.

Jessica could see the arrow sticking out of Chuck's

shoulder, and she shuddered. She'd seen those same arrows shoot down her family; she knew how lucky Chuck was to escape with his life—all because he'd been willing to put himself in danger to rescue her.

"Thank you." The words didn't seem to be enough, but they were sincere, and as she rested her palm lightly on Chuck's dusty thigh and looked up into his eyes, she knew he understood just how grateful she really was.

He didn't answer, he just nodded in response, pain etched deeply across his face. One hand clutched the reins, the other hand held his shoulder, blood oozing out between his fingers and soaking the sleeve of his shirt.

"Let's get you back to camp." Mr. Jordan and Davey flanked Chuck's horse, and Johnny extended his hand down to her to pull her up behind him. As she wrapped her arms around his waist and pressed her cheek into his broad back, she inhaled the scent of him. Dust, cows, sweat… an unmistakable manly scent that had become not only familiar to her, but almost precious; it was the scent of Johnny. The man who had rescued her, twice, and asked for nothing in return. Her hero.

"Monty!" The drover in the lead went cantering into camp yelling for the cook. Chuck had collapsed in the saddle from the pain of the arrow that was still embedded in his shoulder, and Monty with his prairie doctoring skills was his only hope. Mr. Jordan and Davey lifted him down off the horse and carried him over to the fire, laying him down on a blanket that Billy was hastily spreading on the ground.

He's obviously done this before, Jessica thought. *So young, but he's seen so much.*

It occurred to her then how different Billy's life must have been from hers, brought up in the respectable, civilized Boston. What had Billy seen? What had Johnny seen?

Mr. Jordan, Davey, Monty, and a few other men were all crowded around Chuck, doing what they could to make him comfortable, but Jessica was still shivering with cold. The sun was high in the sky now and the day had warmed up, but the bone-numbing chill that pervaded her body hadn't entirely left yet, and the thin petticoat she was wearing didn't provide much in the way of warmth.

Johnny put his arm around her shoulders and led her to the supply wagon. Reaching in, he pulled out a coat and the pants and shirt that she'd been wearing on the trail. "Here, put these on," he said, handing them to her. "Then we'll get some coffee into you, get you warmed up. You still look frozen." The smile he gave her nearly melted her insides—somehow, the ravishing cowboy looked even more ruggedly handsome with stubble on his strong jaw, dust streaked across his face, and sweat glistening on his brow.

Taking the clothes, she turned away, retreating to other side of the wagon to put them on in privacy.

• • • • • • •

"Chuck's in the back of the supply wagon, miss," Mr. Jordan told her quietly as evening wore on. "So I hope you don't mind bedding down with us. But don't worry," he raised his voice. "My men will all be gentlemen; none of them will give you any trouble." He fixed the drovers with a stern stare that made it clear he meant business.

"Oh, I'm not worried," Jessica assured him. "Your men have been nothing but kind to me. Even when I didn't deserve it." She looked around at the gathered men and smiled at them, pleased when Woody and a few others tipped their hats to her. "Besides, I'll be with Johnny. He'll protect me." She reached for his hand then, clutching his fingers tightly with her own, stepping closer to him.

"Johnny will be with the herd for part of the night, we'll be doubling the night watch just in case. I don't think the Indians will be back, but we'd best be prepared. We're down two men—Billy, you might even be needed tonight."

"I can help," Jessica offered. But Mr. Jordan shook his head.

"No. Not on the night watch. It's not safe for a woman.

But you can help care for Chuck, free up Billy and Monty a bit. Can you do that?"

Jessica nodded. "Of course. Mama taught me a bit, and Mr. Monty can tell me what else I need to know. Is he all right?"

Mr. Jordan nodded once. "He'll live."

Sitting down by the fire, Jessica leaned her head against Johnny's shoulder as she sighed and closed her eyes.

"You like me again, huh?" Johnny whispered, squeezing her gently.

She didn't speak; just nodded sheepishly. She did like Johnny—that's why she was so confused. She liked the way he treated her, the way he took care of her, his gentle possession of her. She loved the way he looked. She liked everything about him... he was so unlike any man she'd ever known. All her suitors back in Boston had been refined gentlemen, and Johnny was anything but. He was rough, he could be uncouth, he was always covered in dust. His cowboy ways were so different from what she was used to. But despite all that, she liked him.

CHAPTER SEVEN

"I was so tired," she murmured, as she mopped Chuck's sweaty brow with a damp cloth. "We walked all day, in horrible, uncomfortable shoes. I was exhausted, I was so sick and sore, all I wanted to do was lie down. And I never wanted to leave Boston in the first place." Picking up the canteen from the floor of the wagon, she held it up to Chuck's lips and tipped slowly, frowning as it dribbled unchecked down his chin.

She pushed open the flap of the wagon to let in a bit more light, so she could see what she was doing. Monty had patched Chuck up as best he could, but blood was still soaking through the bandage and it would need to be changed.

"I bet you're thinking 'poor little rich girl, what would she know about hardship?' Perhaps you're right. My family wasn't as rich as some, but it was richer than many. So maybe I have led a somewhat privileged life. What I knew about hardship back then would fit into one of the tin mugs we drink our coffee out of…" She let her voice trail off as she unwound the bandage that was wrapped around Chuck's arm. The stitching Monty had done was crude, but it looked to be effective enough. Folding a clean strip of cloth, she pressed the pad against the wound, then used a fresh bandage to hold it in place, tying it securely.

"I didn't want to come out here." For some reason, talking helped. Chuck wasn't responding, but that didn't matter. In fact, in some ways, it made it easier. "Walking all day then having to do all the domestic work around the camp, all the cooking and washing up and mending… it was hard, back-breaking work. I went to finishing school—I was raised to be a lady, not to traipse along in the dust behind the wagons out here in the wilderness. Ma understood, but not pa. Pa just expected me to work, and when I was tired, he was ashamed of me. His last words to me were angry ones. That's how I remember him." Her voice caught then, and she lowered her head to Chuck's chest as tears fell, unbidden, down her cheeks.

Sitting up, she swiped at her eyes with the back of her hand. Billy was banging on a pot with a spoon, summoning the men to come and eat, and she didn't want them to see her crying. They'd seen enough of her vulnerability as it was.

Last night, as camp had quieted down, she'd barely been able to keep her eyes open. The men had all spread their bedrolls in close around the campfire, not spread out like they often were, and she'd fallen asleep almost immediately when she lay down. She'd been so tired she hadn't even stirred when Johnny had slipped his arm out from around her and headed out to take his turn watching the herd. And when daylight had risen and the camp had begun to stir, she'd quickly come into the wagon to check on Chuck. She felt responsible for his injuries—he'd been hurt helping to rescue her, after all.

Tucking the blanket around Chuck securely, she fastened the lid on the canteen and propped it up against the side of the wagon next to him, before slipping out to join the rest of the men for breakfast.

• • • • • • •

THE WAYS OF THE WEST

"Head 'em up! Move 'em out!" Mr. Jordan yelled, waving his hat in a wide circle above his head. Adjusting herself in the saddle trying to get more comfortable, Jessica joined Johnny at the back of the herd, riding drag again. She'd dispensed with her Boston gown entirely, accepting that the ugly pants were by far the most practical item to wear on the trail. Had she been wearing pants when the Indians had captured her, not only would her night have been a bit warmer, but she would have preserved a lot more modesty and retained her dignity. She was still embarrassed when she remembered being draped across Davey's saddle in her ripped petticoats, clutching frantically at the legs of his pants to keep herself from toppling off. If it hadn't been a matter of life and death, she would have refused to get on. As it was, she'd had no choice. And riding back into camp behind Johnny had been only marginally better—she knew none of the men really liked her, and she'd felt so vulnerable, naked almost, wearing nothing but her torn undergarments.

Eating dust wasn't her favorite way to spend the morning, and when they made camp at midday, she was relieved. Woody had promised them both a reprieve from drag; he'd put them on the roster for a different position the next day. The rest of the drovers took turns riding swing, flank, and drag, as none of them liked being at the tail end of the herd. And she knew she had been assigned to it with Johnny as a punishment of sorts—she'd needed to redeem herself for her thoughtless comment on their arrival. The tanning Johnny had given her hadn't been enough, as far as the men were concerned—they wanted to see her eat dust.

It was hard to believe now, but less than a year ago she'd been studying at Miss Bishop's Ladies' Academy preparing for her first season as a debutante, learning how to attract the best of the eligible young men, learning the airs and graces necessary for a young lady of her social standing to master. If she'd married well, she'd be expected to host dinner parties frequently and attend balls and charity functions. And now here she was, covered in dust from head to foot, astride a horse at the tail end of a cattle drive, dressed in men's pants. Her mouth was salivating at the thought of the bacon, beans, and coffee that would make up their noon meal, fare that she would have turned her nose up at not so very long ago.

Chuck returned to the land of the living later that afternoon. As they all washed up before the meal, drying their hands and faces on the damp towel hanging on the side of the chuck wagon, he was sitting on a log by the fire with his arm in a crude sling, eating a plate of beans with gusto.

• • • • • • •

Now that Chuck was better, Jessica was feeling a lot happier about everything. She still missed her family terribly, she still wanted to go back home to Boston, but she was also starting to feel comfortable with the drovers, and regarded them as friends. She sat around the fire, leaning against Johnny, glad of the strong arm he had wrapped around her.

"What are you going to do when I go back to Boston?" she asked him. "Do you think you'll go back to Missouri, back to your family?"

Johnny shrugged. "I might. If I stay on with this drive to the end of the trail, that's Sedalia, Missouri. Not too far from home. But it depends. I promised myself I would never go back, not till I had something I was proud of."

"I'll miss you," she said simply. She knew she would settle quickly back into Boston society, find herself a nice husband and settle down to raise a family, but she would never forget Johnny. He had, quite literally, saved her life.

CHAPTER EIGHT

"Boss! They're going to run!" Davey yelled as he rode into camp. The wind had been picking up all afternoon and now, in the evening twilight, the recent flashes of lightning had unsettled the beeves to the point of stampeding. Wheeling his horse, Davey cantered back to the herd to help the other drovers try to keep the steers calm.

"Everyone in the saddle!" Mr. Jordan called. He turned back to look over his shoulder at Jessica as he strode away toward the remuda. "Jessica, you get into the wagon with Billy and stay out of the way!"

"But I want to help," she protested, leaping up as Johnny got to his feet next to her.

"No!" Mr. Jordan's order was uncompromising and stern.

"Listen to him, Jessie," Johnny whispered in her ear, planting a kiss on her cheek. He tipped his hat to her, winked, and hurried to his horse.

Chuck was riding with his arm still bandaged up and even Monty, the old cook, was headed toward the horses, so she knew they needed all the hands out there that they could get, to save the herd. *I'm not staying here!* she thought. As quickly as she could, she saddled up the nearest horse and galloped out to the herd. So far, they hadn't stampeded, but they were restless, milling around and bellowing, and she knew that if thunder crashed again, that would be it. She'd never seen a stampede before, but she'd heard the drovers all talking about how to stop one. And how hard could it be, really? From what she'd heard, it was just a matter of getting in front of them, yelling and waving your hat, and milling them, making them turn back. It certainly didn't sound very hard.

She could see the other drovers riding back and forth around the herd, she could hear the ones closest to her singing softly, trying to keep them calm. Mr. Jordan was on the far side of the herd and Johnny was at the back. Knowing she was defying orders by being out here, she deliberately kept out of sight, riding at the side of the herd where she wouldn't be seen by either of them.

The flash of lightning illuminated the ground all around her and she could see the steers quivering in fear. The crash of thunder that followed shook the ground and echoed on and on… then she realized that it wasn't the thunder she heard at all, but the pounding hooves of the stampeding beeves.

Spurring her horse, she galloped alongside them, trying to get in front of them, but it was impossible. They weren't running in an orderly line—they were fanning out into a wide front, they were turning, and they were headed straight for her. Waving her arms and shouting, Jessica tried to get them to turn back but she may as well have been invisible—the steers were running blindly, in a panic. She couldn't see any of the drovers now, and she was frightened.

I need to get out of the way! Twisting in her saddle to look around, she could see that she was surrounded by stampeding steers and there was no escape. Her heart was in her throat as she took in the hundreds of Texas Longhorns bearing down on her, getting closer and closer.

I'm going to die. Tonight, right here in the wilderness, I'm going to get trampled to death by runaway beeves. The realization came as a shock, and she screamed. Reliving her childhood as her life flashed before her eyes, her mind conjured up the image of Johnny. That strong, handsome young man who had rescued her, who had been her strength during the darkest moments of her life… that image stayed with her.

Spurring her horse, she tried desperately to outrun the advancing steers, but the front was just too wide and it was moving too quickly. There was nowhere for them to go—the steers were headed straight for them.

"Jessica!" She heard Johnny yell over the roar of the pounding hooves and she stood up in the saddle to see where he was. *He's too far, he'll never make it!* she thought desperately. Woody was racing urgently toward her from the other direction, trying his best to reach her, and Mr. Jordan was yelling orders at his men to head the cattle off the other way, trying to buy Johnny a few more seconds to get to her. But it was futile. The cattle were out of control and the noise was deafening. The horns clinking together sounded like cymbals and the pounding hooves like drums—the prairie version of the symphony orchestra she'd enjoyed visiting in Boston in her past life.

Suddenly her horse stumbled and went down on one knee. Panic overwhelmed her as she clutched desperately at the saddle horn and yanked on the reins. She fell off anyway, flying over his head in a spectacular somersault to land hard on the ground just in front of him. The breath whooshed out of her and she lay winded, stunned, gasping for breath. In a second, the horse was up and galloping again, leaving Jessica lying in the dust, at the mercy of the herd of frenzied steers.

"Johnny!" she screamed, terror making her voice shrill. With great effort she got to her feet, her body trembling, her forehead drenched with sweat. She could feel the ground rumbling beneath her feet, being shaken by the fast-approaching steers.

"Jessica!" She heard Johnny's voice over the thudding of the hooves, that deep baritone rumble resonating through her, snapping her out of her panic. And behind him was another drover, waving his hat and yelling, trying to mill the herd, to regain control. Further over, galloping along the front from the other direction was Woody, doing the same. But it wasn't working—the steers weren't slowing. They were still headed directly for her, for them, and they were still out of control.

Johnny's horse loomed closer and closer and she reached out for him. Without even breaking stride, he leaned out of the saddle and swung her up behind him, galloping at an angle in front of the herd. Wrapping her arms tightly around him, she pressed her body against his hard back, comforted by his warmth and awed by the muscles she could feel rippling under his shirt. Relieved now that she was safe, she let out the breath she hadn't even realized she'd been holding and snuggled up closer against Johnny.

It took several more long minutes before the drovers finally got the herd under control, and as the steers milled, still bellowing but calmer, Davey rode up next to them.

"The boss is not happy with you, Miss Jessica," he drawled. "But I'm glad you're both okay." Then he turned to Johnny. "As close as I can figure it, we're about three miles southwest of camp. Take them back slowly; it'll be easier to do it now than in the morning." Tipping his hat to them both, he rode off to relay Mr. Jordan's instructions to the other drovers.

Once the herd was on the move and they had fallen into position as swing riders, Johnny swiveled around in his saddle to look at her. "What the hell did you have to go and do that for?" he asked her angrily. "What were you thinking? There's going to be hell to pay when we get back to camp; you know that, don't you? Why didn't you just stay in the wagon like you were told? We'll probably both be fired now."

"I wanted to help." Jessica's voice was small, but there was unmistakable defiance in it. "I thought I'd be needed.

Even Chuck and Monty went out. I'm a drover now too; it felt right that I should be helping."

"But you don't have the experience—you were just about killed!" Johnny snarled. "Me and Woody both could have been killed trying to rescue you! Orders are given for a reason. You need to start obeying them."

They continued riding in silence; the steers were easy to manage now that they'd exhausted themselves and they walked placidly back to camp with Johnny having to do very little to keep them headed in the right direction.

"Do you really think we'll be fired?"

Without turning around, Johnny answered her, his tone hard and cold. "You probably will be. And if you go, I'll be going with you. Someone needs to take care of you and I promised you I'd do it."

"You don't need to take care of me. I don't need you." The instant the words were out of her mouth she regretted them, but she couldn't take them back. The truth was, she *did* need Johnny, and she knew it. Maybe she could make out just fine on her own, maybe she wouldn't. But she *wanted* to be with Johnny. She'd come to depend on his quiet strength, his constant companionship, and she *liked* the way he took care of her. It wasn't an accident that his face was the one that flashed into her mind as she waited to be trampled to death by the herd of stampeding steers. His face was there because she loved him.

Reining his horse to a halt, Johnny slid her down off the horse, only to promptly haul her back up again, in front of him this time. And before she was even properly across his saddle, she knew what was about to happen. He'd had her belly-down across his horse once before, and the experience that had followed hadn't been pleasant. She had no doubt that this one wouldn't be any nicer.

Smack! The flat of Johnny's hand landed hard on her seat, and she yelped. This was definitely worse than last time, much worse. Last time she'd been upended like this, the layers of skirts and petticoats she'd been wearing had afforded her some protection from Johnny's heavy hand, but the man's pants she was wearing didn't absorb very much of the stinging impact at all. *Smack! Smack! Smack!* Johnny's big hand fell hard and fast, his fingers spread out to cover most of her bottom with each blow.

Jessica was debating in her mind whether or not the embarrassment was worse than the pain when Johnny landed an extra-hard swat down low, in the juncture where her bottom met her thighs. She buried her face in Johnny's pants leg to stifle her cry of pain, but the debate raging inside her head was solved; the pain was worse.

"You're hurting me! Please stop!" she begged, wrapping her fingers tightly around Johnny's ankle.

"Do you actually think that's all you deserve?"

"No," Jessica admitted. "But it really hurts. I'm sorry!"

"It's meant to hurt," Johnny snarled, smacking the tops of her thighs again. "You're lucky I'm just using my hand. If there were any trees around I'd be cutting a switch to wear out on your backside." He punctuated that statement with two more hard slaps on each cheek.

He stopped spanking and held her securely as he spurred his horse into a canter to head a runaway steer back into the herd, but the reprieve was short-lived. It took less than a minute for Johnny to herd the steer back to the main mob, then he slowed his horse down and continued his task of making Jessica sorry for disobeying orders, landing another hard swat to her thighs. He took up a steady rhythm, spanking her in time with the horse's strides, alternating between her bottom, her thighs, and the juncture between them.

Clinging frantically to Johnny's legs, Jessica bit her lip to fight the urge to cry out. The last thing she wanted to do was draw attention to herself; she didn't want all the men to see her being spanked like a naughty child again. Twilight had deepened, but it wasn't dark yet, and she had no doubt that many of them would be close enough to see what was happening, if they chose to look. She was trying not to kick or struggle too much for fear of spooking the horse, but her legs were kicking of their own accord, spreading wide as well as up and down, flailing around.

Smack! Johnny landed a swat right up high on the inside of her sensitive thigh, one of his fingers brushing against the crotch of her pants. Jessica gasped in both pain and shock. Surely spanking her right there, so close to her intimate lady parts, was crossing a line? She was outraged! Scandalized!

"You stop that right now, Johnny Truman!" she ordered in a quaking voice. "You've punished me enough!"

Johnny just smacked her again, in exactly the same spot. "I'll decide when you've been punished enough."

Squeezing her legs closed to prevent any further assault in that area, she dug her fingers into his ankle and concentrated on keeping her legs still, as Johnny kept up the unrelenting rhythm of fiery swats.

When they heard the sound of hooves cantering up behind them, Johnny stopped spanking her and reined his horse up, lowering Jessica to the ground. Taking a deep breath, she steeled herself to face the wrath of Mr. Jordan as best she could.

"What the hell did you think you were doing?" Mr. Jordan yelled down at her from his horse. "You were told to stay in the wagon! When I give an order, it's given for a reason." He glowered fiercely at her from under his hat and she wanted the ground to open up and swallow her whole. Instead, she forced herself to hold her head high and look at the furious, stern trail boss as she answered his question.

"I was only trying to help. It's what you pay me for."

"I pay you to follow my orders! Nothing else!" He'd stopped yelling, but his voice was still raised enough for her to be intimidated. "Not only did you just about get yourself killed, you endangered the lives of some good men who had to rescue you. And you ruined a good horse. The horse you were riding got gored; I had to put him down. If you'd just listened and stayed in the wagon like you'd been told, none of that would have happened. When we get back to camp

I'll pay you off—you can leave in the morning."

"No!" Jessica protested. "Please, Mr. Jordan, I know I was wrong, but please give me another chance. If you fire me, Johnny will leave too—he's got it in his head that he needs to take care of me. Please don't make him suffer for my mistake. Please, sir, let me stay with the drive. Punish me in some other way. I'll accept whatever punishment you give me. Dock my pay... anything... just please let me stay."

"So you want to stay with a bunch of filthy, stinking cattle men?" Mr. Jordan asked, using the same words Jessica had used when she'd first been offered employment on the trail.

"Yes, sir. Please," she begged, looking up at him.

Mr. Jordan scratched his chin thoughtfully. "Is she right, Johnny?" he asked. "If I fire her, will you be leaving too?"

Johnny nodded. "Yes, sir. I promised to take care of her. You can't just abandon a woman in the middle of nowhere, miles from the nearest town. She wouldn't last a day. You know that as well as I do."

Inwardly, Jessica grinned, although there was no sign of that on her face. She knew Mr. Jordan well enough to know that he was a man of honor—now that Johnny had pointed out the lack of chivalry in his decision, she knew he would change his mind. She wouldn't be fired.

Mr. Jordan sighed. "I suppose you're right. Okay then, Miss Jessica, you can stay. But this isn't over, and don't you be thinking that it is. I'll be taking a razor strop to your bare backside once we're back in camp. If you'd rather me pay you off instead, you let me know." Whirling his horse, he cantered away, leaving Jessica standing in a cloud of dust.

Johnny extended his hand and reached down, swinging her up behind him on the horse. She inhaled sharply as her bottom came into contact with the horse, then grimaced as she remembered what awaited her back at camp. She knew from experience that Mr. Jordan packed a powerful wallop—he'd already made short work of reducing her to a sobbing mess using just his hand over her skirts. How much more would a razor strop on her bare behind hurt? She didn't want to find out.

Wrapping her arms around Johnny, she inhaled the scent of him, then pressed her cheek against his back. "Maybe I should just let him fire me," she murmured into his shirt as the horse broke into a trot. "You need to stay on though—this is your opportunity for regular work. Don't give up your life for me."

Johnny swiveled around to look at her. "Do you want me to spank you all the way back? I promised to take care of you. I don't go back on my promises."

"But I'm scared, Johnny. A razor strop is going to hurt."

"It will hurt a hell of a lot less than getting trampled to death by steers," Johnny pointed out. "It's only a walloping. No one's ever died from a walloping before."

"I might be the first," Jessica sulked.

"You might," Johnny agreed. "Somehow I doubt it though. Mr. Jordan isn't going to beat you to death."

As they neared camp, Jessica started to tremble. She was truly frightened of the fate that awaited her. She was no stranger to a strap—she'd felt it plenty when she was growing up—but her father's strap was a lot smaller than a razor strop, and her father was a lot smaller than Mr. Jordan. And, more important, her father had loved her, and hadn't wanted to actually hurt her. The same could not be said for Mr. Jordan. Mr. Jordan was a fair man, and she knew he could be kind, but he was tough as nails and very hard. He was furious with her, and he wouldn't go easy on her just because she shed a few tears.

• • • • • • •

Johnny could feel Jessica's fear. She was pressed up against him so tightly that he could feel her heart beating in her chest; he could feel her trembling. The poor girl was shaking so much, he was half afraid she was going to fall off the horse. It wasn't all fear of the fate that awaited her back at camp either; he knew that the bad scare she'd had when she'd fallen off her horse in front of the stampede hadn't helped matters. Had she been hurt when she'd fallen off? He'd been so intent on rescuing her and stopping the herd that he hadn't even thought to ask.

"Did you get hurt when you got thrown?" he asked, without turning around.

"No. Just bruises."

"Good. You're going to be okay, you know," he told her gently, wanting to reassure her. He wished she hadn't disobeyed. More than anything, he wished she had followed orders and remained in the wagon. Oh, he was well aware that she was only trying to help, and he admired her for that, but her defiance wasn't going to remain unpunished. Not when her inexperience had put her in such grave danger. He just wished Mr. Jordan wasn't the one who was going to punish her. Mr. Jordan was tough—Johnny had seen him knock a man down with just one punch. He was a big man, and Jessica was so small. Just as it was her vulnerability that had spurred him to want to protect her after tragedy struck their wagon train, it was her vulnerability that made him want to protect her now. But what could he do?

CHAPTER NINE

After unsaddling his horse, Johnny put his arm around Jessica's waist and pulled her close to walk with her into camp. He knew how scared she'd been out there in the stampede, and he knew she was afraid of Mr. Jordan, and he wanted to comfort her. Her trembling had eased, but she was still tense beneath his hands.

They had the herd bedded down for the night and the night riders were circling, keeping them calm. After their stampede, it was unlikely they would have any more problems tonight—the steers were too tired to run again.

"Come to the supply wagon," Mr. Jordan ordered as they approached, his voice hard, his face stern and unyielding. "I told you what was going to happen. You *will* learn to obey my orders. Are you going to accept your punishment or would you rather I pay you off now?"

Johnny squeezed Jessica's shoulders. She was trying to be brave, but he could tell she was afraid. He watched as she took a deep breath and raised her chin.

"I will accept whatever punishment you give me."

"Good."

Johnny looked around the camp as darkness encroached. The supply wagon was right on the edge, and the men had obviously been given orders to remain by the fire, as they were all hunkered down talking quietly and playing poker. He was relieved. Jessica would have some modicum of privacy at least, although they weren't far enough away for her cries to go unheard. And she would cry—Johnny was sure of that. No matter how hard she fought it, the razor strop would bring her to sobbing and wailing, that was certain.

Hanging a lantern on a hook on the back of the wagon, Mr. Jordan leaned inside and took the razor strop down off the wall. "Take down your britches and bend over the back of the wagon," he ordered gruffly.

Her eyes glistened with tears already but her fingers fumbled with the buttons at her small waist. Johnny's heart constricted with pain, watching her. And surprisingly, he was jealous. Jessica was his girl—his responsibility. He couldn't stand back and let another man punish her. He stepped forward.

"Let me do it. You'll be too hard on her—you don't love her like I do."

Mr. Jordan glared at him for a moment, then sighed and handed the strop over. "Fine. But if you're not hard enough on her, I'll do it again myself." Jessica had wrestled her pants down to her thighs and had bent her body forward to rest her forearms on the back of the wagon when Mr. Jordan leaned down and touched her shoulder. "When I give an order, I expect it to be obeyed."

"Yes, sir," she stammered as he strode back to his men.

In the glowing light of the lantern, Johnny stared at her naked behind. She was stunning—her copper locks trailed down her back, accentuating her slim shoulders. Her waist was slender and her bottom was shapely. Her legs were parted slightly and he could just make out the tuft of curls nestled between her thighs. His breathing changed. His cock was straining at his pants, begging to be let out. He wanted to ravish her, not punish her. He wanted to sink his cock into the dewy wetness of her and make her scream in delight, not scream with pain.

Her pale skin was smudged with pink splotches and he could see the outline of his fingers in several places. He knew she was already sore. She hadn't been punished enough though; Johnny had been intending to spank her all the way back to camp. He'd only stopped because of the walloping Mr. Jordan had promised; he didn't want to make it any worse for her than it had to be.

Steeling himself, Johnny raised the heavy leather strop high and brought it down hard across the crest of her buttocks. She was clinging to the wagon so tightly her knuckles were turning white, but it didn't help. When the strop landed, leaving a bright red stripe in its wake, she arched her back and screamed, a long, drawn-out wail that echoed across the plains.

Johnny put the strop down. He couldn't listen to that noise the whole time. It made him feel too guilty. Besides, the drovers all knew what was happening, but they didn't need to hear the consequences of it. Untying the bandanna at his throat, Johnny pulled it free and folded it over and over, into a pad.

"Here, bite on this. It will help." He placed the cloth between her lips, holding it until she bit down, pinning it securely between her teeth. "Good girl." He traced a circle on her back with his fingers, trailing his fingertips down her spine to the crease of her buttocks, inhaling sharply as the pads of his fingers brushed against the heat of her scorched skin. Grimacing, he raised the strop again and brought it down repeatedly, relentlessly, crisscrossing her bottom with welts. He lashed her from the top of her buttocks all the way down to mid-thigh then back up again, forcing himself to continue the punishment, wanting to throw the strop down and take Jessica in his arms each time her body jarred in response to the blows he was dishing out. Despite the makeshift gag, small squeaks kept escaping her lips and her body had gone limp, hanging over the back of the wagon like a rag doll.

Steeling himself for the last blow, Johnny raised the strop one final time and brought it down as hard as he could, on an angle across the roundest part of her buttocks. He didn't want to give Mr. Jordan any reason to repeat this punishment—he had to make this final stroke count. Although Mr. Jordan was over by the fire with his men, Johnny knew he was watching.

This time, the cloth clenched between her teeth wasn't enough to stifle her screams and as her entire body went rigid with pain, Johnny threw the strop down and took her in his arms. He held her tightly as she collapsed against him, sobbing so hard he thought her heart would break.

"I'm so sorry," he whispered in her ear, "but I couldn't let him punish you."

Twining his fingers in her hair, he massaged the nape of her neck while he held her tightly with his other hand, pressing her in against his chest. Bending forward, he kissed her forehead tenderly as she sobbed into his shirt, her body shaking.

"Shhhhh," he murmured. "It's all over, you're okay now."

Gradually, he felt her relax against him, her sobs easing, and her legs stopped trembling. Still holding her close to his chest, he kissed her forehead again, then he shook out his wet bandanna that she'd been biting on and used it to wipe the tears from her face.

"It's all right now," Johnny whispered again.

Jessica's sobs had eased to sniffles when Mr. Jordan strode over.

"Here comes the boss," Johnny whispered. "Pull your pants back up." Gently, he eased her drawers back up and fastened them quickly. Gripping the waistband of the heavy pants, he pulled them up over her hot, swollen bottom. The rough material chafed and she hissed in pain. He winced on her behalf, a stab of guilt slicing through him. He'd been hard on her, and he knew it. Would Mr. Jordan actually have been any harder on her that what he had been? And if not, why had he insisted on punishing her himself? Why hadn't he just let the boss handle it? He knew the answer to that question though, without even having to think: Jessica was his.

Mr. Jordan stood there with his arms folded across his chest for a moment, just studying them. "You get in the wagon now, Miss Jessica, and you stay there!" he told her firmly. "And you," he said to Johnny, "can take first watch. Starting now."

"Yes, sir." He gave Jessica's hand one final squeeze in reassurance, then he strode away to saddle up his horse.

• • • • • • •

Mr. Jordan was the last person Jessica wanted to see. She knew she looked a mess—she was still sniffling, her eyes were all puffy and red-rimmed from crying, and her bottom was one mass of pain. And she blamed him for the strapping she had just received. Turning away from him, she starting to clamber into the wagon, but Mr. Jordan stopped her. Resting his hands lightly on her shoulders, he spun her around to face him and looked down directly into her eyes. She looked at the ground.

"Look at me," he commanded softly. Hesitantly, she obeyed. "You'll be in no state to ride tomorrow so you can stay in the wagon. But you're still being punished—you're confined to the wagon. You're not to leave without permission. For two days, then you're back in the saddle. I'm docking your pay for the cost of the dead horse, and you won't be getting paid while you're in the wagon. You nearly died out there, and two good men risked their lives to save you. When I give an order, Miss Jessica, I expect to be obeyed." He spoke softly, but there was no mistaking the sternness of his tone.

"Yes, sir," she mumbled, looking down again.

Sliding his hands down her sides to wrap around her waist, Mr. Jordan lifted her effortlessly and placed her gently in the wagon. He gave her a small smile and patted her shoulder affectionately. "I'll get Billy to bring you some coffee," he said, before turning away and striding back to camp, taking the lamp with him, leaving her in darkness.

The bed was still there and she collapsed onto it, stretching out on her front. Burying her face in the blankets, she began to cry again. She was so sore. The strappings she'd endured from her father were nothing compared to what Johnny had just done. Even the smallest movement made the rough fabric scratch painfully against her scorching skin, so she just lay still. *You don't love her like I do* kept swirling round and round in her mind. Did Johnny really love her? Despite the pain in her behind and the tears streaming down her face, she managed a small smile at the realization that yes, he did love her. She loved him, too. Even now, with the scorching pain in her rear end, she loved him.

By the time Billy arrived at the wagon with coffee for her, she was sound asleep, still with the same small smile on her face. Reaching in, he gently covered her with a blanket and left again.

Monty's bashing a spoon against a pot to summon the men to breakfast woke her up. Stretching, she was horrified to realize she was even sorer now than she had been last night. Johnny had set her rear end on fire with the razor strop but now, as well as the burning, was an itching and a deep ache. Reaching around, she touched the seat of her pants gently, then immediately pulled her hand away. Even the lightest of touches hurt. Mr. Jordan had been right—she was in no state to ride today. Even though banishment to the wagon was meant to be a punishment, she was grateful for it; she didn't want to have to face the men today, when every step she took would be agony.

· · · · · · ·

Billy brought her biscuits, bacon, and coffee and

wordlessly handed them to her over the tailgate of the wagon. She could see the sympathy in his eyes as he placed her breakfast gently on the floor of the wagon, but he didn't speak to her. As soon as the plate had left his hand, he turned away and hustled back to the chuck wagon, where she knew he'd be helping Monty serve breakfast to the men.

No one came and spoke to her. She felt the wagon bumping as it was hitched to the team. She heard the ruckus of the drovers moving the herd on. She heard the crack of the whip as Billy set the team moving, pulling in behind the chuck wagon, ready for another day on the trail. The front cover was tied closed so she couldn't see out, and there was nothing to see behind them but dust.

Where was Johnny? Why hadn't he come to see her? How could he claim to love her one day then abandon her the next? What was going on?

Pain coursed through her body with every jolting movement the wagon made. Even the smallest stone on the trail caused the wagon to lurch, making her grit her teeth against the fierce throbbing in her rear end. There was nothing to do but lie still and try to relax and it wasn't long before the rickety rocking motion of the wagon as it made its way slowly across the prairie lulled her to sleep.

• • • • • • •

Johnny knew Jessica was hurting. Not just physically, but emotionally as well. He'd been hard on her last night and he wanted to check on her. To run his fingers over her bruises and make sure he hadn't damaged her too badly. He wanted to wrap his arms around her and kiss her, to make everything better.

"You stay away from that wagon today, Johnny," Mr. Jordan had ordered at first light, when Monty was summoning the men to come and eat. "She's being punished. She'll be in no fit state to ride, so she can remain in the wagon. Alone." The last word was given a harsh emphasis; Mr. Jordan left no doubt in Johnny's mind that her confinement would be enforced.

Johnny was riding swing that day, on the other side of the herd, far away from the supply wagon. He knew it was a deliberate move to keep him away from Jessica, but he didn't fight it. There would be no point; Mr. Jordan had made his position clear. Defying orders would only get him fired, and Jessica had taken one hell of a walloping to avoid that. This job, regular money, was something he hadn't had in a long time, and it felt good.

• • • • • • •

Jessica jolted awake when the wagon stopped for the midday meal. She could hear the sounds of the drovers making a rough camp, and she could smell the fixings of a basic meal. Monty's cooking might not be Boston fare, but she had grown fond of it. She wondered where Johnny was; why wasn't he coming to see her?

She heard footsteps directly outside the wagon, then a head peeped in over the back. It was Monty, with a mug of steaming coffee in the dented metal mug that was now so familiar and a plate of beans and biscuits.

"Where's Johnny? Why hasn't he come to see me?" she asked.

Monty smiled at her kindly. "He's out yonder, with the beeves. Boss won't let him come. You're being punished."

A lone tear trickled down her cheek. She'd been through so much in such a short space of time—watching her family massacred, being kidnapped by Indians, then nearly killed by stampeding steers. She needed Johnny. She needed to feel his arms around her, holding her tight, reassuring her that everything was going to be alright.

As she reached out to take the meal, the rough fabric of her pants scraped across her still-burning bottom and she winced.

"He cares about you, girl, you remember that," Monty

said, waggling his finger at her as he turned and left the wagon.

"If he did, he'd be here!" Jessica cried, but Monty didn't answer.

• • • • • • •

"You need to let that girl out of the wagon," Monty declared to Mr. Jordan once he returned to the rickety table folded out from the back of the chuck wagon. "She's miserable in there. She's been punished enough."

"I'll be the judge of that," Mr. Jordan argued firmly.

"You haven't seen her; I have. She's been through enough. You keeping her in there is cruel. I've known you nigh on ten years, Wes Jordan, and in all that time, you've never been cruel. Tough, yes, but not cruel."

Mr. Jordan sighed and looked toward the wagon. "Johnny!" he called. The young man rose from his spot on the ground and, balancing his cup precariously on top of his plate, carried them over to where Mr. Jordan and Monty were standing.

"Go and get Jessica."

"Yes, sir." Passing his dishes to Billy to save for him, he walked over to the supply wagon as fast as he could, without actually breaking into a run. He was eager to see Jessica; he felt so guilty knowing she was all alone in there.

"Jessica," he called softly, leaning in the back of the wagon. She was curled up in a ball, her meal untouched beside her. "Jessica, it's me, Johnny. Come on out now."

Slowly, she unfurled herself, stretching out her arms then her legs, and hissing in pain when her pants stretched tight across her bottom. Johnny winced on her behalf; he knew she would be sore, but he had no idea she'd be *that* sore. He lifted her gently down to the ground before wrapping his arms around her tightly, pulling her into his chest, burying his face in her hair. He loved her hair—the gorgeous auburn curls had been the first thing he'd noticed about her. The unruly tendrils that kept escaping the pins holding the tresses up reminded him so much of her—untamed, wild, and free, outspoken and beautiful.

Catching her chin in his hands, he tilted her face up to his and touched his lips lightly against hers. She responded instantly. Her fingers went around the back of his neck, pulling him into her, her lips locked with his, her probing tongue exploring his mouth. He could taste the salt of her tears on her cheeks where they had trickled down her face and he kissed the residue away. He wanted no reminder of her sadness.

She pressed her body up against his and he felt himself growing hard as the curves of her exquisite body melded into him. Tracing his fingers in long, delicate strokes down her back, he came to her rounded bottom where his palm gently came to rest. He wanted to squeeze it, pinch it… but he restrained himself. She was too sore; the light touch had made her tense up against him. He moved his hand away. This was to be a positive reunion, not a painful one.

"Come on," he said, pulling away from her, but keeping one hand possessively in the small of her back. "Let's go and eat." Reaching into the wagon, he retrieved her meal and the cup of coffee she had discarded, and led her over to the chuck wagon.

Mr. Jordan, Woody, Davey, and Billy all tipped their hats in greeting to her when she approached the camp on Johnny's arm, but no one said a word. She'd been worried they would, but they had obviously forgotten the events of the night before a lot quicker than she would.

• • • • • • •

"Head 'em up and move 'em out!" Mr. Jordan waved his hat and called the order. Jessica stretched out happily on the bed in the back of the supply wagon and breathed a sigh of contentment as the wheels started rolling. Her banishment to the wagon was voluntary this time—there was no way she could join the other drovers in the saddle, she was still too sore. But she was happy now, despite the fire still radiating from her backside. Johnny still loved her; he still cared.

CHAPTER TEN

"Are you able to sit on your saddle, Miss Jessica?" Mr. Jordan asked. "There's a town just a few miles east of here. I'm going in now, with Davey. You and Johnny can both come along if you want to."

Jessica nearly dropped her plate of biscuits in excitement. Finally, she'd be able to wire the news of her family's passing to her aunt, get some money, and get herself back home to Boston! After everything she'd been through, it almost seemed too good to be true.

"I'll manage," she told him. And she would. Riding would be uncomfortable, but she wasn't going to miss this opportunity. The whole reason they'd joined this trail drive, at least as far as she was concerned, was to get to this point. To get to a town where she could make contact with the only remaining family she had left.

"Woody—take charge of the herd. We'll catch up later."

The ride into town was uncomfortable—Jessica's bottom burned fiercely from the strapping Johnny had given her, and the fast pace at which they rode jolted her around in the saddle mercilessly. *But it will be worth it,* she reminded herself every time tears sprang into her eyes. *It won't be long now until I can go home... home to Boston where I belong*. Despite the pain in her rear end, thinking of home nearly made her smile.

Then her breath caught. What about Johnny? Somehow, Johnny didn't seem like the type of man who would be happy in a city like Boston. He didn't seem like the type of man who would easily find employment in Boston… and he definitely wasn't the type of man who would fit into her old social circle in Boston. What of her old friends? Her old suitors? What would they think of a man like Johnny? Provided she could convince him to accompany her, of course.

"How are you feeling?" Johnny asked her softly, riding close beside her. The tender concern in his eyes made her heart melt.

"I'm managing," she replied, not bothering to try and hide her discomfort. There was no point; Johnny knew she was sore.

"We're nearly there, Miss Jessica," Davey said, swiveling around in his saddle to look at her. "Not much further." The smile he gave her was kind; he knew she was hurting too.

"Look—it's just over that rise," Mr. Jordan pointed out. Slowing the horses to a walk, the group approached the town slowly, checking it out.

Jessica was so excited she thought she would burst. Finally she was in civilization again! Of course, by Boston standards, the little town was nothing; but after so long on the prairie, wearing the same clothes, sleeping mostly on the hard ground, bathing in a cold river, not seeing any buildings, the town was perfect.

"There's the telegraph office." Johnny pointed over to his left, to a little building further down the dusty main street. "You go in and send the telegram. I'll find the stables and get the horses fed and watered."

Dismounting stiffly, Jessica grimaced as pain radiated down her legs when she stood up straight. Her pants chafed roughly on her tender skin when she took the first step, but she pushed aside all thoughts, except those to do with the telegram.

A little bell tied to the door jingled merrily when she pushed it open and a short, fat, balding man frowned over the rim of his thick glasses at her, looking her up and down severely.

"Ladies should look like ladies. Come back when you're dressed properly," he told her stiffly, in a stuffy English accent. The odious little man reminded her of the father of one of her old friends back home—he'd come to Boston from England only a few years earlier and had looked down his nose at her family. They hadn't been rich enough for his expensive tastes, and he had enjoyed pointing that out to Jessica often.

"I need to send a telegram," Jessica informed the man behind the counter. "It's rather urgent."

The man pushed his glasses higher up on his nose and peered at her again, looking her up and down, shaking his head disapprovingly. "Come back when you're dressed properly."

"But sir …"

"Come back when you're dressed properly," he cut her off.

"I'm with a trail herd out that way a bit," Jessica indicated, with a dramatic sweeping of her arm. "I'm a drover. I don't have anything else to wear." Which was sort of true; she hadn't worn her gown since Johnny had snatched her back from the clutches of the Indians.

"There's a shop over there." He pointed directly across the street. *Jim's Mercantile,* the sign read.

"Please, sir, it won't take long," she pleaded.

The man shook his head. Then, ignoring her, he turned back to his desk and began to shuffle papers; papers that Jessica was sure didn't need to be shuffled.

"Ooooooh!" Growling in frustration, Jessica stamped her foot loudly, sending up a cloud of dust from off her clothing. Turning on her heel, she threw the door open, making the little bell jangle wildly, and stomped off down the street. There was nothing else for it; she'd have to buy herself a dress. So she had to find Johnny.

The street was empty. Johnny was nowhere in sight. *I may as well see what they have in the way of dresses*, Jessica thought, crossing the street. As she pushed open the door of the mercantile, there were Mr. Jordan and Davey, talking to the man behind the counter.

"Mr. Jordan?" she approached him, a bit afraid to ask him for money, but knowing she didn't really have any other choice. "I need... I need some money. I-I need a dress," she stammered. "The man in the telegraph office won't let me send a telegram without one."

Mr. Jordan looked at her, astounded. "What?" he exclaimed. He stepped forward and took her by the shoulders, pushing her along in front of him. "You finish up here, Davey; I'm going to send a telegram."

Jessica almost had to run to keep up with Mr. Jordan's long strides, lengthened more than usual because of his anger. He pushed his shoulder against the door, opening it violently, sending the little bell into a ringing frenzy.

"The lady needs to send a telegram," he stated, emphasizing the word *lady* heavily.

The man behind the counter drew himself up to his full height of only slightly taller than Jessica and puffed out his chest, glowering at her fiercely.

"The lady needs to dress like a lady, just like I told her, then she can send her telegram," the man sneered.

Mr. Jordan leaned forward and put his hands on the counter, glaring at the small man hiding behind it. "The lady needs to send a telegram. Now."

Pushing his glasses back up on his nose, the man took a step backwards. Jessica had seen Mr. Jordan intimidate people before with his sheer size and presence; normally it scared her a little bit, but right now she was glad of it. She felt protected and safe. It was a good feeling, having the big, imposing trail boss by her side.

Mr. Jordan leaned closer. The man stepped further back. He looked at his shoes. Then he sighed. "Fine," he said, slapping a piece of paper onto the counter. "Write it down."

Aunt Thelma, everyone killed by Indians. I am sole survivor. No money to return to Boston. Nowhere to live. Are you able to help?

Your niece, Jessica Walsh

"How long will it be?" Mr. Jordan asked, once it was sent.

The man behind the counter shrugged. "Maybe half an hour?" he suggested, sounding frightened.

Mr. Jordan nodded. "We'll be back." Putting his hands on Jessica's shoulders again, he guided her gently out of the telegraph office onto the street, where they saw Johnny heading toward them.

"All done?" he asked, taking her hand.

Jessica nodded. It was done. Now she just had to wait. Closing her eyes, she leaned against the post flanking the step and kicked the heel of her boot against the boardwalk. *Come on, Aunt Thelma*, she begged in her mind. *Hurry up and reply! I want to get out of here!*

• • • • • • •

They didn't have to wait long for the telegram, but after glancing at it briefly, she gasped loudly and let it slip from her grip to flutter to the dusty ground.

"She won't help me!" she cried, collapsing against Johnny and dissolving into tears. "She was my only hope and she won't help me!" She clung to him desperately, sobbing into his shirt, her shoulders heaving.

Holding onto Jessica, Johnny bent down to retrieve the telegram, shaking the dust off it. *Dear Jessica,* it read. *Can't help. Don't return to Boston. Nothing for you here. Letter to follow. Aunt Thelma.*

What on earth does that mean? Johnny wondered. *Didn't Jessica spend her entire life in Boston? There's more to this… has to be.* Frowning, he tightened his hold on Jessica, who was still sobbing into his shirt. "Shhhh," he whispered to her. "It's going to be okay."

"I don't understand," she cried. "Why doesn't she want me to go home?"

Johnny said nothing. What could he say? Instead, he just stood there with her on the side of the street, holding her tightly, doing his best to comfort her.

After a few moments she pushed herself back up off his chest and swiped at her nose and eyes with the back of her hand, wiping her knuckles dry on her pants. "I'm sorry," she murmured, embarrassed. "I... It was such a shock. I really thought she would help me. Now I truly am all alone in the world."

Putting his hands on her shoulders, Johnny gave her a gentle shake and gazed intently into her eyes. "If you weren't already so sore, I would spank you good and proper, my girl. How many times do I have to tell you? You're not all alone—you've got me."

"And why would you want to take care of me?" Jessica retorted. "I've got nothing to offer you. Not even the last of my own family wants me."

One of Johnny's hands left her shoulders and snaked its way around to her buttocks. Grabbing hold, he squeezed gently. Jessica winced. "I love you," he said simply.

"I don't want to be your whore, Johnny."

"I don't want you to be my whore either," he told her, kissing her nose. "I want you to be my wife. I love you, Jessica. Will you marry me?"

He was looking down at her so expectantly, so nervously, that it was all she could do not to burst into laughter of undisguised glee. She smiled. "Do you really mean that?"

"I really do." He took her hands in his, holding them gently, rubbing his thumbs in small circles over her knuckles.

Her smile widened. "Yes, Johnny, yes!" She flung her arms around his neck excitedly and pressed her lips against his, exploring his mouth with her searching tongue, her fingers tangling in his hair at the nape of his neck, her pelvis crushing against him. She fitted into Johnny's body perfectly… this was where she belonged.

• • • • • • •

"Mr. Jordan!" Jessica yelled. "Over here!"

From further up the street, Mr. Jordan turned. He was walking beside Davey, away from them, but at her shout, he spun on his heel and began striding toward them, with Davey by his side.

"Johnny and me, we're getting married!" she announced proudly, as soon as the two men were close enough to hear.

"Congratulations, son," Mr. Jordan said, clapping Johnny on the shoulder.

Quickly, Johnny explained the contents of the telegram and what had happened since. As expected, Mr. Jordan took charge. "You go find a preacher, Davey," he ordered. "And you can go find a ring, Johnny; try the mercantile first." He pointed across the street to the store where Jessica had gone in search of a dress earlier. "And you, Miss Jessica, will need some proper clothes for your wedding. You can't stand up before a preacher in those dusty pants!" He fished some money out of his pocket and gave it to her. "Get yourself something pretty."

She smiled at him, grateful. She was sad that her ma wouldn't be there to see her marry the man she'd fallen in love with, but she was grateful that two men she now considered to be her friends, would be.

"Does this mean you will be leaving us?" Davey asked. "Will you be staying in town now that you're getting married?"

Jessica shook her head emphatically. "I'm not living in no town that won't let a woman in pants send a telegram!" Then she lowered her eyes, and her voice. "I want to redeem myself to the men. All I've done so far is cause problems.

Besides, I'm beginning to quite enjoy being a drover. I'd like to stay on with the drive."

"So you don't think cattlemen smell then?" Davey asked her, grinning.

"No, they do. But I smell now, too."

"What about you, Johnny? Are you happy to stay on with the drive?" Mr. Jordan asked.

"Yes." Johnny nodded. He was happy Jessica had answered first; he wouldn't have insisted they stay if she didn't want to, but he didn't have enough money yet to make a start for them anywhere. He wanted to stay on. If they both stayed on to the end of the drive, that would put them in Sedalia, Missouri, not too far from where he'd grown up. He could take Jessica home to meet his ma; the old woman would like that.

"Great!" Mr. Jordan looked pleased. "I will go and organize for your aunt's letter to be forwarded up the trail," he announced. "Meet me at the saloon in half an hour."

"Can we stay in town for the night, Mr. Jordan? Please?" Jessica begged. "It will be my first night as a married woman. I'd really like to spend it in a real bed. Please?" She gave the trail boss her prettiest smile, trailing her fingers seductively up Johnny's arm as she did so.

"Yeah, boss, you can't expect them to ride back to camp straight after getting married!" Davey agreed.

Mr. Jordan laughed. "Righto then, hotel tonight it is. I'll sort it out."

"Oh, thank you!" Jessica cried, wrapping her arms around the big man in delight.

Mr. Jordan chuckled as he disentangled himself from Jessica's embrace. "Go on," he told her. "Go and find yourself a pretty dress. We'll see you soon."

• • • • • • •

Jessica stood in front of the preacher in a borrowed dress. The mercantile didn't have anything suitable, and the seamstress couldn't make anything at such short notice. She'd been just about in tears when she'd walked into the saloon to meet Mr. Jordan, Davey, and Johnny; she didn't want to get married in her dusty drover's clothes. What kind of bride would she be if she spoke her vows while wearing man's pants?

"What's wrong?" Johnny asked curiously as she approached. Then he noticed her empty hands—he could see she didn't have a dress. "Couldn't you find anything suitable at the mercantile?"

Jessica shook her head, fighting back tears. No way was she going to cry… she'd cried enough already, and shedding more tears wouldn't help. Especially not right before such a happy occasion.

"You come on with me, little missy," a friendly saloon girl with long blond curls invited her. "We're about the same size—you can borrow something of mine, we'll get you prettied up right nice, we will. Give us a moment, lads," she said, blowing the men a kiss. Then she took Jessica's hand and led her from the bar, up the stairs to the rooms above the saloon.

The saloon girl was a young woman called Chloe and she was right, they were the same size. Chloe didn't have a white gown, but she did have a lovely cream one, not quite in the latest fashion, but still beautiful.

Discarding her dusty drover's clothes in a heap by the door, Jessica washed up as best she could, using the pitcher of water beside the basin, and slipped on the dress. She sucked in a breath as she caught sight of herself in the mirror—she looked like a real bride! She sat on the stool in front of the table as Chloe bustled around behind her, pinning her auburn curls up on top of her head, taming the loose tendrils with a mother-of-pearl comb.

"You look perfect!" Chloe declared. "Come on; time to marry that man of yours! He's right handsome, he is," she whispered conspiratorially. "The men with him are mighty fine too!" She threw her head back and laughed then, the bitter laugh of someone who has seen far more than they should, and who accepted long ago that this is as good as it gets.

"Will you stand up with me?" Jessica asked shyly.

Chloe's face broke into a wide smile and she gave a small squeal of glee. "I'd be glad to!" she cried. "I've never been to a weddin' before!"

• • • • • • •

Jessica was enjoying watching the shocked, but delighted, expression on Johnny's face as she stepped out of the borrowed dress to reveal short, sexy drawers that had been the height of fashion back home in Boston, but which were still considered scandalous among decent company. She left the gown and petticoats in a puddle on the floor at her feet and shimmied out of her undergarments, standing completely naked before him in the dim glow cast by the lantern on the table by the bed. She'd never been naked in front of a man before but the excitement of the wedding was making her brave.

Johnny whistled softly through his teeth, stepping forward to place his hands gently on her waist, drawing her into him. "You are beautiful," he whispered into her hair.

Jessica's hands went to the front of Johnny's pants where she urgently fumbled with the buttons with clumsy fingers. She wanted him naked, too. Groaning in frustration at the tight buttons that wouldn't come undone, she moved her fingers to his chest, undoing his shirt instead. These buttons opened easily and she trailed her fingers inside his shirt, along the hard muscles of his chest. Pushing the shirt back off his shoulders, she brushed her lips against the light smattering of hair she found there, pulling his shirt off completely and discarding it carelessly on top of her own pile of clothing.

"Here, let me," Johnny murmured, brushing her hands away from his jeans, undoing them for her. She gasped when his erection sprang free, then reached out to touch it gingerly.

"It's so big," she breathed. "Are you sure it will fit?"

Johnny chuckled. "It will fit. I'll be gentle. Come," he invited, stretching out on the bed, extending his hand to help her lie down next to him.

The room was cold, so Johnny pulled the covers up over them. Jessica grasped Johnny's cock tightly, running her fingers up and down the length of it, twirling her thumbs around the head. She jumped when Johnny moved his hand between her legs, pushing them apart, exploring the moist depths of her gently with long, probing fingers. She wriggled. Surely she wasn't meant to be enjoying these sensations this much? Her mother hadn't told her very much about what happens to a lady on her wedding night; she'd simply said that she should lie back and do her duty. Nothing had been said about pleasure, or the exquisite tingles of electricity firing through her. There had been no hint that Johnny would arouse feelings in her quite unlike anything she had felt before; no mention of the dampness that was spreading rapidly between her thighs as Johnny's fingers circled inside her gently, moving in and out slowly, teasing her, stretching her wide, readying her for his cock.

"Are you ready for this, sweetheart?" he asked her, his voice husky with arousal.

She could only nod.

Gently, he flipped her over onto her back, positioning himself above her, his weight resting on his forearms on either side of her body. His face was directly above hers and he gazed down lovingly into her eyes before dropping his lips to hers for a passionate kiss.

A sharp pain ripped through her as he entered her roughly, and she cried out. Johnny stilled inside her, waiting. As soon as the pain subsided, she let out her breath and smiled. She felt so full. It was exquisite. Johnny moved slowly, gently, at first, his pelvis moving in small circles. But as he picked up momentum his thrusts became longer, deeper, faster, his breathing ragged.

Ma never told me about this! Jessica smiled and arched her back to meet him, moving her hips in time with his thrusts. She could feel a pressure building up inside her, threatening to explode, begging for release, as Johnny drove into her faster and faster. Gripping her shoulders, his fingers dug into her as his hips ground against hers one last time before his whole body shuddered and he fell against her, spent. At the same time, heat was building up inside her to boiling point, and she reached climax the instant he did, calling out his name hoarsely, digging her fingernails harshly into his back, her legs wrapped around his waist squeezing against him.

They lay there like that for several long moments, blissfully trying to catch their breath, then Johnny rolled off her. Jessica sat up, propping herself up on her elbows.

"My mother," she declared, "clearly had no idea what she was talking about!"

Johnny chuckled, pleased. Rolling over, he reached for her, pulling her down next to him, and wrapped his arms around her tightly. Within minutes, they were both sound asleep.

CHAPTER ELEVEN

After a quick breakfast at the hotel, they left town to head back to the herd first thing in the morning. Jessica had enjoyed her night in a real bed; she couldn't remember the last time she had slept in a real bed, with real sheets, in a real room. It had been far too long. And what had gone on in that bed... oh, that had been delicious, and something she would like very much to repeat. And they would have, too, but Mr. Jordan had banged on their door just after sunup telling them to hurry up, so there hadn't been time.

It was obvious from a long way off that the camp was in chaos. For starters, the herd wasn't moving. The beeves were grazing placidly, under the watchful eye of a few drovers, but everything else looked wrong. Men were mingling around, looking busy doing... what? "What's gotten into them?" Mr. Jordan muttered, kicking his horse into a gallop.

Davey followed suit, and after a second's hesitation, so did Johnny and Jessica. Something was clearly wrong, but what could it be?

Leaping off their horses before they'd even stopped moving, Mr. Jordan, Davey, and Johnny rushed into the camp and toward the chuck wagon where the majority of drovers seemed to be gathered. Jessica didn't have the skills they did on horseback, so she drew her horse to a halt first, then dismounted gingerly. She was sore. The effects of the spanking with the razor strop still lingered, but most of the discomfort was from between her legs. Those hours in the saddle, so soon after losing her virginity, had left her aching. Joe, the old wrangler, took her horse from her, and she walked carefully into camp, trying to disguise her pain.

It was Monty. He was lying down on the ground beside the chuck wagon, surrounded by a cluster of drovers who looked both concerned and helpless, and a very harried-looking Billy, who was trying to make biscuits. At least, it looked like that was what he was doing, although it was hard to tell, as he was covered in flour from head to toe, and he was up to his elbows in sticky dough. It was all Jessica could do not to laugh.

"What's going on?" she whispered to Johnny, tugging on the sleeve of his shirt to catch his attention. Mr. Jordan was crouching down beside Monty, but she couldn't hear what he was saying.

"Snakebite. A rattler, I think."

"Oh, no! That's bad..." Snakebite victims had been rare in Boston, but she'd heard stories. Everybody had.

Monty was still conscious, but barely. He was in shock—he was trembling and incoherent, and his leg below his knee was puffy and swollen. His pants leg had been cut off so the bite was visible—Jessica could see where a crisscross cut had been made so the poison could be sucked out. The wound site was red, starting to blister, and looked sore.

"Put him in the supply wagon, make sure he's comfortable," Mr. Jordan ordered. "He'll probably slip into a coma; there's not much we can do, other than keep him warm."

"Come on, Billy!" one of the men yelled angrily. "I'm hungry!"

"Yeah, Billy, hurry up!" someone else agreed. "Let's eat so we can get this outfit movin'!"

Jessica stepped closer to the chuck wagon. "What do you need help with, Billy?" she asked gently. The poor boy looked close to tears. He'd obviously been getting yelled all morning, and clearly wasn't capable of doing what he was now expected to do—put together a meal for all the men, all by himself.

"Everything, miss," he whimpered, sounding defeated. "I can't do anything right. They spat out the coffee, the biscuits won't work…" Billy's voice trailed off.

"I'll put some coffee on, then I'll get started on some bacon. You keep working on those biscuits," she told him kindly.

The big coffeepot was heavy, but Jessica managed to fill it up and hang it over the fire to boil. When she turned around, Billy had managed to wipe even more flour over his face and through his hair and he looked so comical that she had to stifle a laugh. It wouldn't do to burst out laughing now, she knew that. What with breakfast being late and Monty being in danger of dying, laughing would be highly inappropriate.

As she sliced the bacon, Jessica was glad for the hours she had spent in the kitchen in Boston with her mother. They'd had a cook for dinner parties her mother had hosted, but even then, Jessica had been expected to help. Her family had never quite slotted into the elite of Boston society—they hadn't quite been rich enough, so it had fallen to Jessica and her mother to prepare the daily meals. The cook for dinner parties had been a luxury they could barely afford. Her father had been a man of simple tastes, so the meals she had helped her mother prepare had been plain enough, perfect training for the cooking she'd been expected to do while they were traveling with the wagon train, and for the situation she now found herself in. At home in Boston their kitchen had been equipped with a good stove, so there had been a few disasters at first as they had learned how to cook over a campfire, but now Jessica was glad of the burnt dinners; now she was equipped to help Billy feed the men.

Now that he had some help, it looked like Billy almost had the biscuits ready to cook, so Jessica set about frying the bacon. By a stroke of luck the coffee was ready too, so Jessica banged on the side of a pot with a spoon. "Come and get it!" she yelled.

While the drovers were eating, Jessica was thinking. She could remember her grandmother telling her, many years ago, about an old Plains Indian remedy for snakebite—plantain. Did it grow around here? She wasn't sure; she didn't even know what it looked like.

"Do you know what plantain looks like, Billy?" she asked him.

The boy looked at her. "Sure, I know. What do you want it for?"

"Do you know where to get it?"

"There's some not too far from here, I saw it yesterday."

"Can you get it now? I want to make a poultice with it, for Monty. It might help."

Looking around nervously, Billy put down the pan he was washing and scurried off to do her bidding. Jessica was pleased. If her grandmother had been right, Plantain was almost a miracle cure, or so the old Indians had said.

Billy was back with the herb before the men had even finished eating and Jessica made it into a warm poultice. Taking it into the supply wagon, she crouched down next to Monty. He was still conscious, but barely. After wiping his brow with a warm cloth, she quickly applied the poultice to the snakebite wound on his leg. It was ugly—red, swollen, and blistered, and she tried to be gentle, but he groaned anyway.

"I'm sorry," she murmured. "I'm hoping this will help. It's plantain," she told him, hoping to reassure him.

"Good," he gasped. "Good." He seemed to relax then, once he knew what she was doing and she took that to be a good sign. Monty knew most of the herbal remedies around here—if she was doing the wrong thing by putting a plantain poultice on him, he would have told her so.

As they were cleaning up the dishes and packing everything away into the supply wagon, it occurred to Jessica that they should stock up on plantain now—she wanted to apply another poultice at their next camp, and she didn't know how abundantly it grew. So she went off with Billy to where he had found it growing, so he could show her what it looked like. Gathering an armful each, they carried it back to camp and stowed it away carefully inside the chuck wagon.

• • • • • • •

Mr. Jordan was right—Monty did slip into a coma, and nobody knew what else to do. Jessica made him as comfortable as she could in the back of the supply wagon, making sure there was a canteen of water within easy reach in case he did wake up, then she folded up a blanket to put on the wooden seat of the wagon to cushion her bruised, aching bottom. It had been bad enough sitting in the saddle for hours; riding on the bouncing, hard wagon seat would be even worse.

For two days Monty was unconscious, at times confused with delirium, sometimes sweating with fever. Jessica continued to nurse him. She would stop periodically on the trail to check on him, to drizzle whisky or water between his lips whenever she could, and wipe his sweaty brow. She applied the warm poultice three times on the first day and twice on the second, then their stash of plantain ran out and they were unable to find anymore. She had all the men looking, but none of them saw any. All that was left to do now was pray.

When she wasn't nursing Monty, she was helping Billy with the cooking. The meals she served up weren't as good as the ones Monty cooked, but at least the men were getting fed, and fed plenty. It was hard work and she was tired. But as she walked among the men with the coffeepot, and as she spooned stew onto their plates from the table at the back of the chuck wagon, they looked at her with newfound respect. Thanks to Monty's misfortune, it seemed she was redeeming herself after all.

As Johnny pulled her in toward him for a quick cuddle after breakfast and dropped a tender kiss on the end of her nose, she smiled. For the first time in her life, she really felt like she belonged somewhere—she felt needed. It was a good feeling. She wrapped her arms around him, pressing her fingers into his broad back as she snuggled in against his chest. She'd only spent one night sleeping in her husband's arms, but that didn't matter. Becoming Mrs. Johnny Truman was the best thing that had ever happened to her.

• • • • • • •

On the third day, Monty was coherent. He sat up in his bed in the back of the supply wagon and demanded to know what he was doing there. He wasn't the type of man to enjoy being mollycoddled, and he knew he had a crew to feed.

"Who's doin' the cookin'?" he asked gruffly, his face pale.

"Me and Billy," Jessica told him. "Our grub's not as good as yours, but none of the men have starved yet." She smiled at him, then pressed his shoulder gently. "But you need to lie down. You've been very sick, you know."

Monty just grunted.

"Mr. Jordan!" she yelled from the back of the wagon. Mr. Jordan was beside them in a flash. As soon as he saw Monty sitting up, his face broke into a broad grin, his eyes crinkling up at the corners.

"Welcome back," he said, still smiling.

"He needs to lie down," she told Mr. Jordan, hoping the boss would order the old cook to take it easy.

Mr. Jordan just kept smiling. "You listen to your nurse now—she did a great job taking care of you. And a fair job of the cooking too," he added, patting her shoulder.

Grumbling, Monty lay down, but she could tell by the

smile he gave her that he was pleased with her work.

· · · · · · ·

It was a full week before Monty was recovered enough to resume his duties, but as the week wore on, Jessica's workload lightened. She wasn't nursing Monty around the clock anymore, although she was still driving the supply wagon and doing the bulk of the cooking, with Billy's assistance.

"I love you," Jessica whispered as she sat down at the campfire behind Johnny, wrapping her arms around him and nibbling gently on his ear. "And I've missed you. We've been married for a week now and you've only made love to me once!" She laughed as Johnny nearly choked on his coffee, then she looked around, startled. Had any of the men heard her whispered words? It didn't appear so; the men who weren't on night watch were engrossed in a game of poker by the fire. Jessica stood up, relieved.

"Come on," she hissed at Johnny.

Johnny hurriedly swallowed the last of his coffee and stood up too, gently sliding his fingers over her hand.

"Oooooh, where are you two off to?" one of the men teased.

"What are you two going to get up to?" Another jested. Laughter broke out among the men as Jessica's face flushed bright red. Had the men heard her after all?

Ignoring the jeers from the laughing drovers, she felt Johnny's grip on her hand tighten and she had to hurry to keep up with him as he strode away from the campfire. Reaching into the back of the supply wagon, Johnny pulled out his bedroll, and spread it out behind the wagon where they would have a little bit of privacy.

Jessica smiled as Johnny placed his hands on either side of her face, holding her still while he kissed her. His rough lips pressed urgently against hers, sending bolts of electricity through her. She could feel his erection as she pressed her body up against him, devouring him with her lips. Her fingers tangled in his hair and she pulled his face in closer to her, unable to get enough of him.

Tumbling to the ground together, Jessica gasped as Johnny slipped his hand inside her shirt, squeezing her breasts gently as their kiss intensified.

Fumbling with the buttons on his jeans, Jessica finally managed to undo the fly and push his pants down his thighs. Grasping his cock in the palm of her hand, she wrapped her fingers around it tightly and squeezed. Gripping it with both hands, she ran her fingers up and down the shaft, circling the very tip of it with her thumb.

Johnny moaned softly.

"Am I hurting you?" she whispered, concerned.

"No, not at all; I like it," Johnny reassured her, reaching up to brush a strand of hair off her face. Darkness had settled over the camp but the moon was bright enough to see by.

Ripping open his shirt, Jessica continued to explore her husband's body. Holding his cock tightly in her left hand, she traced the fingers of her right hand down his leg as far as she could reach then back up again, over his hips, all the way up over his firm abdomen to his muscular chest. The light smattering of hair there intrigued her, and she brushed her fingers over it, pulling the hairs gently. Lowering her face to his chest, she took his nipple in her mouth, circling it with her tongue, biting it gently. She breathed in the masculine, musky scent, before brushing her tongue across his chest to take his other nipple in her mouth, teasing it with her tongue.

Johnny's fingers had deftly unfastened her pants and untied her drawers and he was pushing them down over her hips, sliding them gently down her thighs. He grabbed her buttocks with both hands and squeezed, digging the balls of his fingers into her bottom, pulling her down on top of him, his mouth nuzzling at the soft skin of her belly.

Jessica knelt over Johnny, trailing her fingers down his

torso and following with her mouth, her lips leaving gentle kisses all the way down. Her fingers skimmed over his cock to hold his balls in her hand and she manipulated them with her fingers as her mouth closed gently around his erect penis. Flicking her tongue across the top of it, she tasted him, licking the head boldly, running her tongue all the way down the side, grasping him firmly with her other hand.

"I want you," he rasped softly. Grabbing her waist, he gently flipped her over so she was underneath him, pinned by his body. "Mrs. Truman," he said, planting a gentle kiss on her pouting lips, "I love you." He kissed her nose. "I want to make you mine, completely mine." He kissed her passionately again, deepening the kiss as he entered her roughly, his mouth absorbing her small cry.

Her hands snaked around him and her fingers found his hips; she moved her pelvis in time with his thrusts, arching upwards to meet him, pulling him deeper inside her. The movements grew faster, more urgent, deeper, and pleasure built up inside her. They moved together, the pleasure continuing to build until her body erupted and she shook with the exquisite waves of bliss as they washed over her. Gripping Johnny tightly, she felt him shudder and then collapse against her, sated and spent. His weight against her was heavy but pleasant, and she didn't want him to move. But after a few minutes, he did.

"My, my, Mrs. Truman, you continue to surprise me," he whispered in her ear, happiness evident in his voice. His hand moved to her bottom and he slapped it lightly, before fixing first her pants, then his.

Too tired to answer, she snuggled up against him happily, holding his hand that was draped over her, and she fell asleep with a smile on her face.

When he got up in the night to take his turn on nighthawk, she smiled happily. She'd have to get up soon herself and help Billy get breakfast ready for the men, but in the meantime she had the memory of Johnny's arms around her, the pleasant, dull ache of him between her thighs, the tingle of his kiss against her lips, and the warmth of his body against hers, which lingered until she drifted back to sleep.

CHAPTER TWELVE

Trouble was brewing—Jessica could sense it. Frank kept staring at her, his eyes flicking from her to Johnny and back again. He'd been the only one of the drovers who had not congratulated them on their unplanned wedding, and he'd been acting bitter ever since. It was almost as though he was jealous, Jessica thought. But why? Usually Frank avoided them completely, but all day he'd been edging closer, watching them closely, especially her. And she felt uneasy. She'd mentioned it to Johnny but he'd thought nothing of it, simply telling her not to worry. But it wasn't that simple—she'd watched her entire family be massacred; she knew that Johnny had killed Frank's brother, and she knew Frank wanted to kill Johnny, as revenge. Knowing all that, how could she not worry? She considered approaching Mr. Jordan with her concerns, but thought better of it. The trail boss had enough to worry about, without playing referee to his men too. And if Johnny was right, and it turned out to be nothing, she'd only be another burden. And she was indebted enough to the trail boss as it was.

As they made camp that evening, Jessica was still on edge. She could feel Frank's eyes following her as she washed up before supper, shaking out her long curls to get most of the dust off them. Just as she hung up the damp towel on its hook on the side of the chuck wagon, she felt a strong arm grip her around her waist and lift her backwards off her feet. A big hand clamped over her mouth to stifle her scream and she felt herself being half-dragged, half-carried out into the open, away from the protection of the wagon. She struggled and squirmed frantically, kicking and punching her attacker as best she could, but her efforts were futile; in the position she was being held in, she simply couldn't reach to do any damage to her captor.

"Johnny!" the man holding her yelled. Jessica groaned. It was Frank who held her; she recognized his voice. Was he going to use her as bait to get to Johnny? Where was Mr. Jordan? Where were the rest of the drovers? Why wasn't someone stopping this?

She felt something cold and hard pressed against the side of her head and she gasped in horror as she realized it was a gun. Frank had her held fast against him; she couldn't escape. He was using her as a shield—there was no way Johnny, or anyone else, would risk shooting Frank now, for fear of shooting her by mistake. Her breath caught in her throat and she started to panic. *Run, Johnny! Run!* she wanted to yell, but she couldn't make her voice work, she was too scared for Johnny. It was Johnny Frank wanted, not her; if Johnny ran, she would be safe enough, and Frank would let her go eventually.

"Let her go." The voice was harsh, spoken barely above a whisper, but there was no mistaking it—it was Johnny. "Let her go, Frank. Your quarrel's with me, not her."

"Is it?" Frank's voice was dangerously soft, and he pressed the barrel of the gun harder against her head. "If I kill her we'll be even—my brother for your wife."

Jessica's heart stilled momentarily and she couldn't breathe—she truly was in danger! Then her heart started racing, beating so hard she could feel it against her forearm that Frank had pinned against her chest.

"That poker game was rigged!" Johnny yelled, sounding

desperate now. "Jessica is innocent in all this! Let her go! What kind of a man kills a woman?"

With a grunt of rage, Frank jerked his arm up under her throat, pulling her head right back, cutting off her air supply. She could still feel the cold metal of the gun pressing against her temple and she couldn't breathe—she knew her time was up. A lone tear trickled down her cheek. With her head tilted right back as it was, the only thing she could see was the sky, but she could hear footsteps approaching. Heavy, running footsteps. Mr. Jordan? She hoped it was—Mr. Jordan was the one man Frank might listen to, the one man who may be able to convince Frank to spare her life. But it would mean Johnny would lose his. Johnny was armed, but Frank already had his gun out with the hammer cocked—in a shootout, Johnny wouldn't stand a chance.

"What's going on?" Mr. Jordan's booming voice rang out. Then she heard him suppress a gasp. "Let her go, Frank. That's no way to treat a woman!" All the authority Mr. Jordan could muster was in his voice, and she felt Frank waver. "I said, let her go!" The order was even more forceful this time, and she felt herself being thrown violently sideways at the same time there was a crash of gunfire—two guns went off almost simultaneously, shattering the silence, echoing across the plains. Time stood still.

Able to breathe now, she screamed in terror as she lost her footing, knowing in her heart that Johnny was dead. Strong arms caught her as she fell, enveloping her, and she pressed her face into the dusty shirt of whoever it was that held her, sobbing in fear with big shuddering, heartbroken wails that caught in her throat and came out sounding strangled. Her legs collapsed beneath her but the strong arms held her fast.

Her heart was shattering, she could feel it—the broken pieces spread, stabbing her insides with a physical pain. Johnny was gone. It was a loss so great she couldn't comprehend it. She'd accepted the fact that she was an orphan, she accepted she was homeless... but now to find out she was a widow so soon after getting married was the ultimate blow. Her body went limp; she didn't want to go on. She wanted to die, but she couldn't stop her tears. She wanted to curl up in a ball on the ground and cry but the man who was holding her up wouldn't let her. He held her on her feet and even though her legs wouldn't take her weight, he supported her, and kept her upright. She tried to struggle against him but she couldn't make her muscles work.

"Noooooooo," she wailed. "Johnny!" Finding strength in her arms that she didn't know she had, she pounded her fists in anguish and frustration against the chest of the man who was holding her, then she looked at him through her tears—Woody.

Gently, Woody enclosed his fingers around her wrists and shook her gently. "He's not dead. Look!" He inclined his head to the left, but her vision was too blurry for her to make out anything. "Johnny is fine."

"Jessica." It sounded like Johnny's voice, but that was impossible. Johnny was dead—she'd heard the gunshot that killed him. "Jessie, it's okay, it's all okay now," the soft voice crooned, and she felt herself being gathered into someone's arms. "I'm fine, not hurt at all." Wrapping an arm around her waist securely, he grasped her chin gently with his other hand and tilted her face up to look at him. "Look at me," he commanded softly. "It's okay."

She did look at him then—and he was speaking the truth; he was unhurt. Then she looked over at the crumpled heap on the ground, blood pooling around the unmoving body.

Panic overwhelmed her as she took in the dead man on the ground. All the ghastly memories of recent events came flooding back to haunt her and her mind was awash with blood, terrified screams, and the sound of gunshots. She opened her mouth to scream but nothing came out. Her hands flew to her face in horror and she spun on her heel and ran.

She had to get away. It didn't matter where she went; she just had to get away. Away from the guns, away from the death, away from the terrible memories that were stuck in her brain and wouldn't leave. Her breath was coming in short, ragged gasps and she ran blindly, as fast as she could, away from the camp. Inside, she was screaming, but outwardly she was silent. The only sound she could hear was the pounding of her footsteps on the dusty ground.

"Jessica! Stop!" Johnny called out from behind her.

"No!" she screeched, hysterical. "Leave me alone!" She ran faster, determined to put more distance between herself and Johnny. She could still feel Frank's arm tight around her throat, the cold steel of his gun pressed against her temple. A stronger wave of panic gripped her and she stumbled, falling down, sprawled out on the dusty ground.

Within seconds she could feel strong hands lifting her up, Johnny's soothing voice whispering words of comfort. She could feel his arms wrap around her, holding her tightly, his lips dropping tender kisses on her forehead where Frank had held his gun to her.

"You're okay now, Jessica, I've got you," he soothed her, rubbing her back softly.

"Leave me alone," she begged through her sobs. "Please just leave me alone. I'm just a burden to you." She was shaking and crying, and Johnny held her fast.

"I'm not letting you go. You're my wife now; I will protect you and care for you always, no matter what. I'm not leaving you out here."

"I'm not going with you, Johnny!" she yelled at him. "You're better off without me! If I stay with you, your whole life will be spent protecting me, fighting for me, killing for me… I don't want that for you. I've seen enough killing. I don't want to be a burden anymore."

"You are not a burden!" Johnny insisted, his voice calm and firm. "I want to spend my whole life protecting you and caring for you. You are my wife—you will just have to get used to that."

Jessica shook her head at the same time as she wrenched herself free of his embrace. "I will *not* be a burden to you," she insisted, as she turned to walk away from him.

She was halted when Johnny took a firm grip of her upper arm. "You are *not*," he told her sternly, "a burden. You are my wife."

"Let me go!" Jessica insisted, trying to shake his hand free of its firm grip on her arm. Instead of releasing her, Johnny half-dragged, half-carried her over to a nearby fallen log. Sitting down on it, he wrestled Jessica down across his dusty thighs and landed a hard swat to her upturned bottom.

Realizing what was about to happen, Jessica started struggling in earnest, but Johnny easily restrained her flailing arms and legs, pinning her wrists behind her back with one hand and trapping her kicking legs beneath his. Reaching underneath her, he undid the buttons on her pants and slid them down her thighs, and smacked her again.

"You put me down!" Jessica shrieked, struggling harder, but her efforts were futile.

"I don't think so. You're going to get what's coming to you. You need some sense spanked into you!" Johnny growled, swatting her ferociously again. Then his hands went to her short, sexy lace-trimmed drawers, loosening them enough so he could slide them down too, baring her bottom.

"Johnny! Don't you dare!" Jessica ordered him, writhing and squirming, but not able to escape. "Put my clothes to rights this instant!"

Johnny just chuckled. "I quite like them like this." He rubbed his hand gently over her bottom and she could feel the rough calluses scratching against her tender skin. *Smack! Smack! Smack!* The harshness of the swats was such a contrast to the tender rubbing of just moments before that Jessica was shocked. His huge palm felt as hard as a board and each time it impacted against her bottom it felt like she was being branded by a hot iron.

"Am I getting through to you?" Johnny asked, giving her

another hearty swat. "You are my wife," he scolded, punctuating his words with another hard swat. "I will always protect you. Get used to it." Johnny aimed four spanks at the juncture where her bottom met her thighs and Jessica clenched her teeth to prevent herself from crying out. They seemed to hurt so much more on the tender skin there; she was truly miserable.

"I'm sorry!" she wailed, clenching her fists tightly against her back where Johnny held them fast. "Please stop, Johnny, I'm sorry!"

He didn't stop. Instead, he increased the force behind the swats, landing them hard and fast, and Jessica's whole bottom felt like it was on fire. She kicked and screamed as Johnny kept up a relentless pace, spanking her hard on alternating cheeks until she truly thought she would die of the pain. It was only when she was hanging, limp and defeated, over his lap, sobbing so hard she couldn't even breathe, that he stopped.

For several minutes she lay there, sobbing, trying to catch her breath, as Johnny rubbed her back. She slowly felt herself starting to relax under his expert ministrations, his gentle fingertips trailing soft circles down her spine, the tenderness he was now displaying was in stark contrast to the harsh punishment he'd just administered with that same hand. Very slowly, her sobs eased to quiet whimpers, her shoulders stopped shaking, and she became aware of where she was: in the middle of the prairie, lying across her husband's thighs, her bare bottom on display.

"Let me up," she pleaded, arching her back, trying to sit up. Johnny released her and she stood up, pulling her pants up gingerly, wincing as they slid over her hot, swollen bottom. Once her pants were fastened, Johnny pulled her down to sit on his lap, kissing away her tears, cuddling her close. Jessica snuggled into him, pressing her face against the hard muscles of his solid chest, calming herself down.

"I'm sorry I had to do that, sweetheart," Johnny murmured against her hair. "But you're my wife and I love you. I will do whatever I have to do to protect you, and I always will. Do you understand that now?"

Jessica sniffed in response. Grasping her chin gently, Johnny tilted her face up to look at him. "Do you?" he repeated, his tone firm.

"Yes," she snapped.

Johnny slapped the front of her thigh hard enough to make her yelp. "Do we need a repeat performance?" he asked sternly, one eyebrow raised.

"No, sir," Jessica quickly corrected herself, her tone demure. "I understand, Johnny. Truly, I do." She looked out over the prairie, then back at him, locking her eyes with him. "I love you. Thank you for protecting me."

Johnny bent his head down and kissed her tenderly, his lips melting against hers in a possessive show of raw passion. They kissed hungrily, deeply, their love for one another evident. When they broke apart, they were both smiling.

Jessica's bottom burned fiercely with every step she took, the rough fabric of the pants scratching horribly, but she tried not to let it show. Instead, she grasped Johnny's hand tighter as they walked slowly back to the camp together, secure in the knowledge that Johnny truly loved her.

CHAPTER THIRTEEN

Mr. Jordan rode into town the next morning to send a letter to Frank's family about his death and left Woody in charge of the herd. They'd buried Frank in a peaceful spot under the trees and the drovers had recited the Lord's Prayer as they stood around the grave, clutching their hats to their chests as a sign of respect. She'd joined in the recitation, her shaky voice drowned out by the deep, solemn voices of the cowboys as they said goodbye to their colleague and friend. None of them bore either her or Johnny any malice; they all agreed that Johnny had done what he had to, but it was still a very sad occasion.

Tears streamed down Jessica's face as she counted up on her fingers just how many people she'd watched buried since leaving Boston just a few short months ago.

Johnny and Jessica were both on drag again, eating dust for the third day in a row. Still, someone had to ride drag, and she knew better than to complain. Woody would just leave her on drag for days on end, if she did. Pulling her bandanna up over her face to shield her nose and mouth from the worst of the dust, she mounted her horse and moved the last of the cattle off, following the rest of the mob down the trail.

• • • • • • •

Mr. Jordan returned just as they were making camp for the night and he had the mail with him. One by one he read the names on the front of the envelopes and passed letters out to the drovers.

"Miss Jessica Walsh," he read, passing her an envelope.

Taking the envelope from him, she tore the flap open. Finally, the answers to the mysterious telegram from Aunt Thelma would be revealed...

Dearest Jessica, the letter read.

I'm afraid your father didn't tell you the real reason you all left Boston. Yes, it was his dream, and had been his dream all his life; but he was happy enough in Boston. He left because he had no choice. Your father was a gambler and he ran up big debts; he lost the house, he lost his job, he lost your mother's precious heirlooms, he lost everything. He was able to salvage just enough money to make a fresh start out west. The Walsh name is not a good name anymore—your father had no friends left. Don't come back to Boston—you are better off to make a new life for yourself however you can, wherever you are. You will be shunned in your old social circle; there will be no suitors, no offer for your hand in marriage. You will not be able to find employment. My dear Jessica, I'm so sorry to be the bearer of bad news but it really is for the best that you never return to Boston.

With love, Aunt Thelma

Jessica stared in shock at the letter, trying to comprehend what she'd just read. It couldn't be! Her father had been a reputable, highly respected man! He'd had a good job; they'd had lots of friends. How could it be true? How could he be a gambler and lose everything they owned? How could their good name be dragged through the mud like that?

Wordlessly, she handed the letter to Johnny. She felt ill. Her father... a gambler? He'd never liked gamblers; he'd always held them in contempt. How could mama have agreed to go with him? Why hadn't she put up a fight?

Mama had never let on… and she must have known. Realization at what her mother had gone through broke Jessica's heart all over again. Boston born and bred, her ma had loved their life in the city. It had never mattered to her that they weren't quite as rich and sophisticated as their peers; she'd been happy. Leaving behind everything she'd known and loved must have been so hard for her. A tear trickled down her cheek and she wiped it away, ashamed. Mama had never cried, at least not that she'd ever seen. She had been brave, meeting each challenge with a smile on her face. And that was what Jessica must do now, she realized. She had to move forward bravely, forgetting her life in Boston and forging a new one out here, with Johnny.

"I really do have nothing left," she murmured, turning to Johnny and burying her face in his chest. "No family, no inheritance… nothing." Then she looked up at him and smiled. "All I have in the whole world is you. I love you, Johnny."

"And I love you," Johnny replied simply, returning her smile. "And my family will love you too, I promise you. Now that I've got something I'm proud of, we can go home at the end of the trail."

"What are you proud of?" she asked him, puzzled.

Johnny's smile widened and he kissed her gently. "You."

EPILOGUE

One year later

"Are you nearly done out there?" the older woman bellowed from the door of the little log house that was now Jessica's home. For such a small woman, she sure had a loud voice!

"Nearly, ma!" Jessica called back. She leaned against the door to the chicken coop and placed her hand on her swollen belly, smiling contentedly. The baby kicked inside her; it was due any day now.

Jessica could still remember the day that Johnny had brought her home to his family, once they'd brought the cattle to the end of the Sedalia trail. Two full days' riding had brought them to the small ranch where Johnny had grown up, and she'd been nervous the whole time. What if they didn't like her? What if she didn't like them? Small-town Missouri was so different from Boston; what if she wasn't happy here?

She needn't have worried. The second they had turned in the ranch gate, the front door of Johnny's childhood home had flown open and a short, rotund lady wearing a red and white checked apron had come running down the path to meet them. Jessica had called her ma right from the start, and the kind-hearted lady with the booming voice had immediately filled the empty space her own mother had left in her heart.

The small, two-roomed log house was very different from the house she'd grown up in back in Boston, but it was home. Johnny and pa had just finished building it last week and ma had been busy in there ever since, helping Jessica hang curtains and getting it all ready for the new baby. The little crib pa had carved was in the corner next to the rocking chair, filled with blankets that ma, Jessica, and Johnny's sisters had knitted. The little stack of gowns the women had sewn was sitting on the shelf above it, and everything was ready.

The house was perfectly positioned—they had chosen the building site carefully. The front window looked out over the yard to the corral where Johnny broke in the horses, so Jessica would be able to sit on the porch rocking the baby, watching her husband work. It was far enough away from the old house, where ma and pa still lived, for them to have privacy, but close enough for ma to visit daily, if she wanted to. Ma had been lost ever since Johnny's sisters had all gotten married and moved away recently; the baby would be good for her. She needed someone to take care of.

The delicious aroma of the chocolate cake Jessica was baking wafted outside. Very soon Johnny would smell it and he would come inside for dinner. She couldn't wait to see him.

Making sure the gate on the chicken coop was latched securely, Jessica picked up the eggs and made her way slowly inside, still smiling. She was home.

The End

The Code of the West

CHAPTER ONE

The sound of hoof beats outside startled Jedda-Lyn Cross out of her reverie and she put down her sewing. Who on earth would it be at this hour? Since their parents had died two years ago in a buggy accident, no one ever visited their tiny ranch on the edge of a tiny Texas town. People had, once, but her alcoholic brother Neil never made visitors welcome, he was always drinking and rude. And it wouldn't be him—he wouldn't be home for another hour, at least. Standing up, she looked out the small window and groaned. The man dismounting from his fine gray gelding was the last person she wanted to see. But, always polite, she rose to her feet and opened the door to let the man into her house.

"What can I do for you, Mr. Robinson?" she asked, not wanting to appear rude, but really not wanting to welcome him in, either. She'd be in trouble with her brother if she sent him away, but she certainly didn't want him to stay. It would be better if he left of his own accord, then she wouldn't have to face her brother's wrath.

"Call me Cal, please."

"I haven't called you Cal yet, Mr. Robinson, why on earth would I start now?"

The man standing in her kitchen looked her up and down with a sleazy eye. "We've known each other for a long time, Jedda-Lyn; I'd hoped we could move past the formal stage and treat each other as friends. Companions."

Jedda-Lyn snorted. "I don't think so, Mr. Robinson. Look, Neil's not home. He might be a while yet. Why don't you come back later?" Cal Robinson was the last person she wanted to be alone with. He might be her brother's best friend, but she didn't like him and she didn't trust him. Many of the local girls thought him handsome, but she didn't. She knew him too well for that. She knew that his smile and charm could be turned on and off at will. She also knew his reputation: he was known about town as being handy with his fists, and he seemed to enjoy brutalizing his women. Her brother's best friend or not, she had no desire to put up with him any more than she absolutely had to.

"I think I'll stay, if you don't mind," Cal said, leaning casually against the door frame.

"I do mind, actually," Jedda-Lyn told him quite forcefully.

"That's a shame. I'd hoped we could be friends, you and I."

"We will never be friends, Mr. Robinson. Please leave."

"Maybe we could be more than friends, Miss Cross?" Cal advanced toward her, a menacing look on his face. The man looked positively evil. Jedda-Lyn shuddered as she took a step backwards, only to find the rough edge of the wooden kitchen counter pressing into her back. She was trapped. She cringed as he reached out for her and touched her face with a dirty finger. The skin on his hands was rough and scratchy and when she tried to pull away from him he laughed.

"Just relax, girl," he snarled. "This ain't gonna take long."

She was backed into the corner of the kitchen pressed up against the cupboards, and Cal held her there with his body while he fumbled with his pants. She knew what he was about to do, but she was powerless to stop him. Screaming would be pointless—there was no one around to hear her. Desperately she fought him with hands and feet, kicking him, scratching at his face with her long fingernails, trying to get away. But he was too strong. She saw him draw back his fist and although she tried to turn her face away, the blow landed squarely, solidly, on the side of her face. Momentarily everything went black, but she didn't pass out completely. The room was spinning, and there was a searing pain in her jaw, but she could still see. She was still conscious. She was aware of every movement that hateful man made; she was aware of everything he was doing to her, as he tried to wrestle with her skirts and petticoats. Dazed, she lay back against the kitchen counter while he tried to force himself on her, unable to summon any more energy to resist him.

"Get off my sister!" The order came low and clear from the doorway and the anger in her brother's voice was unmistakable.

Quickly, Cal moved off her and she crumpled to the floor, sobbing. All she could think of was how glad she was that Neil had showed up when he did, before Cal had the chance to finish what he'd started.

"Get up," Neil ordered her, his voice still harsh.

With great effort, she struggled to her feet, righting her clothing as she did so. The triumphant smirk on Cal's face as he stood there in her kitchen, staring at her possessively, made her want to vomit.

"Don't you have a shred of decency in you?" Neil was yelling at her. "Doing that right here in the kitchen where anyone could have walked in on you?" He slammed his fist down on the counter next to where she stood and she jumped.

"Do you think I did that by choice?" she asked him incredulously.

"Well, I didn't see you resisting," he retorted.

"Before he hit me I was resisting!" she yelled, holding her sore jaw. Blood trickled from the corner of her mouth, out between her fingers, so she grabbed the tea towel off the stove and gently pressed it to her face. She could see Neil's penetrating gaze switching between Cal, still looking smug, and herself; it was obvious he didn't know what to believe.

"You'll have to marry her," Neil told Cal.

Cal nodded. "Of course."

"No!" Jedda-Lyn screamed. "I won't marry him!"

"What do you mean?" Neil asked. "Of course you will!" he affirmed. "No one else is going to want you now."

"I don't care!" she yelled. "But I won't be marrying him." Turning her back to the men, she leaned against the cupboards and tried to stop shaking. When she turned around again, she was alone. Her solace didn't last long though—within minutes she heard heavy footsteps outside, then Neil stood before her in the kitchen.

"Cal will marry you next week."

"I'm not marrying Mr. Robinson. Stop trying to make me!"

"You don't have a choice." Neil's voice sounded so hard and cold. She'd never been close to her brother, and their parents' death had only served to push them further apart, but she had thought he at least cared a little bit. His tone right now proved otherwise.

"He forced himself on me! I'm going to the sheriff," she declared.

"The sheriff won't believe you. Don't be ridiculous, Jedda-Lyn. The Robinsons are the most powerful family in town—hell, they own most of the town! They control the sheriff. There's no way the sheriff is going to believe you."

Jedda-Lyn sighed. Neil was right. He often was right, when he was sober. The trouble was his sober moments were rare. "Do you believe me?" she asked him.

He paced back and forth across the kitchen a few times, then stopped and looked down at the floor. "I don't know," he mumbled. Then he straightened, and his expression brightened. "It will be good being married to Cal, you'll see. Think of the money, Jedda-Lyn! You'll be able to have whatever you want! I'll be able to get this place paying again…"

"You'll have someone to pay for your drinking habit, you mean," she accused him angrily. Thanks to Neil's addiction, the little ranch was mortgaged to the hilt—if something wasn't done soon, the bank would foreclose and they'd both be homeless. But surely marrying Mr. Robinson wasn't the answer. No, there must be another way…

"No." She was determined. She was not marrying Cal Robinson! "I'm not marrying him. He treats his women roughly, you know he does!"

"Only whores. Everyone treats whores roughly," Neil defended him.

"No, Neil. Not just whores. He won't take care of me and you know it. I'm not marrying him and there's nothing you can do to make me!"

"Jedda-Lyn, you have to!" Neil shouted.

"No, Neil, I don't. And I won't."

Reaching up to the high shelf where the whisky was, she slammed it down on the kitchen table, placing two glasses beside it. Maybe a drink would help ease the throbbing pain in her head. The pain stretched right across her temples, down the side of her face, and culminated in a climax of pulsing agony in her jaw where Cal had slugged her. Already, her jaw was swollen and it hurt to open her mouth, but she only had to open it enough to have a few small sips. Pulling the crystal stopper from the decanter, she filled both glasses.

"Broaden your mind, brother—come and have a drink."

• • • • • • •

She'd lain awake in bed for hours that night, trying to decide what to do. She would have to leave—she knew that much. By tomorrow the whole town would know that she was Cal's betrothed. If she stayed, and refused to marry him, he would tell everyone that he'd ruined her, and that would be it. She'd be left on the shelf. But what could she do? She could run away… but where would she go? The stagecoach left every day, but she had no money for a ticket, and she didn't know anyone she could borrow money off. Neil's drinking habit had made sure of that. She felt utterly hopeless. Heartbroken, she eventually cried herself to sleep long after Neil had drunk himself into a stupor at the kitchen table.

She woke up to the sound of Neil snoring and immediately she remembered her predicament. Hopelessness threatened to overwhelm her again, and then she remembered: there was a large cattle drive due to leave town in just a few hours, heading north on the Sedalia trail, led by a highly respected trail boss by the name of Weston Jordan. This was her chance! Working for Mr. Jordan, she would be safe, out of the clutches of Neil and Mr. Robinson, and she'd be earning a wage. By the time they got to Sedalia, Missouri, she would have enough money to make a fresh start somewhere new and leave her Texas life behind. It wasn't really as far-fetched as it sounded—all she had to do was convince Mr. Jordan she was a boy, and that should be easy enough. She'd spent her entire life on their small ranch so she was used to steers, and she could ride, rope, and brand—if she made a convincing enough boy and managed to get the job, she would make a fine drover. As long as Mr. Jordan agreed to give her a job… if he wouldn't hire her, she didn't know what she would do.

CHAPTER TWO

Jedda-Lyn watched the drovers as they congregated in the street. She nervously fingered her hair at the nape of her neck, hoping that the rough job she'd done with her dressmaking scissors just that morning was enough. She'd nearly cried, watching her beautiful black tresses dropping to the floor, but it had to be done. There was no way she could have passed for a boy with hair like that. Now it stuck up at odd angles all over her head, currently squashed flat by her hat. She hoped her hat wouldn't fall off; her haircut looked ridiculous. But then, her whole ensemble looked ridiculous, if she were honest. She'd had time to do a quick alteration of the waistband of the jeans she'd stolen off her brother, but they were still baggy, and she'd rolled them up at the bottom because she hadn't had time to shorten them. The shirt was baggy too, and the sleeves were far too long, but it hid her womanly figure well, so she couldn't complain. Farm boys wore clothing that was too big all the time—everyone just made do with what they had.

It would be now or never. Adjusting her brother's gun belt that was holding the Colt she'd stolen off him, she leapt down off the railing and hurried across the street to where the drovers stood.

"Excuse me," she called out, roughening her voice. "I'm looking for the trail boss. Is he here?"

"I'm trail boss," a big man stated, looking down from his horse. He was huge! It was difficult to tell exactly how tall he would be, considering he was on horseback, but he was definitely plenty tall, and solid, with jet black hair and kind eyes. "Wes Jordan. What can I do for you?" he asked politely.

"I, uh… I'm looking for work, sir," she told him, trying to sound more confident than she felt. "I've been riding the range all my life." That was close enough to the truth—their small ranch didn't exactly count as a 'range' but a little white lie wouldn't hurt, surely?

"What's your name, boy?"

"Jed."

"Jed, huh?" Mr. Jordan scratched his chin thoughtfully, looking down at her with one eyebrow raised. "And how old are you, Jed?"

"Fifteen, sir," she answered, her voice quavering. "But I'm as good as any man; you give me a chance to prove myself and I'll show you!" Fear was making her brave. What was she going to do if Mr. Jordan didn't give her this job? Neil would wake up soon, he'd notice her gone. He'd find her note and then… What would happen after that just didn't bear thinking about. She *had* to get this job. She just had to!

"Hmmmm." Mr. Jordan didn't look impressed.

"Please, sir!" she begged, trying to keep the desperation out of her voice.

"Do you have a horse?"

She shook her head.

"A saddle?"

"No. But I can ride! You give me a chance! Please!"

She stood there while Mr. Jordan looked her up and down. She saw his gaze linger on the ugly, discolored bruise on her swollen jaw and she unconsciously moved to touch the tender skin. It still hurt.

"What are you running away from, son?" Mr. Jordan asked kindly.

Jedda-Lyn shivered. *How on earth did he know?* Then it occurred to her—he believed she was just a boy. He didn't know she was really a soon-to-be-married woman of nearly twenty-two years old. She folded her arms across her chest in what she hoped was a gesture of defiance, and scowled. Boys liked to scowl, didn't they? The bandage she'd wrapped tightly around her breasts to squash them down was doing the job well. She could feel the thick strip of material under her forearms.

"Nothing!" she announced. "Ma just needs the money, that's all. She's got a lot of mouths to feed at home and pa's not well. And I'm the oldest…" She let her voice trail off, hoping Mr. Jordan would believe her. And not only that, but he would take pity on her and offer her a job. All the way to the end of the trail, if possible. She needed to get as far away from here as she could possibly get. Once she was at the railhead, destinations were limitless. And by then, she'd have her wages, so she could move on. She'd never have to be under a man's thumb ever again.

"Well, I do need another man," Mr. Jordan conceded. "But I need to know that you can take care of yourself. Can you ride? Shoot? Do you know cattle?"

"Yes, sir," she told him. "I can do all of that." And it was true—sort of. She was an excellent rider, she could shoot straight, and she knew one end of a steer from the other. How hard could it be? Besides, even if it was hard, it was better than the alternative. Anything was better than the alternative.

"And I need to talk to your parents."

"You can't, sir, they're way out of town. But here—" She pulled a folded piece of paper out of her pocket and handed it to him. A note from a mother giving her son her blessing to get work on the cattle drive headed north. It was signed in an illegible scrawl, but the name 'Hetty' could just be made out.

"That's fine, then," Mr. Jordan said as he pocketed the note. "Have you got all your belongings? Old Joe there will sort you out a horse and a saddle." He pointed to a man who looked to be in his forties with graying hair, whom she assumed was the wrangler.

Old Joe acknowledged the boss's order with a curt nod, ignored her completely, and went about finding her a suitable horse.

"Right here," Jedda-Lyn said, patting her bedroll. She'd managed to wrap up everything she wanted to take inside her blankets—just a spare change of clothes, her mother's locket, and a coat. She'd had to leave everything else behind. Not that it mattered—nothing she owned was more precious than the prospect of freedom.

Jedda-Lyn couldn't contain her smile. She'd done it! She'd really done it! Writing that note from her 'mother' had been a stroke of genius, she knew. Without it, she probably wouldn't have got the job. But now she did, and by the time Neil woke up and recovered from his hangover she'd be long gone. And the last place he'd think to look for her would be on a dusty cattle drive with Mr. Jordan's outfit. Mr. Jordan was well known, he had a reputation as a top trail boss, and no one would expect him to hire a woman. Especially not a woman who was meant to be getting married to one of the town's wealthiest gentlemen. No, she'd be safe enough on the trail.

• • • • • • •

"I'm Woody Carlson, ramrod." The voice right next to her made her jump, but she tried to hide her fear. This drive would be hell if she was going to react to every man who snuck up beside her. Taking a good look at the handsome young man to her left, she noticed that he was only a few years older than she, with a rugged, boyish appearance.

Dirty brown hair peeked out from under his battered gray-brown hat, and he was at least six feet tall.

"Jed," she introduced herself, smiling. *If I'd known cowboys this good-looking were working as drovers I would have done this a long time ago!* she thought, pleasantly surprised at just how attractive Woody was.

Her smile was not returned. Woody clearly wasn't impressed with Mr. Jordan's decision to hire on a boy as a drover. "You're on drag."

"Yes, sir," she answered briskly. She didn't mind being on drag. Sure, there were better things to do than spend all day eating dust behind a herd of cattle, but the alternative was much worse. At the tail end of the cattle drive, trying to keep three thousand steers moving in the right direction, she'd be safe enough from Neil, at least. Taking a firm grip on the reins, she swung herself up into the saddle, ready to move out as soon as Mr. Jordan gave the order.

· · · · · · ·

Wiping the sweat out of her eyes again, Jed exchanged her tired horse for a fresh one. It was hard work, keeping the steers moving. They kept trying to turn and go back to their home range, and even though two other drovers were helping her on drag, she was exhausted. She'd underestimated how hard it would actually be, being a drover. She'd thought that working on the ranch at home would have prepared her; it hadn't. Not really.

Her jaw was aching from where Cal had struck her, and she rubbed it absentmindedly. "That's a nasty bruise you've got there."

She looked up to see a drover just behind her, bringing back a couple of strays. He didn't look to be very old, in his mid-twenties maybe, and he had a striking black moustache. He was twirling the ends of it between his fingers, which muffled his words slightly, making him difficult to understand.

"Yes," she agreed. "It's still sore." She had no idea what this drover's name was; she hadn't managed to sort out who was who yet, besides Joe, Mr. Jordan, and Woody.

"I'm Chuck," he said, smiling timidly. He had a nice smile, and his moustache accentuated his even, white teeth.

"Jed."

"You're a bit young to have left home, aren't ya?" Chuck questioned.

"I'm fifteen," she told him. "Plenty old enough. Besides, ma needs the money. Pa's not well, and I'm the oldest…" She trailed off as she discreetly pressed her arm against her chest, making sure the bandage she'd wound around it that morning was still there. Her shirt was big and loose, but it wouldn't do for the bandage to slip, all the same.

"So that bruise there, how'd ya get it?" Chuck asked, moving his horse in closer to her. "You're not running away from nothing, are ya?"

"That's not…" She'd been about to tell him it wasn't any of his business, but she stopped herself just in time. She was meant to be a boy just starting out in the world, not a grown woman who was full of sass and opinion. And she was pretty sure that a young boy on his first job wouldn't be talking back to drovers. Not if he wanted to stay in one piece, anyway. She sighed, touching her jaw lightly again. "My brother did it," she said. "I'm the oldest, but he's the biggest."

"Well, you be careful," Chuck told her. "Don't go hurtin' it again. And if it gets any sorer you go talk to Monty—he's the cook—and he'll doctor it for ya. He's got all sorts of medicines in the chuck wagon yonder." He indicated with his thumb to the far edge of the herd, right up near the front, to the two wagons traveling together.

"I will, thanks." She smiled, then winced. She'd been jolting around in the saddle for so long that even smiling hurt. She stared after Chuck's retreating back as he rode away from her. So far, he was the only drover to show her any kindness. The others had either ignored her or yelled orders at her. They certainly didn't bother to introduce themselves or stop and chat, or ask how she was. As far as they were concerned, she was just a boy to be ordered about. And remaining meek, as a boy should, to those shouted orders was a struggle for her. It had been a long time since she'd had to be obedient—she'd been making her own decisions and helping to run the ranch for years. The treatment she was getting now at the bottom of the pecking order was a challenge she hadn't considered.

Chuck seemed nice. She picked him to pieces in her mind as she herded steer after steer back into the mob, keeping the stragglers moving. Although she didn't consider him to be a handsome man, especially not with that moustache he'd been fiddling with, he had a nice smile and she'd liked him.

As the day wore on and she grew tired from hours in the saddle and weary of taking orders from the drovers, she started to wonder if she'd made the right decision after all. Could this—bone-numbing exhaustion, dust covering her body in a light film, and getting yelled at by all the men—really be any better than life as Mrs. Calvin Robinson? She knew how bad it would have been with Cal—she knew his reputation, she knew how he treated women. But this drive was only just starting and already she was struggling. She didn't take orders well; how much longer was she going to be able to keep her temper in check? How long would it be before she fell out of the saddle with weariness?

• • • • • • •

"Jed, you can help Billy collect firewood," Woody told her as soon as they made camp. She'd barely handed the reins of her horse over to Joe and she was exhausted. Bent over with her hands on her knees, she ignored Woody's order for the moment—she needed a breather. "Jed!" The raised voice made her jump. "The next time you hesitate when I give you an order, you'll be getting a whuppin'. Now get out of here!"

"You ain't got no right to whup me!" she declared vehemently. "I'm a gro…" She stopped herself just in time, frustrated. Exhaustion was making her careless already and they'd barely started. How was she going to keep up this charade over fifteen hundred miles?

"You're a boy who needs to listen," Woody growled.

Scowling, she glared at him, but there was nothing she could say.

"Who's Billy?" she asked.

"Cook's louse," Woody snapped, pointing at a young man, not much older than the age she was pretending to be, wandering off into the trees at the edge of camp.

"I'm Jed," she greeted him as she approached.

The young man stood up from where he was crouched picking up wood, and looked at her. "Billy," he announced. "Helper to the best range cook in the west. The cook is my uncle." He gave her a broad smile, clearly pleased to have a peer within the team.

"What's Woody like?" she asked Billy as soon as they were out of earshot. "Does he treat you fairly?"

"Oh, he's all right," Billy drawled, picking up a broken branch. "This is my third drive so he's okay now. He was a bit rough at first but Uncle Monty told him to leave me be. He's been all right since then."

"Rough on you?" Jedda-Lyn questioned. "In what way?"

Billy straightened up. "Well, he…"

"Jed!" Mr. Jordan yelled from camp. "Come in and get some coffee!"

"Here, take this." Billy dumped the firewood he'd collected into her outstretched arms. "It will keep Woody happy."

Jedda-Lyn smiled gratefully at him; she'd been so busy talking she hadn't collected any wood at all, and she didn't want to give Woody any reason to make good on his threat.

"What were you doing out there?" Mr. Jordan asked as she walked back into the camp, laden down with Billy's wood.

"Woody told me to help Billy. Where do I put it?" she asked.

Mr. Jordan indicated the chuck wagon. "In the possum belly, under the wagon. Then you can come and have a break—you've earned it." The smile he gave her lit up his whole face, little creases appearing around his eyes. Her gut tightened as she noticed how good-looking he was. Young, too, for a boss. Much younger than she had expected he would be. She'd heard all about Mr. Jordan; nearly everyone in the cattle business knew of his reputation as one of the best trail bosses around. He'd never lost more than a handful of steers in any herd, in all the drives he'd led. It was rumored that he'd encountered it all out there on the trail, and no matter what, he always got the cattle through, on time, in peak condition, and got the best prices. He was fearless and tough, but an honest man, and he had an air of authority about him that had made her think he was older than he was. But looking at him now, it was clear he wouldn't be thirty. A couple of years off it still, probably. His smile melted her. Was he married? The question gnawed at her insides, but she forced it down. It didn't matter who was married to whom—she wasn't looking for a husband. She was trying to escape from one.

The boss is much kinder than Woody, she decided as she headed to the wagon to offload the wood. She could see Woody watching her as he stood in line for his meal so she glared at him defiantly. There was nothing he could do to her now—she'd done what he'd asked her to do; now Mr. Jordan had given her a break. And she meant to enjoy it.

• • • • • • •

The first few days were rough. Really rough. Woody kept her on drag the entire time, rotating the other men to help her keep the steers heading the right way, cutting back the ones who managed to wander off and head back toward home. She kept waiting for Woody to give her a spell from the tail end of the drive, but he never did. It was intentional—she knew it was—he clearly had a problem with a 'boy' being given a job as a drover, and making her stay on the drag was the worst thing he could think of to do to her. Especially this early on in the drive when it was the worst, the hardest position to be in, with the steers constantly breaking out of the mob. She'd really had no idea it would be this tough, being a drover. And the long hours spent on drag day after day were wearing her down. More than once she considered turning around and going home, to let Cal do his worst.

Breaks were rare, and sleep even rarer. The noon meal was often sandwiches, eaten in the saddle. Twice they even pushed the beeves all through the night. She was beginning to worry that she would fall asleep in the saddle if she didn't get a rest soon.

"Is it going to be like this the whole way?" she asked Joe, the wrangler, as she exchanged her weary horse for a fresh one. She didn't want to question the pace or complain, but she knew that she couldn't keep it up for much longer—she was exhausted. It was her fourth day with barely any sleep. Even the men were complaining about being tired.

"Naw, it will get easier soon," Joe reassured her. "The boss always starts out like this, gotta trail-break the herd, he says. Keep them tired, push them hard, and they're easier to manage. If they're too fresh they get out of control and scatter all over Texas, heading back home, and we'll never round them up again."

She smiled her thanks at him, pleased. She remembered how Joe had made a point of ignoring her that first day, and had only grunted at her on the second. Now, she could actually hold a real conversation with him. It was a definite improvement.

She squinted into the sun at the rider coming toward her. From this distance, he looked an impressive specimen of manhood. He sat tall and straight in the saddle and had the broadest shoulders she'd ever seen, and he looked to be lean and muscular. He looked as fine and natural on horseback as the boss did. She felt her pulse race as the man drew closer.

"How are you holding up?" he asked her, turning his horse to ride beside her. "We'll be stopping for a rest soon—you look like you need it!" he chuckled. "You're covered in dust!"

"A rest will be good," she agreed. "What's your name?"

"Oh, I'm Davey, I'm the scout. It's my job to find the water, know what danger is on the trail up ahead, find the bedding ground, that sort of thing."

As Davey spoke, Jed looked at him. This cowboy was attractive too, but not as handsome as the big trail boss. She guessed them to be around the same height; both lean and tough. Light brown curly hair peeked out from under his hat to touch his collar and he had deep brown eyes. *Stop thinking about the attractiveness of the cowboys,* she scolded herself. *You're meant to be a boy! It doesn't matter how good-looking the drovers are, they're out of bounds!* Suddenly, she found herself hoping that she would get found out one day, and she could be free to ogle the men properly.

Davey nodded to her as he rode away, continuing on up the other side of the herd.

At noon, they stopped for a break and a hot meal. She lined up with the men while Monty and Billy ladled hot stew onto plates and once she'd eaten, she put her head on her saddle and lay back under the hot sun.

• • • • • • •

Woody watched Jed while she slept. He hated the idea of the boy being given a job on the drive—it was too hard for a kid, and far too dangerous. Boys of that age belonged at home with their mothers. He shook his head in frustration as he tipped the dregs of his coffee on the ground. He'd only been twelve when his brother had left home the day after he turned fifteen—was going to make a life for himself, he said. He was sick of playing by the rules of the house, sick of following their old man's orders; he was going to do what he wanted. And so he'd left. Pa had pretended he didn't care, but he did. And ma had taken to her bed and cried for nearly the whole of the first week, then she'd gotten up and carried on as though nothing had happened. Things had changed though, with Adam's leaving. Woody had been left to bear the brunt of their father's temper and he'd had to take over all of Adam's chores. He had to stop going to school most of the time; he was needed at home.

A few months later, a telegram arrived to say that Adam had been killed by a mustang he'd been trying to break. Ma had taken to her bed again and pa had turned to drinking and gambling; it had been left to Woody to milk the cow and do the chores and keep his little sister Cecelia fed. He didn't mind taking care of Cece; at just six years old she was a cute little thing and she hung on his every word, following him around, smiling a gap-toothed grin. But it was hard work, and he blamed Adam. If Adam had stayed at home where he belonged, he wouldn't be dead, and none of this would have happened. Ma wouldn't stay in bed all the time, pa wouldn't be constantly drunk, and he wouldn't be taking care of Cece.

One day pa didn't come home. The sheriff had knocked on the door and gone in and talked to ma, who still refused to get out of bed, and that was that. Woody never did find out what happened to pa, and there wasn't a funeral. In the end, ma had taken Woody and Cecelia back home to Philadelphia to live with her brother and his wife, and Woody's hate toward Adam for leaving had grown more, festering inside until he was hard and bitter.

Woody threw a disgusted look in Jed's direction as he tossed his cup in the wreck pan. "That boy shouldn't be on the trail," he muttered to Monty, the cook. "I wonder how many lives he is wrecking by running away from home at his age?"

"What makes you think he's wrecking any?" Monty asked, sounding disgruntled.

"Look at that bruise on his face. He's running from something, for sure!"

"You don't know that it's family responsibilities he's runnin' from," Monty argued, packing the last of his things away in the chuck wagon. "You leave that boy alone."

"Right, back in your saddles!" Mr. Jordan gave the order and the men around him sprang to life, grumbling and stretching.

"You too, boy!" Davey, the scout, called. He was nearest to Jed, and he squatted down beside her and shook her gently. "Hey!" he called gently. "Wake up!"

• • • • • • •

Cal had found her! She was awake instantly, her gun clearing its holster even as she scrambled to her feet. She couldn't let him take her! She wouldn't go!

"Hey, it's just me, Davey, scout for the trail drive, remember?" He spoke softly, calmly, his palms up in a submissive gesture.

Jed's vision was blurry from sleep, but before she could focus properly, someone grabbed her wrist in a tight grip and the gun was wrenched from her grasp.

"You give that back!" Jed cried, but Woody held it out of her reach.

She gasped. "Oh no!" Her vision cleared, and she could see that it wasn't Cal that she was threatening at all, but Davey, a man who had shown her nothing but kindness. And next to her, towering over her threateningly, holding her gun, was Woody.

"You pull a gun on us again and I'll take a switch to you, boy!" Woody snarled.

"Let him be, Woody," Davey ordered. "He just got a fright, that's all."

Shocked, Jed stood there with her hands over her mouth, hardly able to believe what she'd done. How had she mistaken these men for Cal? "I'm so sorry," she apologized. "I was… I was having a nightmare," she stammered. "I'm so sorry."

Woody and Davey both fixed her with a stern glare when Mr. Jordan appeared in front of them. "What's going on?" he asked, his deep baritone voice rumbling angrily.

Woody continued to glower at her, breathing hard. "If you want to survive out here, boy, you better learn the code of the west." He handed Jed back her gun.

"You never pull a gun on a man unless you're willing to use it," Davey scolded. "Unless you want to get dead, you keep your gun in its holster." Frowning, he turned and walked away.

"Give me your gun, Jed," Mr. Jordan demanded, stretching out his hand.

She shook her head. She couldn't be out here unarmed! What if Cal really did come? Her grip tightened around the butt of her Colt, but Mr. Jordan fixed her with his sternest stare, with one eyebrow raised ever so slightly, and he looked so fierce that her resolve crumpled. When he reached for her gun, she relaxed her grip and let him take it.

"You can have it back when you've proven to me you're responsible enough to handle it," he told her. "You're lucky it was mild-mannered Davey you pulled the gun on," he said. "Other men would have shot you as soon as you started to draw. Your gun wouldn't have cleared the holster and you'd be on the ground, dead."

Jedda-Lyn looked at her boots. How could she have stuffed up so badly, so soon? This wasn't going at all like she'd hoped. She'd had no idea that being a drover would be so hard! Not a week from home and already she was in trouble.

Mr. Jordan turned to Woody, who was still standing there, watching, looking annoyed. "Where is Jed riding?" he asked.

"Drag," Woody snapped, glaring at her.

"Right, get going," Mr. Jordan ordered. "Both of you."

CHAPTER THREE

Wes Jordan took a swallow of his coffee and let out a tired sigh. He was getting sick of being a trail boss, always on the move. He wanted to settle down, try his hand at running his own place. At the end of this drive he would have the money together to buy a ranch and put together his own herd, instead of driving cattle for others all the way across the west. This was no life for a man, not for long. Sleeping on the ground, constantly on guard against the many threats to the lives of men and herd, battling weather, searching for water... he'd done it for long enough.

"Mr. Jordan!" Woody called.

He looked up to see three men riding into camp, all of them looking weary. They'd obviously been riding hard to catch up to the herd. As the men got closer he could see that one of them was wearing a badge. The sheriff and two deputies. His heart sank. What did the sheriff want? The last thing he needed this early on was trouble with the law. Out of the corner of his eye he saw Jed quickly ducking out of sight behind the supply wagon. So... the boy *was* running from something.

"You the boss of this here outfit?" the sheriff asked as he rode up, flashing his badge. The two deputies with him looked sullen.

"Yep, Wes Jordan."

The sheriff plucked a picture from the pocket of his vest and handed it to Mr. Jordan. "You seen this woman around anywhere?" he asked. "She's missing. Her fiancé is offering quite a generous reward for her safe return. Jedda-Lyn Cross is her name."

Mr. Jordan scanned the photo quickly. The woman was beautiful, with jet black hair pinned up high on her head. He knew who it was instantly. Even dressed as a boy with that ugly bruise on her face, the likeness was unmistakable. What on earth was Jed running from?

Mr. Jordan shook his head. "No women around here, sheriff. A trail drive is no place for a woman, you know that."

The sheriff looked unconvinced, but he nodded, pocketing the photo again. "You let us know if you see her then," he snapped, wheeling his horse abruptly and spurring him into a canter, the deputies hot on his heels.

Mr. Jordan took off his hat and ran his hand through his hair in frustration. What was he going to do now?

"Jed!" he bellowed, anger coursing through him. What was he going to do with a woman on his drive? How was he going to ensure her safety? And what was he going to do when the jilted fiancé came back? Come to think of it, why *was* there a jilted fiancé? What had the man done to Jed to make her run, and disguise herself as a boy? She must have been desperate to have cut off all that beautiful hair. And there was the yellow bruise still coloring her jaw. Had the fiancé done that?

Jed was scurrying toward him, wringing her hands nervously in front of her, looking scared. Actually, she looked more than scared. She looked close to tears.

"Care to tell me your *real* name, Jed? And why you're on the run? The sheriff was just here looking for you—your fiancé is offering a reward for your return." He drew himself up to his full height, folded his arms across his chest in an intimidating manner, and fixed her with a stern stare. Her eyes never left the ground. "Well?" he demanded. "I'm waiting."

"I don't have a fiancé," she insisted, trembling. She still didn't look up, and her body shook with fear. "I... I'm sorry, sir," she stammered. "I'll go. Please don't turn me in to the sheriff, please just let me go. Please!" her voice quavered. "I'm begging you, please just let me go! Let me borrow a horse, I'll get you the money to pay for it somehow... but please, don't turn me in. Just please let me go." Her eyes glistened with unshed tears. It was clear that, whoever her fiancé was, she was afraid of him.

"You won't be going anywhere," Mr. Jordan assured her. "Just tell me the truth, that's all I'm asking. *All* of the truth." He put a hand on her shoulder in what he hoped was an encouraging gesture. Maybe his size was more intimidating to her than he realized. He relaxed his posture somewhat and smiled kindly. "I can see that bruise on your face; I'm guessing your fiancé was a cruel man. I'm not sending you back there. But I do need to know the truth."

"My name is Jedda-Lyn Cross," she told him timidly. "But please call me Jed, I like it." Taking a deep breath, she told him the whole sordid story. Her voice broke when she started to describe what Mr. Robinson had done, but she took a deep breath and bravely carried on. "So I cut off my hair, stole some of my brother's clothes and his gun, and here I am. Destitute and homeless."

She broke down then, seeming completely broken. Sobs wracked her body, her shoulders shook, and she buried her face in her hands.

He admired her bravery. Not many women would have the courage to do what she'd done, or the skill and stamina required to keep up with the men on the trail drive. Especially not the way Woody had been pushing her. Her face was contorted in anguish and he felt sorry for her. Her head fell forward as she sobbed and came to rest gently against his chest. Her small fists closed around his waistcoat as she cried. Gently, he reached up and put a hand on her back, hoping to comfort her. It took a couple of minutes, but eventually her sobs subsided and she stood up.

"Have you got any family anywhere? Is there anywhere you can go?" Mr. Jordan asked her. He couldn't keep her on the drive; it wasn't safe.

She shook her head. "No. It was just Neil and me. And I can't go back to Neil."

"Look, we're a just bunch of rough cowboys pushing cattle north to the railheads. There's no place for a woman on a trail drive." But as he said it, he remembered the last drive, and Jessica. She'd gotten along fine. But she'd had Johnny there to protect her. A single woman, a beautiful single woman, was another matter entirely. She would cause all sorts of tension in the camp, cause rifts between the men… no, she couldn't stay. But he couldn't send her away, either. Not now that he knew her story. His hands stayed by his sides but he clenched his fists in frustration. What on earth was he going to do?

• • • • • • •

Inwardly, Jed was panicking. She'd known when she first started out that Mr. Jordan might discover who she was, but she'd hoped they would be a little further north, in a place where she could start afresh. If she left the drive now not only did she have no money, but she was too close to home. It would be too easy for Neil and Mr. Robinson to find her. And if there was a reward for her return, how long would it be before someone discovered her whereabouts and took her back? But as soon as Mr. Jordan said the words, "You won't be going anywhere," she relaxed. It was clear by the tension in Mr. Jordan's body that he wasn't happy about having a woman along on the drive, but for now at least, she was safe.

"So you'll let me stay then?" she asked him hopefully.

Mr. Jordan sighed. He took off his hat and ran his fingers

through his hair, before replacing his hat on his head. "Yes, for now," he agreed. "But you'll need to remain a boy. It's not safe for a woman in camp. I barely know half of these men. If they know there's a woman around there'll be tension… fights." He shook his head, a worried frown on his face.

"Thank you." Her voice was quiet, but it was filled with gratitude. She was relieved. But she was concerned too. How was she going to keep her secret all the way to Sedalia? She'd already come close to blowing her cover more than once, and the drive had barely started. What would happen when—if—the men discovered she wasn't a boy after all, but a grown woman?

• • • • • • •

"Take Jed off night watch," Mr. Jordan ordered as Woody read out the roster for the night. She'd been assigned to second watch.

"Why?" Woody asked, confused.

"He's too tired. Just do as I say!"

The light was dim, but even from across the other side of the fire she could see Woody's face contort with anger.

"It's okay," she objected. "I can do it." But Mr. Jordan held up his hand to silence her.

"He's signed on as a man to work a trail drive, he can do a man's work!" Woody argued.

"But he's not a man, is he? Take him off." Mr. Jordan's deep, gravelly voice was raised slightly, his body taut, his fists clenched by his sides.

"That's not fair, boss!" someone called out. "We're all tired!"

"Yeah!" someone else agreed. "If he can't do a man's work, he shouldn't be here!"

There were echoes of muffled agreement throughout the camp. Jed could feel her body going tense. What was going to happen now?

"I pay you to follow my orders," Mr. Jordan shouted. "Any man who doesn't want to do that is free to leave. I'll pay him off and he can leave tonight. Woody, take Jed off night watch. Now."

She watched as several of the men stood up, clearly ready to quit their jobs. And she understood why—Mr. Jordan had a reputation as being a fair man, yet right now, he wasn't being fair to his men; one of his drovers was getting special treatment.

"Hold it!" she called out, scrambling to her feet. "Listen to me, please!" she commanded, not roughening her voice this time but instead trying to sound like the woman she was. "I'm not a boy. I'm a woman. Mr. Jordan kept my secret to protect me, but it's not fair on you all for him to do that." She caught the fierce glare he gave her, out of the corner of her eye, but it was too late. She'd just have to deal with the consequences of letting out her secret—it wasn't fair to Mr. Jordan for him to lose half his drovers because of her. She looked around. The men had stopped moving, halting in mid-stride, to look at her disbelievingly. She heard a few gasps of astonishment, a few outraged murmurs.

"I was... attacked," she told them, "by one of my brother's friends." Reflexively, her fingers rubbed her jaw, where the fading bruise was still visible. "Mr. Robinson is rich—his family owns most of the town," she continued. "I couldn't go to the sheriff, he wouldn't believe me. As far as my brother was concerned, marriage to Mr. Robinson was the only option." She choked back a sob. This was much harder than she'd thought it would be. Telling Mr. Jordan was one thing. But telling a whole bunch of men she barely knew about her ruination was quite another. She heard Mr. Jordan come up behind her, and felt him lay his hand gently on her shoulder, giving her strength. Taking a deep breath, she continued with her story, not daring to look at the drovers who had gathered closer to hear her words.

"Mr. Robinson is not a kind man," she told them. "His reputation is well known—he's arrogant, a dirty fighter, and violent with his women. Neil—my brother—wanted me to marry Mr. Robinson as a way of financing his drinking habit, but I couldn't do it." She shook her head, still not daring to look up. "I couldn't marry a man like that."

The camp was deadly silent. None of the men moved. She didn't dare breathe. What was going to happen? She looked at the men, wondering how they were reacting to her story. They looked shocked. She turned to Mr. Jordan. "I'm sorry," she whispered. "I couldn't keep it a secret. I couldn't let you lose all your men, just to protect me." He didn't answer.

She looked back at the ground, then heard Chuck clear his throat. "I'm happy to do Jed's night watch," he said.

"So am I," Davey spoke up.

"Me too," agreed another drover. "Night watch isn't safe for a woman."

"Leave me on night watch, please, Woody," she spoke clearly and directly. "It isn't fair on any of you men for me to be treated any differently. I will pull my weight."

Mr. Jordan slapped his hand against his chaps in frustration and blinked rapidly as dust flew up off them. "No woman in my camp is doing night watch duty. You're doing a fine job as a drover. But you're not doing night watch and that's the end of it. Disobey me, and you'll be cutting me a switch."

Jed gasped. "What?" she exclaimed in outrage. "I just ran away from an abusive man, I'm not staying here with more of them! I think I'll get my stuff and move on."

"Giving a deserving woman a spanking isn't the same thing as abusing her," Mr. Jordan explained. He touched the bruise on her jaw gently. "I would never do that to you."

She snorted and shrank away from his touch. "Thanks all the same, I think I'll move on now. Have I earned enough money yet to pay for a horse and saddle?"

"You lot, get back to what you were doing!" Mr. Jordan snapped at his men who were still hanging around, watching the proceedings with interest.

Jed gulped. What on earth had she gotten herself into? What had she been thinking, coming out here disguised as a boy? Maybe it wouldn't be so bad, life as Cal's wife… not that she was left with a choice. If she left the drive she would have to go back; she had no money and nowhere to go.

"Look, Jed, you're a woman. There isn't a man here who would let you do the night watch. Not now that we know. We protect women; we don't have them do the protectin'."

"Threatening to spank me doesn't sound very protective," she countered, still not yet willing to back down.

"If it helps to keep the woman safe, sometimes it's necessary." Mr. Jordan spoke softly, his tone a gentle one, unlike the brusqueness in which he'd issued orders to his men just seconds before. He swept a stray lock of her hair back off her face. "There is a job for you here for as long as you want it. All the way to Sedalia. You're a good drover. But now that I know you're a woman, I will put in place measures to protect you. And I will expect you to obey them." His deep baritone voice rumbled through her, sending waves of heat to her loins. It was so gruff and commanding, even though he was speaking quietly. What was it about his voice that affected her so?

She sighed, giving in. "Thank you," she murmured.

"Are you happy bedding down on the ground with us or would you rather spread your bedroll in the supply wagon?"

"The ground is fine. I don't want any special treatment, Mr. Jordan. I signed on to this drive to do a job. The fact that I'm a woman doesn't change that."

"Good." Tipping his hat to her, Mr. Jordan turned and walked away, leaving Jed to her thoughts. They were tumbling around in her brain, confusing her. Why did she find Mr. Jordan so attractive? Threatening to spank her like that—he was no more than a callous brute! And yet she couldn't get him out of her mind. His spanking threat intrigued and excited her, and much to her shame, she found herself mildly curious as to what a spanking from the handsome trail boss would feel like.

• • • • • • •

Once the men knew she was a woman, they treated her differently. No more did they bark orders at her as they'd done when they'd thought she was a boy. They didn't swear around her so much either—not that Mr. Jordan allowed much in the way of cussing in his camp, but now that there was a lady present, he was even stricter about it.

She remained on drag, helped by whatever drover happened to be rostered on drag that day. On horseback, she did her job, and was treated as one of the men. Every so often Mr. Jordan, Woody, or Davey would come and check on her, as they had always done, but they spoke to her with more respect now. Especially Woody—his tone was cheerful, almost flirty, and he always had a ready grin for her, which enhanced his boyish good looks. She wasn't interested in him, though. He hadn't treated her with any kindness when he thought she was a boy; why would she want to have anything to do with a man like that? As far as she was concerned, boys were deserving of kindness too.

The evenings were spent playing poker quietly around the campfire, and she enjoyed it immensely. It had been lonely at home with just her and Neil. And he hadn't always been home. She had friends, of course, but they were all married now, with their own lives to lead. She should have been married too, but their parents' tragic death had changed all that. And so here she was, out in the middle of nowhere, spending her days chasing beeves and her evenings gambling on her pile of matchsticks with a bunch of rough, dusty drovers.

• • • • • • •

The stranger rode into camp three days later, just as they were starting to eat the evening meal.

"Hello, the camp!" he called out as he approached.

Instinctively, Jed turned her body away from the stranger and kept herself hidden between the men around the chuck wagon. Likely as not the stranger was purely just a stranger, but since she'd dispensed with the tight, uncomfortable bandage wrapped around her chest, it was obvious to all that she was a woman and she didn't want to take any chances until Mr. Jordan had checked him out.

She watched as Mr. Jordan talked to the man at the edge of the camp, then smiled and invited him to eat with them. When she saw his face she gasped in horror—she recognized him! She'd only seen him a few times around town, but she knew he drank with Neil and Cal. He was a scruffy man, scrawny, with a hang-dog look about him, much older than Neil and Cal—he'd be in his mid-forties easily. What was he doing way out here? Had Mr. Robinson sent him? Or was it chance that had brought him here?

She pressed herself closer up against Davey, trying to hide from the stranger. She didn't think he would recognize her, not unless he was looking for her, but Davey's tall, strong body make her feel safe. Chuck moved closer to her other side so she was sandwiched protectively between the two men. She started to relax.

"Son-of-a-bitch stew is it, tonight, boys?" the stranger asked, looking around at the men, then threw back his head and let out a great guffaw of laughter. "That's the only thing we get on the trail, isn't it? Old son-of-a-bitch stew? No one joins a trail drive for the cooking!" He laughed again.

Monty straightened up and banged his spoon against the side of the pot. "Look here, mister, if you're just here to complain about the cookin', you can be moving right along. The drovers complain enough without you adding to it."

"And you can watch your language while you're at it," Woody announced. "There's a lady present."

Shut up, Woody! she wanted to scream at him, but it wasn't Woody's fault. He didn't know that she knew this man and that possibly, he was looking for her.

"Lady? On a cattle drive? Where?" The stranger looked around and his eyes fell immediately on Jed. "Oh, that? You call that a lady? She ain't no lady. She's just a whore trying to be a saddle tramp, done cut off all that beautiful hair. Is that what classes as a lady in these parts?"

She felt Davey stiffen beside her, but he didn't move to defend her. He could see the two guns the stranger wore just as well as she could, and although Davey was no stranger to gunfights, no drover wanted to risk unnecessary gunshots and set off a stampede.

"She's not a whore," Chuck spoke quietly from beside her, but he didn't move.

"Oh, she's a whore all right," the stranger argued. "She's used goods!"

"I am not!" Jed defended herself, taking a step forward, leaving the protection of Davey and Chuck.

The stranger gave her a lecherous smile. "It's all over town that Cal ruined you! Come on, let me take you back. He's waiting for you." He stopped talking and looked her up and down, his eyes lingering on her chest where the man's shirt she wore was stretched tight across her ample bosom. He nodded approvingly. "You sure are a pretty little thing; no wonder he's willing to pay so much for your return."

"I'm not going with you." She felt brave with the drovers standing so close to her.

"I'll give you half the reward money," he offered. "You'll be earning it on the way back. Everyone knows you're ruined, Cal won't mind too much if I try you out too, before the wedding."

Jed gasped. How dare he suggest such a thing? Furious, she raised her hand and slapped his face as hard as she could. Her palm stung satisfyingly and she shook it, as the outline of her fingers appeared on his cheek. The stranger blinked, then looked at her, shocked, for a fraction of a second, then he raised his own hand to strike her back.

"Get out of my camp. No one speaks to a lady like that

in this camp." Mr. Jordan's voice had a menacing coldness in it she'd never heard before. He grabbed the stranger's wrist in mid-air from behind and spun him around, punching him with so much force that he crumpled to the ground.

Now that the threat had been removed, Jed realized how frightened she was—her legs were like jelly and she was wobbling on her feet from shock. Davey stepped toward her and she clutched at his shirt, afraid of falling down.

"Get up," Mr. Jordan snarled, reaching down and yanking the stranger up by the lapels of his coat. Still holding him by his coat, Mr. Jordan marched him briskly backwards toward his horse. Woody followed, his hand on his gun.

Davey wrapped an arm around her tightly, holding her upright. "It's alright, I've got you," he murmured. Instantly, she was surrounded by concerned drovers, and it was only then, when she was completely shielded by them, that she began to feel safe enough to relax. She had managed to calm down enough to let go of Davey by the time Mr. Jordan and Woody returned to camp after escorting the stranger away, but her heart was still pounding rapidly in her chest and her breathing was rapid and shallow.

"Are you alright, Jed?" Mr. Jordan asked.

She nodded. "I am now, yes. But that man knows Neil. He'll go back and tell them where I am, and they'll come after me. I need a horse, Mr. Jordan. I need to get away. When they come here, I need to be as far away as possible."

Mr. Jordan shook his head. "You just stay here with us, we'll keep you safe," he assured her. "If your brother comes, we'll be waiting."

She started to panic again. "You don't understand!" she cried. "I need to get away from here! I can't risk being here when Neil comes, I can't go back there!"

Mr. Jordan put a steady hand on her shoulder. "I can't let you leave and put yourself at risk," he told her. "Besides, you're a good drover and I don't want to lose you. But I promise you, if Neil turns up here, every man here will fight to protect you. We won't let him take you. I give you my word on that."

"So my staying here will mean everyone is in danger!" she cried. "Please, Mr. Jordan, you have to let me go!"

"You need to get that damn fool notion right out of your head," Mr. Jordan growled. "Or I'll turn you over my knee right here and spank it out of you!"

She gasped, shocked. How dare Mr. Jordan threaten to spank her for leaving! She was a grown woman! If she wanted to leave, she would leave!

"You have no right to make me stay here," she informed him. "I'm a grown woman; I can do what I like."

Mr. Jordan looked at her sternly and raised an eyebrow. "Sassy, and no regard for your safety? Looks like I've got my work cut out for me," he sighed. Wrapping his arm around her waist, he bent her forward over his forearm and lifted her up so her fingertips and toes barely touched the ground. She dangled there helplessly, watching the drovers around the campfire upside-down.

"Pass me that spoon there, will you, Billy?" he requested, pointing at the big wooden spoon Monty used for stirring the stew, sitting on the rickety table.

Too late, Jed realized what Mr. Jordan was about to do—her sass had gotten her in big trouble! "No!" she cried, struggling to get away, but Mr. Jordan held her fast. He took the spoon Billy proffered and with a quick flick of his wrist, snapped it hard against the seat of her pants. It stung like fire!

"Owwwwwww!" she shrieked, increasing her struggles.

Mr. Jordan flicked his wrist again, scorching her other buttock with the spoon. She gasped. It felt like there were hot embers on her bottom! Those two swats were enough to satisfy her curiosity—there was nothing exciting about getting a spanking from Mr. Jordan, it just hurt!

"Let me go!" she yelled, struggling to get away again, but Mr. Jordan's strong arm held her fast. He smacked her twice more, putting the whole weight of his arm behind these swats instead of just flicking his wrist, and Jed howled.

"The correct response when I told you to stay here, was 'yes, sir,'" he told her sternly, punctuating his words with another smack of the spoon. "I'm offering you protection here, and safety." He brought the spoon down hard again. "Be grateful for it—don't turn it down." He landed a flurry of six hard smacks alternating on each cheek, and Jed cried out with each one, struggling frantically, desperate to get away. He brought the spoon down hard again, twice more, and Jed sobbed. Then he flicked his wrist again and threw the spoon lightly onto the chuck wagon table.

"I am grateful!" she managed to gasp between sobs.

"Good."

Putting her feet back down on the ground, Mr. Jordan took her by the shoulders and looked deep into her eyes, wet with tears. "I'm sorry I had to do that, ma'am," he told her. "But you must stay here, so we can keep you safe. Neil can't hurt you here, I promise you. And sassing me is never wise." He wrapped his arms around her and embraced her tightly, comforting her until her sobs subsided.

Jedda-Lyn was mortified. Mr. Jordan had just held her upside down and spanked her in front of all his men! She buried her face in her hands, wishing she could die. "Your men…" she whispered.

"My men will never mention this incident again," he told her, looking sternly at his men. "It's not the first time they've seen a deserving woman get spanked."

"Oh," she squeaked, still embarrassed.

Mr. Jordan swiped a rag from the chuck wagon and dipped it in the dishpan full of hot water. Wringing it out, he wiped her face gently, holding the back of her head with one hand.

"Are you okay now?" he asked, his deep voice full of concern.

"Yes." She smiled up at him. "Thank you," she told him simply. "I appreciate what you are offering."

Mr. Jordan returned her smile and patted her shoulder.

"Good."

Monty had a plate of stew waiting for her and Billy was pouring coffee. The rest of the men were all eating, their eyes fixed on their plates. Taking her meal, she carried the plate and dented enamel mug over to the fallen log where Davey was sitting and sat down next to him. She winced as her hot bottom came in contact with the log, and shimmied back a bit so the sorest part of her anatomy was hanging over the edge.

"You all right?" Davey whispered softly. "The boss was pretty hard on you."

She nodded, then winced again as the log moved under her as Mr. Jordan sat down beside her. Flanked by the big men, she knew she was safe. It was a good feeling.

"What if he comes back?" she asked, frightened, as she spread her bedroll out before the fire.

"You'll be safe," Mr. Jordan assured her. "I'm on first watch, Davey's on second. Davey will spread his bedroll close to you; when he goes onto night watch I'll take his place. You only need to whisper our names if you're scared and we'll wake up."

Surprisingly, she did feel safe. Knowing her fears, the men had all spread their bedrolls nearby, much closer together than normal, and their presence was enough to assuage her worries. She fell asleep watching the steady rise and fall of Davey's chest and listening to his gentle snoring.

CHAPTER FOUR

After being escorted from Mr. Jordan's camp, the man had ridden hard all night to get back to town just two days later. He hadn't been able to stem the flow of blood from his nose, so his one and only shirt was ruined. Still, the money Cal had offered him for information would pay for a new one several times over. He walked into the bar where the two men were waiting for him.

"She was there all right," he announced.

"I told you that's where she'd gone!" Cal snarled at Neil. "You're supposed to be my mate—why would you tell me she wasn't there, when she was? Are you trying to protect her? Don't you want her to marry me?"

Neil leapt up from the table and backed up, holding his hand palm up in front of him submissively. He didn't want to fight Cal. "The sheriff checked," Neil insisted. "I sent him out there; he came back and said she wasn't there."

Cal snorted. "That useless sheriff couldn't find the nose on the end of his face!" He pulled a wad of money out of his coat pocket and peeled off three notes, slapping them down onto the table. He glared at Neil, then turned back to the other man. "North on the Sedalia?" he questioned. "Are you sure?"

"I'm sure," the other man said, pocketing the money. "It was her. There's a fair few of them though, I counted twenty, there could even be more. And the trail boss is pretty tough." He touched his battered face gingerly, remembering. The trail boss had only punched him once, but he'd done some damage.

Cal just laughed. "I'm not scared of no trail boss." He looked at Neil. "Are you with me?"

Neil nodded, just once. "I'm in."

• • • • • • •

As the days turned into weeks and Neil didn't come, Jed started to relax. The days were busy and long, but the evenings were fun again. The poker games using match sticks as chips were a good way to relax as the men smoked and told stories, and she put her fears of Cal aside. Most of the time the men seemed to forget she was a woman, treating her instead as one of them, but she knew that Mr. Jordan had spoken the truth when he had promised that every man there would fight for her if necessary. It felt good, knowing she had that security.

Now that Jed wasn't looking over her shoulder every few seconds, she was looking over the remuda for a horse to call her own. All the drovers had their favorites, and while most of them belonged to the outfit with which they rode, Joe seemed to know every man's preferences. So far, Jed hadn't found one she really liked. Except for the sorrel filly that caught her eye now. She was stunning—her golden coat gleamed, and she had four white socks and a white blaze down her face. She was at least half Arab—her beautiful flaxen high-carried tail streamed out behind her, and she didn't just trot, she pranced. She held her head loftily, and she was full of spirit.

"Stay away from her, Jed," Joe had warned her. "She looks pretty, but she's a vicious one. She bites, and she's a bucker. You keep yourself clear of that one. We'll sell her next time we go to town."

"But she's beautiful," Jed had crooned, stretching out her hand to touch the velvety muzzle. "I want to ride her."

Joe shook his head. "No one's to ride that one. Boss's orders."

Woody had promoted her to swing position and from there, she had a clear view of the remuda. Now that they were trail-broke, the beeves were easy to drive—they grazed as they meandered along, taking their time, slowly ambling after the leaders. Every so often one would break away and she'd have to go after it, but the rest of the time she gazed at the sorrel filly, plotting a way to gain her trust.

It took her a week of trying, but Jed finally got the filly to respond to her whispered voice. "Goldie," she called her, and the filly would look up and knicker quietly. She would approach Jed too, when she wasn't tethered, and stood calmly while Jed rubbed her body and even picked up her feet. She was perfect! "We understand each other, don't we, girl?" she crooned to the horse. It felt good, forming a bond with the filly. Although the men were kind to her, she felt so alone being the only female on the cattle drive, and her future was so uncertain. She had no idea what she would do once she reached Sedalia—she didn't know anyone there, and although she would have some money, she had nowhere to go. If she could tame Goldie so she could ride her, perhaps Mr. Jordan would let her buy the filly, then at least she would have a friend. And she would need a horse—being without transportation in a strange place would not do at all. The filly didn't even flinch when Jed bounced up and down at her wither, then on the upward bounce she grabbed a handful of mane and swung herself across the horse's wide back. Sliding off, she pulled the strands of long flaxen hair from her fingers. "You'll let me ride you, won't you, girl?" she whispered.

Riding on swing was so much better than riding drag. For starters, she wasn't eating so much dust. Aside from that, she could see much better what was happening with the herd, and the men. She watched Davey ride off with Mr. Jordan; scouting for water, she supposed. The watering hole they'd been relying on the day before had been dry, but she'd overheard Davey talking last night by the campfire about another watering spot he knew of up ahead about eight miles. Now was her chance!

When her mount grew tired, she rode up to the remuda to exchange him for a fresh one. "Goldie!" she called, and the beautiful filly came running over. Quickly, she swapped the saddles over, and slipped the bit between the filly's teeth before Joe saw her. The horse didn't react at all.

"What do you think you're doing?" Joe growled. She jumped. "You're not allowed to ride that horse! Here, let me take the saddle off for you and put it on a more suitable one."

"No, this one is fine," she assured him, checking the cinch again.

Joe clutched her shoulders tightly in both hands, forcing her away from the horse. "Mr. Jordan said no one is to ride that horse," he told her forcefully, pushing her backwards again.

"Please, Joe!" she begged him, flashing him her prettiest smile. "I'll be careful, I promise." She could see Joe was relenting. "Please?" she asked again, using all her feminine wiles to try to charm him. "I want to ride Goldie."

Joe sighed, and stepped back to let her go.

"Thank you!" She smiled at Joe again, then turned back to the horse. "We understand each other. Don't we, girl?" she crooned, putting her left foot into the stirrup and swinging herself up into the saddle.

"Well, you be careful!" Joe admonished, looking worried. "I'm going to lose my job over this. Especially if you get hurt," he muttered.

The filly's paces were exquisite. The high-stepping prance at the trot was unlike Jed had ever felt before, and the lope was as smooth as riding in an armchair. "You're as perfect as I imagined," Jed murmured, rubbing the filly's neck happily.

Suddenly, with no warning, the filly started bucking. Jed rammed her feet home in the stirrups and kept her seat, but once the bucking stopped, the horse bolted. The bit was a vicious Mexican one, but the filly had it in her teeth, so no amount of sawing on the reins was enough to bring her under control. Even during this uncontrolled run, the filly's gallop was a smooth glide, and as they streaked across the plains, Jed was surprised to find she was enjoying herself, even if she had no way of stopping, or even turning. Goldie wasn't a big horse, but she was fast. As they hurtled along at breakneck speed, Jed knew she'd never ridden a horse this fast before. She'd spent all her life on horseback, but none of them could run like this. It was exhilarating! She kept trying to turn the filly back to the herd, using all the tricks she knew, but nothing worked. They kept going, at full gallop, northwest—exactly the direction Davey and Mr. Jordan had ridden out in that morning! Turning around in the saddle, she saw no sign of the herd. She couldn't even see their dust. How far had they traveled? Goldie was showing no signs of slowing down, she was barely even breathing hard; how much further would they run? Starting to panic just a little bit, she sat down hard in the saddle, pushing her feet forward in the stirrups and hauling back on the reins as hard as she could, but it was no use. The filly was out of control!

In the distance she could just make out two riders coming toward her and she recognized them instantly. Even from this far away, it was obvious who they were. No one else had shoulders as broad as Davey, and no one else sat as tall and proud in the saddle as Mr. Jordan. She was filled with a mixture of relief and trepidation. Mr. Jordan and Davey would rescue her, but she knew she would be in trouble—Mr. Jordan had expressly forbidden her to ride the sorrel filly. That was why she had waited until he wasn't there before she did it. Mr. Jordan had already shown he had no qualms about spanking her when he thought she deserved it—would he do it again now?

Davey and Mr. Jordan had obviously seen the runaway horse and both were racing to her rescue. They spread out, so each was coming from a slightly different angle, effectively trapping them. Mr. Jordan cut them off and Davey reached out and grabbed the reins of the now blowing horse, bringing her in a tight circle to a halt. As Davey rested a calming hand on her neck, the filly quieted instantly.

"What the hell were you thinking?" Mr. Jordan growled, clearly angry.

Jed gulped. She'd never seen Mr. Jordan this angry before, and at her! A shiver ran down her spine and her bottom cheeks clenched involuntarily. He was furious—she would definitely be getting spanked.

"Get down off that horse and give Davey the reins. He will take her back to the remuda."

She took her time taking her feet out of the stirrups and dismounting. When she handed the reins to Davey he nodded his assent at the order, and headed back the way she'd just come, leading the filly behind him.

"Did you find water?" she asked Mr. Jordan, standing at the wither of the big chestnut gelding. She watched Davey's retreating back as he rode away at a brisk trot, his figure getting smaller and smaller.

"Don't try to change the subject," Mr. Jordan snapped. "You've got a reckoning coming."

"I'm not a child!" she protested.

"No," Mr. Jordan agreed, sliding down off his gelding. "I wouldn't do to a child what I'm about to do to you. What were you thinking? There's no doctor within two hundred miles—you could have been killed!"

"But I wasn't," she pointed out. "We were fine."

She watched in morbid fascination as Mr. Jordan took off his gun belt, draping it over the saddle of his horse. Then he rolled up his sleeves to the elbows to expose corded, muscular forearms. He was really going to do it! There were no wooden spoons out here—was he just going to use his hand? The thought intrigued her. She took in his sheer size, his incredible strength, his powerful muscles and well-toned body. She took note of his huge, calloused hands, and gulped. Somehow, she didn't think Mr. Jordan would need anything other than the palm of his hand to ignite a fire in her backside.

"I gave you an order," he told her sternly, but so quietly that she could barely hear him.

"I'm not much good at taking orders." She waved her hand dismissively. "It was just me and Neil for a long time. I'm not used to being obedient."

"Well, you're about to learn."

Taking her by the hand, he led her over to a log that lay on the ground nearby. She could feel the strength in his fingers as they enclosed around hers, and she knew there would be no use fighting him. She knew he would be able to restrain her easily.

Putting his left foot up onto the log, he hauled her across his dusty thigh, his hard leather chaps digging into her stomach. She squirmed, trying to make herself a bit more comfortable, dangled as she was in such a precarious position, but Mr. Jordan held her fast.

When the first swat fell, it took her by surprise and she cried out, but more from shock than pain. It didn't hurt at all, not really. Not as much as she'd been expecting, anyway. Even the lighter swats from Monty's big wooden spoon had hurt far more than that!

Several more swats fell. She squirmed again. She felt all funny inside, breathless. She was aware of a throbbing between her legs and a moistness gathering there, and a dull achy feeling in her breasts. Unrestrained by the bandage she'd kept tightly wrapped around them initially, they were now falling free under the man's shirt she wore, and she could feel them puckering in response to the rise and fall of Mr. Jordan's palm connecting with her backside.

Her breath hitched as Mr. Jordan increased the power

behind the swats, and she yelped involuntarily. Now it was actually starting to hurt, and wasn't so enjoyable after all. She squirmed, and was rewarded with a hard swat to the back of her thighs, which made her yelp again.

Mr. Jordan stopped holding back as he found his rhythm and he spanked her again and again, harder and harder, igniting a fire in her bottom with every smack. Those exquisite pleasurable feelings subsided as the spanking continued on and on, and she started to writhe and squirm in pain under his punishing hand. He focused the hardest smacks to the rounded crest of her bottom, putting so much force behind his hard hand that her body jolted forward with every blow.

Her curiosity was well and truly satisfied. She now knew what a spanking from Mr. Jordan's hand felt like—it hurt! His big, hard hand hurt almost as much as that wretched spoon he'd used on her last time. The tightness in her breasts had gone, replaced with a dull ache that left her wanting.

Tears welled up in her eyes as Mr. Jordan's hand landed viciously hard, over and over, making her kick her legs in protest. Not that kicking had the desired effect—Mr. Jordan concentrated the swats to the back of her thighs instead, the tips of his fingers burning the inside of her thigh right up high near where the pulsing throb was.

"You let me go!" Jed yelled, her voice breaking. "You're nothing but a brute!" Mr. Jordan stopped spanking her and stood her up.

"I can see this isn't getting through to you," he growled. He held her arm tightly as his other hand went to her waist. "We'll take your pants down and try again."

Jed struggled with all her might, kicking at Mr. Jordan's shins, desperately trying to get away, but her attempt was futile. She was no match for the big trail boss's strength. Having undone the buttons on her pants, he slid them down her thighs, bunching them around her knees. She kicked at him again in a downward stomping motion and saw him wince when the toe of her boot connected with his ankle.

"Right," he snarled. "You've just earned yourself a bare-bottom spanking."

"No!" Jed yelled, trying to pull away, but Mr. Jordan held her fast as he untied her drawers and let them fall.

Mortified, she tried to cover herself with her hands. This wasn't right! It wasn't proper! But Mr. Jordan didn't seem to notice her nakedness as his big hand enclosed around both her wrists and he bent her back over his thigh.

The flat of his hand scorched her bottom again, the tips of his long fingers landing inside the crevice of her bottom cheeks.

She let out a shriek. She'd been hurting before, but it was nothing like the pain Mr. Jordan was inflicting on her now. With nothing between her tender skin and Mr. Jordan's rough, calloused hand, each smack stung like fire. She kicked and struggled, well aware that he would be able to see everything between her legs, but powerless to stop fighting. As his hand landed again and again, she blushed furiously at the thought of him looking at her most intimate parts. Would he be able to see the wetness she could feel gathered there? Was he aware of her arousal? If he could, how was that affecting him?

Mr. Jordan's hand continued to land in a fast rhythm, the staccato of swats deepening the ache she could feel between her legs as surely as they were reddening her bottom. Jed was getting desperate. Her bottom felt like it was on fire! How could Mr. Jordan's hand not be stinging? She let out a sob.

"I'm sorry!" she cried. "I'm sorry! I will listen to your orders from now on!" she assured him through her tears, truly miserable and contrite now.

With one more hearty swat, Mr. Jordan set her on her feet. "See that you do," he growled, but his voice was husky, and through her tears, she could see passion dancing in his eyes. As quickly as she could, she pulled her drawers back up, tying the drawstring tightly. Mr. Jordan had seen enough! She hissed in pain as she eased the heavy canvas pants up over her stinging, swollen bottom. Jed danced around on her toes, trying to douse the flames in her rear end, and both hands went to her bottom.

"Quit rubbing," Mr. Jordan ordered. "There's to be no rubbing after a spanking."

"But it hurts!" she whined, tears streaming down her face.

"It's meant to," he said dryly.

She watched as he flexed his hands, opening and closing his fist several times. She got a perverse satisfaction out of knowing that his hand was sore too, and she barely managed to stifle a grin.

"Are you ready to go back now?" he asked her gently, his eyes sparkling, his breathing ragged.

"No!" she exclaimed, horrified. How on earth was she going to sit on a horse after what she'd just endured? "I'm far too sore!"

"Well, we can't stay out here forever," Mr. Jordan told her.

"You didn't have to spank me so hard," she sniffled. "It really, really hurts!" She knew she looked a mess—crying never did good things to her, so she tried to avoid it wherever possible.

Mr. Jordan took a step toward her and put a comforting hand on her back, his outstretched fingers against her shoulder blades. He rubbed his hand gently up and down, stepping closer to her so their bodies were touching. Reaching around her with his other hand, he wiped her tears away gently with his thumb. Mr. Jordan slipped his arm around her waist and pulled her in close to him, smiling down at her tenderly. Her heart melted. The man might be a brute—the fire in her bottom was evidence of that—but he did have a soft spot.

"Come on," he said, guiding her over to the gelding with his arm still wrapped around her. "You'll just have to tough it out. We have to be getting back to the herd."

Still sniffing, she followed.

It was torture sitting atop the horse, and she wriggled as much as she could, trying to ease the burning ache in her bottom.

"Hold still," Mr. Jordan snapped. "You earned that spanking, now you can put up with the pain of it as we go back to the herd. Keep up the squirming and we'll get off and do it again."

"That's not fair!" Jed protested. How could the man be so cruel? She didn't want to test him, though, so instead, she wrapped her arms around his waist tightly and leaned into his broad back, resting her cheek on his right shoulder, taking as much weight off her bottom as she could. It was comforting there, feeling his hard body against her, and her breasts tingled in response, growing tight and puckered again.

Suddenly, Mr. Jordan reined up. Startled, Jed looked up and watched him twist around in the saddle to face her, taking his right foot out of the stirrup and hooking his ankle around the saddle horn for balance. Taking her face in his hands, he looked deeply into her eyes and Jed saw the desire burning there. She opened her mouth and tilted her face up to him. Slowly, he moved closer to her, his lips lightly brushing hers, then he crushed his mouth against hers and swept her up in a kiss so passionate she went dizzy. All she was aware of were different sensations swirling around in her brain. She could feel his tongue in her mouth, feel his teeth against hers. He nipped her bottom lip gently, and she responded in kind, grasping the back of his head and pulling him into her. A soft moan escaped her lips. The kiss seemed to go on forever as their lips melded. When they eventually broke away, her heart was racing.

Without a word, Mr. Jordan turned away and spurred the big gelding into a canter, and she pressed her face into his strong back once again.

The whole way back to the herd, Jed remembered the way the ruggedly handsome cowboy's chapped lips had felt on hers as he had kissed her urgently, the tender way his fingers had tangled in her hair while his other hand had caressed her cheek. She couldn't stop smiling as the ache in her breasts deepened, electricity coursed through her, and the drumming throb between her thighs returned. Even the pain in her bottom was deliciously sore now, instead of the fiery, torturing burn of before. Mr. Jordan was the man she'd been waiting for—the man who was able to take her in hand and make her content to be his woman. So unlike Cal in every way—handsome, tough and courageous but gentle and kind, commanding, assertive and stern but fair and honest. She understood what he had meant now when he told her that a spanking wasn't the same thing as abuse. The spanking had hurt, the amount of pain Mr. Jordan had ignited in her bottom was right up there with the pain of Cal hitting her in the face, but when Cal had hit her, she'd been terrified. When Mr. Jordan had spanked her, she hadn't been frightened. Not really—she somehow knew that he wouldn't harm her. And now that the fire in her backside had dulled to a tingling sting, she felt cherished and safe, which was the exact opposite to the aftermath of Cal's treatment of her.

Mr. Jordan helped her down off his big gelding as they returned to the remuda on the outskirts of the herd, and she was pleased to see the little filly safely back where she belonged.

"Joe!" Mr. Jordan bellowed. The wrangler hurried over, looking worried.

Oh, no! Jed knew she couldn't let Joe lose his job because of her. That wouldn't be fair at all! She stood and listened to Mr. Jordan cussing him out, waiting for Joe to defend himself, but he was standing silent, not saying a word. It was obvious he wasn't willing to put the blame on Jed.

"Please don't blame Joe!" Jed begged. "He tried to stop me, but I insisted. None of this is his fault!"

Mr. Jordan fell silent. "Is that true?" he asked.

Joe nodded. Then he looked at Jed and frowned. "If you

wasn't Mr. Jordan's woman, I'd-a taken you across my knee and whupped you good," he told her.

Mr. Jordan's woman? Since when? Jed wondered.

"You shoulda done that anyway," Mr. Jordan growled. "Then I wouldn't have had to do it."

"Hang on, just stop," Jed ordered, holding both her hands up in front of her. "Mr. Jordan's woman? What are you talking about, Joe?" she asked.

"I've seen the way he looks at you," Joe smiled. "Go on, tell me I'm wrong."

Jed felt her face growing red with embarrassment. After that kiss, how could she tell Joe he was wrong? At least, he wasn't wrong as far as her feelings were concerned. But did Mr. Jordan really find her attractive? She'd certainly never noticed any sly looks coming her way, and she knew she wasn't pretty anymore since she'd cut off all her hair and dressed in dusty, shapeless drover's clothes. She looked across at Mr. Jordan and he winked at her rakishly.

"Righto, back to work," he ordered in that rich, deep baritone voice of his. "Choose an appropriate horse this time, Jed," he told her, smiling. "And you're back on drag. You can go and relieve Chuck. He'll be glad of the break from eating dust."

"But I was on swing!" she protested.

"You were," Mr. Jordan agreed. "Until you disobeyed. Now you're back on drag."

"But you've already punished me for that!" she argued.

"Not well enough, it seems, seeing as how you're arguing with me." Mr. Jordan flexed his hands. "If you don't want me to give it another shot right here in front of Joe, I suggest you start doing as you're told."

Scowling fiercely at the handsome trail boss, she took the reins of the horse that Joe was saddling up for her, and pouted.

"Pout all you like, I'm not changing my mind," Mr. Jordan chuckled, and tipped his hat to her as he walked off.

CHAPTER FIVE

Jed pulled her shirt out from her pants at the back and flapped it open, trying to get some cool air inside. She was drenched in sweat. It was so hot! She looked around. Where was Mr. Jordan? It had been more than a week since he'd kissed her and she kept hoping he would do it again, but so far, he hadn't. She knew he was thinking of her—sometimes he caught her eye and tipped his hat to her, or winked rakishly, giving her that dazzling smile that melted her heart. And in the evenings as they gathered around the campfire once they had the beeves bedded down for the night, he would come and sit next to her. But there hadn't been anything more than that. It was clear to her that the men were all aware of the attraction that was building between her and the trail boss. Woody had stopped flirting with her, and the drovers treated her with a kind of reverence that hadn't been there before.

She turned in the saddle at the sound of hoof beats coming up beside her. It was Woody.

"I'm taking over for you here," he told her. "Mr. Jordan wants to see you." He indicated Mr. Jordan riding toward them on his big gelding. Kicking her horse into a canter, she rode out to meet him.

"Fancy a swim?" he asked her, his eyes twinkling. The river wasn't very far away; they'd been riding alongside of it for several days. He extended his hand to her, and she rode up next to him, entwining her fingers with his. What was going on? Smiling shyly at him, she felt a shiver run through her body. He turned to her. "When we're alone like this, you can call me Weston, or Wes," he said. "It's still Mr. Jordan in front of the men, but out here, when it's just you and me, it's different. Out here, I'm not your boss."

"Oh?" She was confused.

He smiled mysteriously. "Out here, I'm your lover."

She blushed clear to her roots. "Oh!" she laughed.

He raised her hand to his lips and kissed the back of it gently. "Joe is right," he told her softly, smiling. "You're my woman. I'm going to lay my claim on you today."

"And if I don't want you to?" She looked up at him cheekily.

Wes Jordan faltered. "Don't you? I thought…" His voice trailed off and he frowned, letting go of her hand and reining up his horse. She could see the myriad thoughts racing through his brain, pain etched all over his face. Immediately, she felt guilty.

She laughed. "Of course I do! I was just teasing you," she giggled. "You should see the look on your face—you look so disappointed!"

He shook his head, a smile creeping onto his lips. "Such a sassy girl! You really do like being spanked, don't you?" He reached for her hand again and laughed. "And that's good, because you have such a spankable backside!"

They rode around behind the boulders and the beauty of the scene took Jed's breath away. Framed by the cliff faces in the distance, a small stream, an offshoot of the main river they'd been following, meandered through a patch of green, shaded by willows. It was perfect—secluded and warm. Tying his horse to a tree, Wes dismounted and held out his hand to Jed.

"Come," he invited. "Let's have a swim."

Jed was shy, now. Quickly, Wes shed his shirt, and she couldn't take her eyes away from his torso—it was muscled to perfection, with just the lightest smattering of dark hair dusting his chest. His abs rippled as he moved, and a line of dark hair trailed its way down past his navel, disappearing tantalizingly inside his pants. He was gorgeous!

Reaching for her, his big fingers fumbled at the buttons of her shirt, undoing them all the way down, before he slipped the fabric off her shoulders. "Mmmmmm," he murmured, nuzzling his mouth against her nipples, licking them, teasing them. He held her breast in his right hand, squeezing it gently, and he moved his face up her chest to her throat.

She wrapped her arms around him, kneading his back with her fingers, feeling her nipples growing hard against him. Her breasts felt tight and hot, and there was an ache between her legs, slowly building in intensity as Wes teased her nipples with his tongue.

He kissed his way down her body, slowly lowering himself to the ground as his kisses trailed lower and lower. When he reached the waistband of her pants, he was on his knees before her and she had her head thrown back in a wanton display of lust, her back arched, her breasts thrust out, her fingers tangled in his hair. He stopped kissing her and she groaned.

"Patience, little lady," he admonished, chuckling. "Let me get to the rest of you!" He stepped out of his pants quickly, discarding them in a careless pile with their shirts.

Her eyes went to his erection. It was so big! She reached out and touched it, wrapping her fingers tightly around the shaft, sliding them up and down, smiling at him seductively.

"Help me," he murmured, his voice husky with arousal. His big fingers were too clumsy to unfasten the buttons on her pants, so she brushed them out of the way and deftly unclipped them, sliding the pants down her thighs. Stepping out of them, she kicked them carelessly in the general direction of their other clothes, and wrapped her arms around Wes again, pressing her body up against him. His erection pressed against her belly and his big hands held her bottom tightly, squeezing her buttocks.

Her heart was racing; she was breathless. She squealed with laughter as Weston hoisted her over his shoulder and slapped her bottom playfully.

"I owe you a spanking," he declared, laughing, as he slapped her naked bottom lightly again. His skin was damp with sweat and she stuck to him when she tried to wiggle.

"No!" she protested, still laughing.

He ran then, with her still over his shoulder, to the stream, then he dumped her in the water, splashing her, kicking water at her with his feet. "Wait here," he said. "I have soap in my saddlebags. We can have a wash."

She watched him as he ran. He was exquisite! There wasn't an ounce of fat anywhere on his toned, lean body, his bottom and thighs were hard muscle from hours spent in the saddle. Even the muscles in his back rippled as he moved.

He came back with the soap and a towel, and he washed her meticulously, rubbing the soap between his hands and spreading the lather all over her body, his fingers probing every crevice. Then he handed her the soap and she washed him, taking delight in exploring his body with her hands, massaging his skin with her fingertips. She jumped up, her hands around his neck, and wrapped her legs tightly around his hips. Their bodies fit together perfectly; they kissed deeply, his chapped lips igniting passion within her that she had only dreamed about.

Exiting the water, Wes spread the towel on the ground in the sun and lay her down on it. The sun warmed her skin, drying the droplets of water that remained on her body, softening her nipples that the cold water had hardened. Gooseflesh covered her body, and Wes trailed his rough fingers over the bumps with the lightest touch, tickling her. Straddling her, he lowered his lips to hers, devouring her hungrily, but before she was sated, he moved his body lower, kissing her throat, her shoulder, trailing kisses all the way down the middle of her body. His hands encircled her breasts, squeezing them gently, as he kissed lightly between them, moving his lips further down her body, kissing away the remaining droplets of water from the stream. He circled his tongue around her navel, tickling her, teasing her.

Her breasts were tight in his hands, tight and hot, as though they would burst. The dull ache between her legs intensified, pulsing in rhythm with the rapid beat of her heart. Her breaths were coming in short, shallow gasps as he pressed her back against the towel. What was he doing to her?

He moved his lips down between her legs, nudging her thighs apart with his chin, nipping her upper thighs lightly when she didn't respond quickly enough. Little squeaks of pleasure escaped her lips and her whole body shivered in anticipation. Still holding her left breast, his other hand trailed down her body to join his mouth at her pussy, and he inserted one finger, probing gently. She gasped, arching her back to meet him. He lowered his mouth to her pussy, the stubble on his jaw scratching her lightly, and she shivered again as he licked away her wetness. He flicked his tongue over her clit, probing deeply within her mound. She couldn't breathe, she couldn't think, she could only feel…

Squeezing her breast again, his other hand brushed against her pussy, tugging gently at the hair he found there. He separated her pussy lips with his fingers, holding her wide open, pushing his tongue deep inside her, exploring her innermost crevice. He nibbled at her pussy lips, tormenting her, driving her wild with desire. He flicked his tongue across her swollen clit, then rubbed the sensitive nub between his fingers, rolling it gently. Raising his hand, he slapped her wet pussy gently with the tips of his fingers, smiling as the look of first shock, then pleasure, spread over her face.

"Do you like that, you naughty girl?" he whispered huskily, slapping his fingers against her pussy again. He drummed two fingers in a staccato pattern against her clit, then lowered his mouth to blow gently across it. She arched her back and moaned, a long, deep, drawn-out moan that showed him just how pleasurable she was finding his ministrations. He slapped her pussy again, slightly harder this time, one finger slapping her clit, and her body shuddered.

She couldn't hold back any longer. She reached for his cock, taking it in both hands, grasping it between her fingers and thumb, and ran her hand up and down the length of him.

Moaning, he stretched up to her mouth, crushing his lips against hers urgently. She could taste the musky saltiness of herself on his lips.

In one swift move he rolled her over, sliding underneath her, pulling her down on top of him. She straddled him, still grasping his cock, and lowered herself slowly onto him, guiding his erection into her with one hand. There was a momentary pang of pain, then the most exquisite sensation of fullness; he was so big, she was full to bursting of him. Rolling her hips in a circular thrusting motion, she could feel his cock deep inside her. Kneading his chest with her hands, she continued to ride him, smiling when his hands slipped under her hips and he met her with upward thrusts of his pelvis, grinding together in perfect unison. They came together explosively, moaning in pleasure, calling each other's names, shuddering as waves of sheer bliss washed over them.

They lay there for a few minutes, both of them breathing hard, his arms around her and Jed's cheek resting on his chest. They were spent, but sated.

"You're mine," Wes told her, kissing her nose. "All mine." He nibbled her lower lip and she smiled in response. She could lie there in his arms, under the hot sun, forever. But all too soon Wes stood up. "Come on," he said. "Let's wash up and get back to the herd. Woody will send a search party out looking for us otherwise!"

The dull, pleasant ache between her legs remained with her for the rest of the afternoon, and she sat gingerly in her saddle, but if any of the men noticed, they didn't say anything.

As she sat next to Mr. Jordan around the campfire that evening, she felt content. The man she loved had claimed her in the most primal way possible, and she felt happy and safe. Obviously the man who had ridden into their camp and destroyed her false sense of security wasn't a spy for Neil and Cal after all; it had just been coincidence. If he had been looking for her, Cal would have turned up here by now, she was sure of it.

CHAPTER SIX

"Where's the boss?"

Jed jumped. She hadn't heard anyone ride into camp, and now it was too late to hide. She'd recognize that voice anywhere—it belonged to the one man she'd hoped never to see again. The one man she was trying to escape from.

"I'm the boss. Wes Jordan." Mr. Jordan was already on his feet, striding toward the newcomer, his tin cup in his hand. "What can I do for you?" he asked.

"You've got something of mine," Cal snarled. "And I want her back."

Mr. Jordan shook his head. "There's nothing of yours here."

"My fiancée," Cal stated. "I've come to take her home."

"Jed!" Mr. Jordan called. Scrambling to her feet, she hurried over to stand next to the trail boss. He put his hand on her shoulder reassuringly, possessively. Automatically, she stepped in closer to him—she was frightened of Cal, but Mr. Jordan made her feel safe.

Cal glared at her, and she glared right back at him defiantly, feeling brave now that she had the big trail boss for protection.

"I've come to take you home," he told her.

"I'm not going home," she stated, shaking her head. "I'm not going anywhere with you." She felt Mr. Jordan's big hand squeeze her shoulder, encouraging her.

"You heard the lady," Mr. Jordan growled. "Get out."

"Lady?" Cal sneered. "She ain't no lady! I took that away from her, right on her kitchen floor. She put up a fight, but I know she enjoyed it."

"You lying bastard!" she screamed, about to launch herself at him, but Mr. Jordan held her fast, gripping her upper arms firmly.

"Get out of here," he repeated, his voice hard and cold.

"Not without her." Cal pointed at Jed.

"She doesn't want to go with you," Mr. Jordan snarled.

"Well, that's a shame, isn't it?" another familiar voice called from behind them. Jed turned to see Neil holding Billy in a headlock, a gun to his temple. "I don't think she has a choice. You give me back my sister, I'll give you back your man."

Mr. Jordan was silent. He looked from Cal to Neil, then from Jed to Billy, and back again. He was obviously thinking. The men were all watching curiously, their hands on their guns, ready to back up their boss the instant the order was given.

Jed looked at Billy. He looked scared—he had no idea what was going on, or why he was being used as a pawn in such a dangerous game.

She could see Cal looking around the camp, counting up the men. The odds were not in his favor, so she knew he would be cautious. He was an experienced fighter, but he fought best when he had the advantage.

"Are you willing to fight for her?" Cal asked venomously.

Mr. Jordan stepped forward. "I'll fight for her."

Immediately, Neil pushed Billy sideways, and the boy stumbled against the side of the chuck wagon. Monty hurried to him, but Billy was unhurt.

"No! Weston!" she screamed; she knew Cal's reputation.

He was a fighter, a dirty one, and he'd never lost a fight. At least, not that she knew of. She knew he would have a knife stashed somewhere—he didn't fight just with his fists. This would not be a fair fight, there would be no rules. Cal was a master at this. Mr. Jordan would get hurt, and all because of her. "Stop!" she screamed again. "Cal, stop!" she pleaded. "I'll go with you!" she cried, desperate. She couldn't watch the man she'd come to care so much about get hurt.

"No, you won't!" Mr. Jordan yelled. "Davey, hold her!" he ordered.

Frantic, she tried to run to Mr. Jordan to intervene, but strong arms caught her and held her fast and although she kicked and struggled, she was no match for his strength; he restrained her easily.

"Be still, boss's orders," Davey commanded her softly.

Cal threw the first punch; she held her breath. So far, Mr. Jordan was dodging all Cal's blows and landing a few of his own, enthusiastically cheered on by the drovers. But Jed's heart was in her throat. She knew Cal; she'd seen him fight before. He wouldn't be an easy man to beat. Mr. Jordan was tough, and he was bigger, but Cal was the better fighter. She flinched at every punch Mr. Jordan took, wishing more than anything that someone would put a stop to this. Why wasn't someone doing something? Why were two grown men fighting over her?

Mr. Jordan landed a combination of solid punches to Cal's body and face and he crumpled to the ground. Thinking it was over, Mr. Jordan started to turn, and that was when Cal pulled out his knife. He staggered to his feet and brandished the knife in front of him, advancing toward Mr. Jordan with a triumphant gleam of victory in his eyes. Jed gasped as Cal thrust the knife at Mr. Jordan, slashing his arm. She saw Mr. Jordan grab his arm in pain, blood trickling out between his fingers. Horrified, she turned and buried her face in Davey's shirt. She couldn't watch. She could hear the beat of Davey's heart as he wrapped his arms tightly around her in a protective embrace, pounding in an erratic rhythm, getting faster and faster as the fight wore on. She didn't need to see the fight to know what was happening—she could hear it in the groans of the men. She could feel it in the grip Davey had on her, the grip that kept getting tighter and tighter even though she remained still.

The minutes ticked by. She could hear blows landing, accompanied by muffled grunts. Davey's arms held her tightly. She was clutching his shirt in one hand, her other fist was stuffed into her mouth to stifle her screams. Suddenly, Davey loosened his grip. Something was happening! Cautiously, she peeked back over her shoulder just in time to see Woody passing Mr. Jordan a knife, the blade small but sharp. She breathed a sigh of relief. Now the fight was even, and Cal hated fighting under those odds. Mr. Jordan had taken a beating—blood oozed down his arm, it stained his shirt, his face was swollen and bruised, one eye was partially closed already. How much more of a punishment could one man take? She closed her eyes again, pressing her face back into Davey's shirt, clutching the fabric tightly in both hands. She couldn't watch.

Then there was silence. "It's over," Davey whispered in her ear, spinning her around so she could see. Sure enough, Cal was lying on the ground, wounded and bleeding but alive, and Mr. Jordan was on his feet, but barely. Woody and Chuck both moved to help him over to the supply wagon where Monty was already laying out his medicine bag.

Jed stood there in horror, shocked, looking at the scene before her, unable to believe it. Woody and Chuck were on each side of Mr. Jordan, supporting him as he staggered over to the wagon, trailing blood behind him. Cal wasn't moving. In a flash, Neil was by his side, examining him briefly, then he drew his gun.

Davey moved so fast that she didn't even see it. Instantly, he'd pushed her sideways, cleared his gun from its holster and shot the gun from Neil's hand. Neil dropped to his knees, clutching his wrist, blood covering his hand and dripping to form a puddle on the ground.

"Neil!" Jed screamed, running to him, crouching down beside him. "Here, let me have a look," she said, picking up his wrist gently.

But Neil jerked his hand away. "If you'd been at home where you belong, and married Cal like you should have done, this wouldn't have happened," he hissed at her venomously. He groaned in pain. "Are you happy now?" he spat at her.

Jed couldn't believe it. Neil was actually blaming *her* for this? His best friend forced himself on her in their kitchen, hunted her down when she ran away, used his dirty fighting tactics to try to get her back, and he actually expected her to marry the man? What kind of brother was he? Tears streaming down her face, she got to her feet hurriedly.

"Get lost, Neil," she snarled at him. "You're dead to me." She turned and crashed into the solid mass of Davey's chest. Instantly, he put his arm around her shoulder and led her away, back to the safety of the supply wagon, where Monty was tending to Mr. Jordan.

"Woody, can you take that useless bastard out there a bandage? He'll bleed to death otherwise," Davey said. "While you're there, help him get Cal back on his horse. They can clear out."

Jed knelt down beside Mr. Jordan. Monty had dosed him up on whisky and he was lying back on a blanket, a piece of wood between his teeth, while Monty stitched up the gash in his arm and tended his other cuts and bruises.

"He's busted up bad," Monty told her. "Broken ribs, all these stab wounds, bruises everywhere. He'll be out of action for a few days. Make him up a bed in the supply wagon."

She nodded once, then went to do Monty's bidding with a lump in her throat. Maybe Neil was right. Maybe she should have just married Cal after all. Mr. Jordan was hurt pretty bad, and it was all her fault.

"I'll be back!" Neil's shouted threat echoed across the prairie and a shudder went through her; she knew what she had to do.

· · · · · · ·

Jed sat on the log down near the creek and tried to muster up the courage to do what she knew she must. She'd washed up as best she could, combing out her short hair with her fingers to try to make it look a bit more feminine and pretty. They were as close to the nearest town now as they would ever be—in the morning they would move off and leave it far behind. If she were to set off now, she'd hopefully be there by daybreak. She knew it would be dangerous by herself, but she didn't have a choice.

Her shoulders shook with sobs as she thought of leaving Weston Jordan and returning to her brother and Cal. How could she do that to herself? How could she willingly leave the one man she'd ever loved, and go back to where she knew she would be treated harshly and be truly miserable? Cal had already proved the sort of man he was—he was a violent rapist, a fighter, quite possibly a killer… yet because of his family's financial position in the town he was able to get away with all of it. There would be no justice for her as Cal's wife when he beat her up or worse… but his money would save their ranch, her childhood home. Was it enough? It wasn't, she knew it wasn't, but she knew she had it do it, regardless. She had to protect the man she loved, and this was the only way she could think of to do it. If she remained here, Cal and Neil would see him killed.

Mustering all the strength she could, she stood up, stretched, and crept over to the remuda. The horses were all line tethered, and she could see the night hawker right at the very end. He didn't look to be very alert; she was safe. The horse at the close end of the line was a bay mare she'd ridden many times before, a solid horse with plenty of stamina and enough speed to put a good distance between herself and the camp, before she was discovered. As quickly and quietly as she could, she threw the saddle over the mare's back and was tightening the cinch when she felt a hand on her shoulder. She jumped.

"What do you think you are doing?" Davey growled. He spun her around to face him and shook her gently. "You can't take off in the middle of the night like that!" he scolded.

"Let me go," Jed snarled. "I don't have a choice, don't you see? Cal and Neil will be back. And next time, they'll kill Mr. Jordan. I have to leave—it's the only way for me to keep him safe!"

Davey didn't let her go. Instead, he hoisted her over his shoulder. "You're coming with me. You can explain your logic to Mr. Jordan. I think he deserves an explanation, don't you?"

"Put me down!" she hissed. She pounded his back with her fists and kicked her legs as hard as she could but he held her fast.

"Stop that!" he told her sternly. When she didn't comply, his hand crashed down hard on her backside.

She yelped, but didn't stop fighting. In fact, she fought more desperately, pounding her fists against his back again and again. She'd always respected Davey—he was a kind and patient man. Why couldn't he understand her desperation now? Davey stopped walking. She felt his body tense up as he prepared to put all his strength into spanking her again. Too late, she stopped fighting. His big hand crashed hard against the seat of her pants three more times, setting her backside on fire, and she went limp over his shoulder, sobbing quietly. She was beaten, and she knew it. She'd barely mustered the courage to follow through on her decision to leave—there was no way she could do it now. Not now that Davey was delivering her into the arms of the man she loved.

Davey kept one arm wrapped securely around her legs as he edged aside the canvas cover at the back of the wagon. When he'd made a space, he set her down gently inside.

"Boss!" Davey called quietly.

Slowly, Mr. Jordan sat up. "What's going on?" he asked, his words slurred, his face etched with pain. "Can't a man sleep in peace?"

"You might want to hear this," Davey told him, standing right at the back of the wagon blocking Jed's escape. "I found her trying to run away," Davey explained. Then he looked at Jed. "How about you tell him why?"

Jed gulped. Her reasoning had seemed sound, when she'd convinced herself she was doing the right thing. But now that she was standing there in the wagon with the man she loved, she couldn't believe she'd been willing to go through with it.

"I wanted to save you," she explained.

"By running away?" Mr. Jordan asked.

"Yes. No! Well, I wanted to stop Neil coming after you and the only way I can see to do that, is for me to leave, and to go back there. Neil's an alcoholic—Cal is his ticket to remain that way. And Cal hates losing, so he'll be busy plotting something right this minute. They'll be after you—they'll kill you! I couldn't let that happen!"

Mr. Jordan propped himself up on his good arm, wincing at the effort. "So instead of coming to me with your fears, you thought it best just to leave? And break my heart?"

"Break your heart?" Jed looked confused. "I didn't think of that."

"Thank you, Davey," Mr. Jordan looked at his scout. "You can go now."

Tipping his hat to her, Davey strode off, back to his position on night hawk, watching over the remuda.

"Come here, lie down." Mr. Jordan winced again as he moved over a bit, making room for her beside him on the makeshift bed. She snuggled up against him, being as gentle as possible, but he still groaned in pain.

"This is a really bad idea," she told him, sitting up. "I'm hurting you."

"Lie back down," Mr. Jordan ordered. "You deserve a

spanking for trying to sneak off like that," he growled. "You're lucky I'm too sore to give you one."

"Davey did," she told him, as she lay back down, taking more care this time not to hurt him.

"Davey spanked you? For running away?" Mr. Jordan sounded disbelieving. "Mild-mannered Davey?"

"Well, no, technically he spanked me because I wouldn't keep still. He was bringing me here to you and I was fighting him. So he walloped me a couple times. It hurt, too! My bottom still hurts."

Mr. Jordan chuckled, then groaned. "It hurts to laugh," he moaned. "So you still deserve a spanking for trying to run away, then. I'm glad he found you." He reached for her hand and entwined his fingers tightly around hers. "You know, there is another way to stop this: I could marry you. If you were my wife, your brother would have no choice but to tell his friend to leave you alone. And I did take quite a beating for you—the least you could do would be to marry me!"

Jed sat up again. "That is the most unromantic proposal I've ever heard!" she exclaimed.

"I'm a trail boss, not a romantic."

"Are you serious?" Jed asked him. "Do you really want to marry me?"

"I want to marry you."

"But why? I've got nothing to offer—I'm homeless, destitute… I'm not even pretty anymore, not since cutting off all my hair. Why would you want to marry me?"

Mr. Jordan squeezed her hand. "Because I love you," he said simply.

"I love you too, Weston." Snuggling back down gently beside him, she laid back, her small hand clutching his big one, listening to the wheezy rasping of his chest as he struggled to breathe. And within minutes, she was asleep.

• • • • • • •

They laid the herd over for two days, to give the boss a chance to recover—there was no way Mr. Jordan could ride, and even the bouncy wagon would have been too much for his injuries. The whole time, Jed remained at his side, nursing him through his fever, wiping his brow with a damp cloth, bringing him whisky whenever he started to groan in pain, lying next to him and chatting when he felt up to it. He told her stories about life on the trail: challenges faced by the weather, outlaws, Indians, and stampedes. He told her he was ready to give it up. He'd been droving for more than ten years; he'd been trail boss for six of those years, and he wanted to settle down. Get married, have a family, raise beef on his own piece of land. No more riding the trails, no more sleeping on the ground, under the stars in all weather… no more risking life and limb for the beeves.

Like her, his parents were dead, both victims of cholera years ago. The family ranch had been sold years ago, and his brothers had dispersed; he didn't know where any of them were. He knew he would probably never see them again.

• • • • • • •

On the third day, the boss got up. The swelling in his face was starting to go down but one eye was still half-closed, bruising still colored his jaw, and he walked gingerly, his arm still bandaged thickly.

It started to rain that afternoon, big, heavy raindrops that dripped off the brim of her hat and ran down her chin. She was wearing a long oilskin coat that kept most of the rain off her, but the cool was a welcome respite from the hot sun.

Billy and Monty were hard at work supervising the erection of the roof tenting over the camp when she came in from bedding down the herd. They kept long poles in the supply wagon for that very purpose—to rig up a makeshift roof extending out from the chuck wagon to cover the campfire and make a dry eating and sleeping area for the drovers.

"You should go back to bed," Jed admonished Mr. Jordan. "You're not healed enough to be up and about yet! Tell him, Monty!" she pleaded with the cook. "Make him go back to bed!"

"I'm all right," Mr. Jordan insisted. "I'm going mad staying in bed like that. I'll take it easy, don't worry," he assured her.

"See that you do," she bossed him. "You only got hurt because of me. The least you can do is stay in bed and let me take care of you."

Mr. Jordan smiled and patted her shoulder affectionately. "Don't you go getting all bossy," he told her. "I'm not too sore to give you a good tanning if you need it."

Jed snorted. "Yes, I think you are, actually. But don't worry, I'll be good." She stood on tiptoe to kiss his swollen lips gently, brushing her mouth ever-so-softly against his. Reaching down, he clasped her bottom in his huge hand and swatted her lightly, before squeezing gently. "See that you do," he ordered her, smiling.

• • • • • • •

"Why isn't the herd moving?" Mr. Jordan asked Woody. The young ramrod pulled off his hat and ran his fingers through his wet hair, exhausted. He'd just got back from scouting the trail with Davey and what they'd found didn't look good.

"We were waiting for you to heal, boss," Woody told him. "Monty said you were too sick to be moved. But if you're well enough now, we have to get moving. There's another herd just three days behind us, they came up from the left fork yesterday. The river is flooded, but Davey's found a crossing he thinks we can make. We'll lose days if we wait for the river to go down."

Mr. Jordan looked thoughtful. Woody hated swollen river crossings—a bad experience on his first trail drive had put the fear of God into him as far as raging rivers were concerned—and part of him wanted the boss to hold the herd a bit longer, even though it would mean the other herd would catch them up.

"Start the herd moving then," the boss ordered. "I'm okay to ride."

Woody nodded. "Yes, sir," he answered. "We should reach the river crossing by noon tomorrow."

CHAPTER SEVEN

"What's the most important thing to a trail boss?" Cal asked Neil over dinner that night. He was still injured—he had a black eye, a bandage across his broken nose, bruising colored his fractured jaw, and his whole body was bruised and cut. He was bitter about the beating he'd taken from the trail boss, and now was out for revenge.

"His reputation, I guess," offered Neil, still nursing a bandage around his hand from where Davey had shot him.

Cal thumped the table triumphantly. "Right!" he agreed. "He can't be allowed to get away with this—he must be stopped!"

Confused, Neil nodded in agreement. "So what do you have in mind?"

"I'm going to destroy him," Cal snarled venomously. "No one takes my woman," he declared. "I'm the laughing-stock of the town! Everyone knows she left me." He slurped his whisky noisily, then coughed. "The Rogan gang: hired guns, outlaws. They're going to kill him and lose the herd. He'll be remembered as being incompetent, as well as dead."

"What about my sister?" Neil asked. "I don't want anything to happen to her."

"They'll bring her back to me," Cal insisted. "Once

they've gotten rid of the trail boss and scattered the herd, they'll bring her back."

Neil downed his whisky in one long swallow. He shook his head. "I don't know…" He sounded doubtful. "Maybe you're better off forgetting the trail boss and leaving Jedda-Lyn alone. The Rogan brothers aren't the type of people I want around my sister."

Cal laughed; a callous, heartless laugh. "She should have thought of that, then, shouldn't she? I always win, Neil. Always."

Neil refilled his whisky glass from the decanter on the table. Cal was right—he did always win. And if he won this time too, Neil's alcohol supply would be guaranteed, far into the future. There wouldn't be any more dry nights, as he tossed and turned, sweating, craving the fiery liquor. The money stream, and therefore the alcohol, would be never-ending. Yes, Cal was right. Mr. Jordan must be brought to justice, must be shown the error of his ways. And the Rogan brothers were the men for the job.

• • • • • • •

The gently sloping bank leading down to the swollen river was muddy.

"Anyone who can't swim, get on the wagons, we'll take them across first," Mr. Jordan gave the order. He was still sore, Jed knew, but he insisted he was well enough to ride, and well enough to organize the negotiation of the treacherous river crossing. It took experienced men, he said, and they couldn't wait—there was another herd catching up to them.

Jed could swim—somewhat. She'd done a bit of swimming in the creek that ran through their small ranch, but their small creek was entirely different from the raging river they were about to cross now. But none of the other men were riding the wagon, save Monty and Billy, and she wasn't about to opt out of the most challenging work they'd encountered yet. It was bad enough that she didn't help out on night watch—she wasn't going to accept any special treatment by riding on the wagon across the river. She resolved to just hang onto her horse real tight and hope for the best.

Hitching both teams of horses to the chuck wagon, Monty drove it down the bank and through the river. Jed watched in fascination as the wagon went in deeper and deeper, water slowly swallowing the big wheels. When it got to about halfway across, the water was so deep that the wagon started to float while the horses swam in front of it uselessly. Quickly, some of the men entered the water, guiding the wagon across to the other side until the wheels touched the bottom again. Then those same men, already wet, led both teams of horses back through the river and hitched them to the supply wagon, repeating the process over again.

Jed was starting to get worried. This rushing river was far different from what she was used to, and the current was strong. The drovers who had assisted the wagons across were already tiring, and they were much stronger swimmers than she. Had she made a mistake by not going across on the wagon? *Well, it's too late now,* she decided.

The first part was easy. She was upstream from the cattle and they were going across easily enough, swimming swiftly once the river got deeper, and scrambling up the bank on the other side with no problems. But it didn't take long for chaos to start—beeves were milling around in the middle of the river, churning it up, turning back, getting swept downstream, and starting to panic. Jed got knocked off her horse.

"Help!" she screamed, struggling to keep her head above the swirling water, fighting against the current. She felt the reins slipping through her fingers; she couldn't touch the river bottom with her feet.

"Just swim to shore!" Mr. Jordan yelled from the riverbank. "Monty will help you up the bank."

"I can't!" she yelled back, fighting desperately against the raging river. "I can't swim!"

"What the hell are you doing in the water then?" he yelled. "Why didn't you go across on the wagon?" He tried to stop any more beeves from entering the water, giving Jed a chance to right herself, but the drovers were pushing them from behind, and they couldn't hear his shouted instructions over the noise of the bellowing.

Jed went under the water. She came up coughing and spluttering, spitting out mouthfuls of dirty river water, but the current dragged her down again. She was knocked sideways this time, and trampled underfoot by the panicking steers, and all she could feel was their legs as she fought her way to the surface. Every time her face found the surface, she would manage to take one gasping breath then she would be dragged down again, dragged under the surface of the water, knocked and trampled by the steers. She was upside down, she was sideways... everything was black, she didn't know which way was up, all around her were steers. She was going to die. Right there in the river, in the middle of the trail drive, she was going to meet her maker. "Help!" she yelled, but she got another mouthful of filthy river water. Her lungs were burning. She couldn't see. Her legs felt heavy. Then there was nothing in front of her, and she felt herself moving. Fighting with everything she had, she struggled to the surface of the water and breathed in a lungful of air. She was being swept away downstream and she couldn't find her footing, but at least she could breathe. Then she felt herself tumbling, being swept over and over and sideways, and she thought she would die again. Then she was snagged. She could feel the water rushing all around her, but she wasn't moving with it. She was held fast. She felt herself being lifted up into the sunlight... she could breathe! She lay on the river bank coughing, gasping, and retching up water while whoever it was who had rescued her thumped her on the back. It was several long minutes before she was able to breathe properly; several long minutes of coughing up water, gasping in huge breaths of air, trying to fill her screaming lungs. Finally she was able to sit up and she looked straight into the face of Woody—the last person she would have expected to rescue her.

"Are you okay?" he asked, his voice full of concern. "I didn't want to cross the river today, it's flowing too fast, but it wasn't my decision to make."

She nodded. "I'm okay now, thank you."

"My first trail drive, a boy got drowned in the flooded river. I've hated river crossings ever since. You're lucky—you should have gone over on the wagon. There's no shame in it," he told her.

She propped herself up on her elbows as she heard hoof beats approaching.

"Mr. Jordan?" she asked.

"Yes, ma'am," Woody told her. "You're in for it now. He was worried about you."

"Thank you, Woody, I'll take it from here," Mr. Jordan said gruffly as he approached. Woody nodded and headed back up the river to where the herd was continuing to cross. Jed couldn't see the herd from where she was, they were around a bend in the river, but she could certainly hear them. The bellowing of the cantankerous beeves, the whistles and shouts of the drovers as they urged the herd down into the river and up the other side. And she could see the smoke from the cooking fire Monty had going, both to dry out the wet drovers and to serve them hot coffee as they went back and forth through the river.

Mr. Jordan dismounted and squatted down beside her, leaving the reins of his horse dangling. "Are you okay?" he asked, his deep voice husky.

"Yes," she nodded. "I'm not hurt." That wasn't quite true—she was battered and bruised and her lungs were still burning, her throat was sore, and her head hurt; but she was alive.

"Good." Mr. Jordan stood up and hauled her up too, turning her to face him. He looked intently into her eyes for a moment, then his hands went to her waist. Fumbling with the buttons on her pants, he managed to get them undone and slide them down over her hips, pushing them down her thighs to her knees. Then he untied the string fastening her drawers, pushing them down too. The wet garments clung to her, resisting Mr. Jordan's attempts to bare her, but he yanked them down roughly, holding her arm to prevent her from toppling over with the harshness of his movements.

"What are you doing?" she asked him, horrified, clutching at her clothing, trying to prevent him from tugging them down. He slapped her hands away roughly. Taking her by the hand, he guided her the few steps to a big rock, and she waddled along after him hurriedly, hindered by her pants that were bunched around her legs, the extra weight of them wet feeling like she was dragging a stone. Sitting down on the rock, he lifted up the front of her shirt so it wouldn't get him wet, then hauled her across his thighs, pushing her pants down further.

"Don't do this, Wes," she pleaded with him. "Isn't it enough that I nearly drowned? You don't have to do this. You're too sore!"

"Yes, I am sore," he admitted. "But a bare-bottom spanking is exactly what you need. If you'd followed my orders you wouldn't have nearly drowned," he scolded. "I told everyone who couldn't swim to go over on the wagon. Cowboys die at river crossings, they drown. You could have drowned. You would have, if it wasn't for Woody."

Mr. Jordan put a hand in the small of her back to steady her, and raised his other hand high. He brought it down with a resounding slap that made her yelp and jump. "Stay still," he ordered. "This has barely started."

She was surprised by how much it stung. She knew Mr. Jordan was still recovering from his injuries, she knew he couldn't put much strength into spanking her. Yet on cold, wet, bare skin, his hard hand felt like a branding iron.

He spanked her hard and fast on alternate cheeks, spreading them out to cover her entire bottom and the tops of her thighs. With each smack, Jed yelped and wriggled, kicking her feet, trying to escape the stinging smacks that just kept landing. Mr. Jordan kept up the assault on her backside, spanking her in a steady rhythm, until Jed was limp over his lap, sobbing hard. Her bottom was one big mass of pain; she wasn't even aware when Mr. Jordan stopped spanking and instead just rested his hand lightly on her burning bottom.

She lay there, sobbing wretchedly, as Mr. Jordan kneaded her bottom with the balls of his fingers, digging them deep into her reddened skin, squeezing the tender flesh, rubbing her back gently with his other hand. Inhaling deeply, she sniffled, whimpering in pain, not even caring that her bare bottom was still on display.

"Come on, stand up." Mr. Jordan patted her bottom lightly, helping her to her feet. She just stood there helplessly while Mr. Jordan fixed her pants, first tying the drawstring on her drawers tightly, then fastening the buttons on her pants. Her eyes were tight and sore from crying; she knew she looked a mess. Using the tail of her wet shirt, she wiped her face and sniffed several times in quick succession, then took a deep breath.

Mr. Jordan put his arms around her gently, tracing small circles on her back, not seeming to bother that she was dripping water all over him. "Are you ready to go back to the herd yet or do you need a few more minutes?"

"I'm okay," she told him.

Riding was uncomfortable, but it only took a few minutes to get back to the herd. Hurrying across the river alongside the steers, Mr. Jordan helped her down from the saddle. "Get yourself dried off," he ordered. "Get some fresh clothes, have some coffee. Then you can help keep the herd calm on this side of the river. Keep them here—it will take most of the day to get the rest across, we'll bed them down here tonight."

Monty smiled kindly at her when he handed her fresh clothes and told her to get dressed in the supply wagon. She winced as she moved—every step she took, her wet clothing chafed against her scorched bottom, hurting her all over again.

Tears were in her eyes as she mounted the horse Joe had saddled for her. He had retrieved the one she had fallen off in the river and it was grazing contentedly on the picket line at the edge of the camp. As the steers clambered up the river bank they were restless and milling around, bellowing, but they soon calmed down and grazed happily with the herd that was on this side of the river. She circled them with another drover, singing softly to keep them calm, thinking that, now that she was dry and warm, life would be just about perfect, if it weren't for the deep ache in her bottom that made sitting in her saddle uncomfortable.

Mr. Jordan was right—it did take most of the day to get the herd across the river, and as the afternoon wore on, drovers slowly rode in, weary, wet, and bedraggled, to dry themselves by the fire and drink hot coffee.

• • • • • • •

They spread their bedrolls side by side, and Jed snuggled carefully back against Mr. Jordan, mindful of his injuries. He wrapped his arms around her and held her tight, and kissed her forehead gently as she relaxed against his warm body. She felt her breasts tighten and her nipples harden, and there was a tingling between her legs. She ran her fingers lightly up his thigh, but he caught her hand in his and squeezed it gently.

"As much as I want you, it will have to wait—I'm too sore," he murmured softly. Then he kissed her deeply. "Goodnight, my darling," he whispered.

CHAPTER EIGHT

They noticed the strange riders as they broke camp from the noon meal. There were heaps of them—at least fifty—and they outnumbered the drovers at least two to one. They had the outfit completely surrounded. Jed gulped. She didn't know how, but somehow she knew that those riders were something to do with Neil and Cal—they were there because of her.

"What are we going to do about them, boss?" Davey asked. "I think they're led by the Rogan gang. They're all outlaws. I recognized Rafe Wilson, the gunfighter."

Mr. Jordan was silent a moment, then he shook his head. "There's nothing we can do at the moment. They're not harming us; we'll just keep the cattle moving. When it comes time to fight, then we'll fight."

"They're here for me," Jed announced quietly. "Why did I ever think Cal would just let me go?" she moaned. "I should never have left! I've been nothing but trouble since I joined up with this drive." She took a deep breath. "Maybe I should ride out there, get the Rogan brothers to take me home. Then this can all end, and you can take the cattle on to Sedalia."

"You're staying here!" Mr. Jordan snarled furiously.

"What do you think the Rogan boys would do to you if they got their hands on you?" His voice softened then, and he wrapped his arm around her shoulders. "Besides, you're mine. I'm going to marry you. And I need you here with me, for me to do that."

"But we're outnumbered here! There's twice as many of them, at least!"

Mr. Jordan just smiled down at her. "I've got the best men in the business. One of my men is worth two of them, maybe more. Don't you worry none." He dropped a gentle kiss on her forehead.

Jed relaxed into his embrace and smiled. How could one man be so tough one minute, and so kind and gentle the next? He was an enigma. But she loved him.

The riders watching them didn't make any hostile moves; they just rode along near them, about half a mile distant, following the herd, watching the men. The drovers were all on edge; being followed was making them nervous, and they were eager to fight. But Mr. Jordan held them back. He wanted the outlaws to make the first move.

It was just on dusk, once they'd bedded the cattle down for the night, when Mr. Jordan rode out with Davey to get a better look at the outlaws surrounding them. Camp was quiet, everyone was tense. Half the men were out with the herd, circling it, keeping watch. The usual camaraderie, the laughing, joke-telling, and poker games were all absent; the men remaining were sitting quietly, their eyes focused on the edge of camp, watching for anything suspicious.

A shot rang out in the distance, just one, and Jed gasped. Her whole body went rigid with fear. She'd heard Davey name the infamous gunfighter—she knew of Rafe Wilson's reputation. Who had been shot? Was it Mr. Jordan? She stood up, feeling faint.

"Just wait, Jed," Woody spoke to her softly and calmly, but she could tell he was worried too; he was clenching and unclenching his fists at his sides, and he was frowning. "They'll be okay, they're good men."

Woody was right. Just a few seconds later, Jed could hear the sound of hoof beats galloping back to camp. Mr. Jordan and Davey rode in fast, dismounting before their horses had even stopped running, just dropping the reins on the ground. Joe moved in quickly to take the horses and secure them with the remuda.

Mr. Jordan ran up to Jed. "Get into the wagon and stay there!" he ordered her briskly.

Jed shook her head. "No. I'm not hiding away. I'm fighting too."

Mr. Jordan grabbed her by the shoulders and shook her. "If you never obey another order again, obey this one! Get in the wagon and stay there! I need to know you are safe!"

"No." Jed's refusal was firm. "I'm going to be out there fighting alongside your men. They're fighting for me—I'm going to be fighting with them."

"Get in the wagon before I take a razor strop to your bare backside!" Mr. Jordan snarled, his eyes flashing with frustration.

"Take a razor strop to me if you feel you must, but I won't be hiding in the wagon. This is my fight, Weston. Let me fight it." Jed had never been more frightened in her life, but she had also never been more determined. She knew exactly why the outlaw Rogan gang was out there—it was because of her. And there was no way she was going to hide while men she had come to respect and care for were risking their lives fighting in a battle that technically wasn't theirs.

Mr. Jordan released her and clenched his fists, holding them rigidly by his sides. "You can be the most aggravating, stubborn young woman, Jedda-Lyn!" he snarled through clenched teeth. "Why won't you just listen?" Spinning her around quickly, he landed a ferocious swat to her backside. "Get in the wagon!"

"No."

He swatted her twice more, even harder than before, stinging slaps that made her flinch and hiss in pain. Jed's eyes filled with frustrated tears. Why couldn't he understand, just this once?

"Boss!" It was Davey. Breathing a sigh of relief as Mr. Jordan let her go, she fought back the tears and straightened up. "We need to move, they're closing in fast."

"Right." The expression on Mr. Jordan's face was a serious one; it was clear he meant business. "Jed, there's rifles and ammunition in the supply wagon, Monty's passing them out now. Get your Colt off him while you're at it. Woody will tell you where to go."

Jed couldn't hide her smile. "Thanks!" she told him. But Mr. Jordan didn't return her smile. He looked too worried.

Monty looked serious as he stood in the back of the supply wagon, handing out rifles and ammunition to the drovers. He passed Jed a rifle and ammunition along with her gun, the one she'd stolen off her brother, and she belted on her gun belt briskly. She was terrified, but excited at the same time. She'd never been in a gun battle before, and she knew the danger she was in, the risk to her life. But she felt useful—she didn't feel like a helpless woman any more, she felt like a warrior!

• • • • • • •

Mr. Jordan watched helplessly as the outlaws stampeded the herd, scattering them across the plains, yelling and whooping, shooting their guns in the air, chasing through the herd and sending them running. The drovers out with the cattle tried to hold them, to turn them, but there were too many outlaws, and the steers kept running. He saw one of his men fall; he couldn't see who it was, but there was nothing he could do now. Hopefully, the drover would survive, and they could doctor him once this was all over.

Once the thunderous pounding of the hooves of thousands of stampeding steers had gone, the outlaws turned their attention back to the drovers. He had chosen their night camp well—his men had protection, cover in the form of rocks and trees, while many of the outlaws were out in the open. Mr. Jordan managed a small smile. Maybe the Rogan brothers didn't deserve their fearsome reputation? It certainly wasn't good planning on their part to have attacked the drovers without enough cover. They obviously thought their sheer number would be enough to win the battle, but Mr. Jordan knew the outlaws had badly underestimated his men. It would take more than being outnumbered for them to lose this fight.

One of the outlaws raised a rifle to his shoulder and pulled off a shot—a bullet kicked up dust just in front of him. Scrambling for the wagon, he threw himself down on the ground underneath it and crawled up next to Jed. She was obviously capable with a weapon—she handled her rifle expertly, balancing it on a stone carefully. He watched as she took aim and fired, then smiled as the outlaw who had shot at him toppled off his horse and fell to the ground.

The gunfire was deafening. There was shooting all around. So far, it didn't look like any of the men in camp had been hit, but that could change. Looking around at his men, he was pleased to see they had taken cover well, biding their time, waiting for the outlaws to make a mistake so they could get off the perfect shot. They were too experienced at this sort of thing to give away their positions by firing without a sure target.

He turned back to the task at hand. Jed had her pistol in front of her and was reloading her rifle. She was a good shot, but he noticed something else about her as well, something important. She was courageous—she had openly defied him to fight alongside his men, and she was doing it well. She was level-headed, calm, and gutsy. She kept loading the rifle methodically, her aim was sure and steady; when she squeezed off a shot, she usually hit what she was aiming at. He watched her kill another outlaw.

A bullet hit the ground right in front of the wagon, spraying up dust into her face. She didn't even flinch, but calmly let off another shot. She didn't appear to be afraid, although he knew she was. They all were. She wasn't even aware that he was watching her, as she fired off shot after shot, calmly and methodically reloading, taking aim and firing… but he was watching. And as he watched, he realized what a good wife she would make him. She was so brave, so loyal, so willing to do whatever was necessary. He was more determined than ever to marry her once this was all over.

It seemed like the gunfire went on forever; shot after shot rang out with no break. The outlaws were dropping, and some of the drovers were wounded. But no one risked going to their aid—to leave the protection of the little cover they had was suicide.

The gunfire continued. As he raised his rifle and let off another shot, he wondered if anyone would get out of this alive.

• • • • • • •

"Look, someone's coming!" Jed whispered, watching the rider approach with a scrap of white fabric held up in front of him. He wasn't holding a rifle, although in the dim light she could see he wore a gun.

"Rafe Wilson," Mr. Jordan muttered. "What does he want?" Crawling out from underneath the wagon, he stood up and waited for the gunfighter to ride up.

"Got a message from Dan Rogan," Rafe Wilson announced. "It's getting dark; senseless for this fight to continue on all night." Rafe's voice was carrying easily in the still night, now that the shooting had finished and there was silence. She wondered what Dan Rogan was proposing. For a brief moment she contemplated going out and giving herself up, but then thought better of it. The drovers had been fighting for her; some of them may have died fighting for her. For her to give up now would be letting them down. She had to stay beside them, fighting beside them, until the end. However it ended, she would be with them.

Mr. Jordan nodded. Neither side would be able to do

much shooting in the dark, but neither side would get much sleep, either. Even sleeping in shifts, those sleeping would be restless and nervous.

"So here's the deal: you and me. Shoot it out. If you win, Rogan will go. You'll be left in peace. If I win, we get the girl and the cattle, but we won't harm your men."

Jed gasped. Surely Mr. Jordan wouldn't agree to that?

Mr. Jordan shook his head. "No. If you win, you get the cattle. Not the girl. She stays with my men—they'll take her to the next town and make sure she's safe."

Rafe hesitated. Then he raised his hand over his head and waved, a signal for Dan Rogan to ride up. Jed watched nervously. She was only semi-hidden under the wagon; she crawled closer to Davey, who was at the other end of the wagon. She felt safer beside him.

Dan Rogan eyed Mr. Jordan as he rode up, and Jed watched in terror as the men stared at each other, their faces expressionless. They spoke, but their voices were too low for her to hear the conversation. She didn't want Mr. Jordan to agree to the gunfight—she knew Rafe Wilson's reputation. Everyone did. He was fast—quite possibly the fastest gun in the west. He was a hired killer—he'd killed three men in Wyoming, and several more in Texas. Killing one more would be nothing to him. But she also knew, if Mr. Jordan didn't agree to it, the battle would continue. It might halt for a time overnight, but it would continue on in the morning. There would be more bloodshed, the cattle would be scattered all over the continent and impossible to round up, and many of the drovers might die. She might die.

With her heart in her mouth, she watched both men face each other, then turn and stride away. They turned at the same time and stood there eyeing each other. Jed couldn't breathe. The air felt heavy and thick; it stuck in her lungs. She heard Davey's sharp intake of breath and glanced at him—he looked worried.

Davey reached out to still her trembling hands. He gave her a weak smile. She looked around the camp; the other drovers were still hidden, but they were watching Mr. Jordan closely too, their expressions anxious.

Both men stood there staring at each other, unflinching, not moving a muscle, their hands hovering above the butts of their guns. Suddenly Rafe moved. A shot rang out in the stillness. Jed stifled a scream and buried her face in her hands, her eyes tightly shut. She heard Davey let out a breath beside her, but the night remained still. There was no answering shot. Was he dead? Had Rafe killed him? Or was he merely wounded? She had to know. Scrambling out from underneath the wagon, she started to run toward him, but stopped dead in her tracks. Mr. Jordan was standing tall and proud, still holding his cocked gun in front of him, and Rafe Wilson was lying on the ground in a pool of blood. He was dead. Jed couldn't contain her glee. Letting out a shriek, she ran toward him again, and he caught her in his arms. Raising her face to his, she kissed him deeply, passionately, as tears streamed down her cheeks. When they broke off from their kiss, she looked up to see the drovers surrounding them, smiling widely.

"Come and get your man," Mr. Jordan invited Dan Rogan. "If you keep your guns holstered, none of you will be shot. Get your man and ride away; you won't be harmed."

Still clinging to Mr. Jordan, Jed watched as Dan walked slowly up to the body on the ground, glaring at her fiercely the whole time. She could tell by the expression of sheer hatred and misery on his face that he knew he was beaten, and she hoped that would be the end of it. He'd said it would be, but what good was the word of an outlaw? It was the code of the west for a cowboy to always keep his word, but did that apply to people like Dan Rogan? She hoped so.

Safe in Mr. Jordan's arms, she watched as Dan Rogan's hired outlaws collected their dead and wounded and silently rode away into the twilight.

· · · · · · ·

Many of the drovers were wounded. Monty set to doctoring them as best he could by the light of the oil lamps hanging from the back of the chuck wagon, but it was hard work. Mr. Jordan rode out to the fallen drover—the one who had been shot right at the beginning—and brought back the body of Chuck.

Jed was distraught—if it hadn't been for her, he would still be alive! She sat beside him and wept loudly, inconsolably, clutching at his shirt, burying her face in his chest, apologizing to him over and over again.

She felt a hand on her back, but she shrugged it off. "Leave me alone," she gasped between sobs, heartbroken over the death of the first drover who had shown her kindness. But Mr. Jordan didn't leave her alone; instead he squatted down beside her, picked her up in his arms, and carried her away, laying her gently on the bedroll someone had spread in the back of the supply wagon. He lay down beside her and held her close, rocking her gently, trying to soothe her, but she wouldn't be comforted. She felt too sad, and too guilty. Women were forced into bad marriages every day; why had she decided she wasn't willing to do that? What made her think she was better than any other woman in that exact same situation? She wasn't… and now Chuck had paid for her mistake with his life.

"I killed him," she sobbed.

Mr. Jordan brushed her hair back from her face. "No." He shook his head. "You didn't kill him. The selfishness and bitterness of your brother and his mate Cal Robinson killed him. You are innocent in all of this. You mustn't blame yourself!"

"I should have just married Cal," she choked out.

"No." Mr. Jordan was emphatic. "No woman deserves to be married to a man like that. You did the right thing, running away. Chuck liked you; he knew you did the right thing."

Struggling out of his embrace, Jed pounded his chest

with both fists, blinded by her tears, taking out her anger and distress on the man she loved. Mr. Jordan caught her wrists and held them tightly in one hand, drawing her to him in the other, holding her tightly while she continued to cry and fight against him. She felt overwhelmed with hatred toward Cal. "I hate him! I hate him!" she cried. "And now Chuck's dead!"

She cried for what seemed like hours, and the whole time Mr. Jordan just held her. Eventually, when she had no more tears left, she hiccupped and sat up. Mr. Jordan gently wiped her face with his bandanna and kissed her forehead softly, then extended a hand to her and helped her out of the wagon. There were things they had to attend to.

The grave had been dug, and Chuck's body had been laid gently in it. The drovers who had been watching the herd when it stampeded had arrived back in camp with about half the herd, and they were all gathered around the grave. She entwined her fingers in Mr. Jordan's and they hurried over.

Once the grave was filled in, the men stood clutching their hats to their chests and began to pray.

"Our father who art in heaven," Mr. Jordan led in his deep voice, the somber moment making the timbre even deeper.

"Hallowed be thy name," the other drovers chimed in.

Quietly, Jed joined in as the men recited the prayer, but she didn't let go of Mr. Jordan's hand. She felt that if she let go, she would fall into the grave with Chuck and die too.

The men heaped the grave with stones, banging a crude wooden cross into one end. Jed stood there watching them, helpless, until Mr. Jordan led her away. "Come on," he murmured softly. "There's no more you can do here. But we've got wounded drovers to take care of; do you think you can help them?"

Jed worked until well into the night, helping Monty clean and bandage the drovers' wounds and dosing them up on whisky when the pain became too much. Most of the men had been shot in the arm or shoulder, none were serious injuries; the bullets had just grazed them. But they would be sore for a few days until the wounds healed. She tucked blankets around them securely and kept the fire stoked up so they would stay warm.

She felt ready to drop with fatigue when Mr. Jordan came up to her and put his hand on her shoulder. "Come to bed, Jed, you're exhausted," he said. "You've done a good job here; all these men will be fine until morning." He led her to the other side of the fire where he'd spread their bedrolls and he lay down beside her, holding her tightly. Within moments, she was asleep.

· · · · · · ·

As soon as breakfast was finished, those who could ride mounted up to go in search of the missing cattle. Jed stayed behind; there were bandages that needed to be changed and Monty also had to cook. Billy rode out with the drovers, so it was just Jed and Monty tending to those who needed it.

"I'm so sorry," Jed apologized to each man as she changed his bandage and gave him more whisky. "You only got hurt because of me." But none of the men bore her any malice, and she was overwhelmed with gratitude to them.

The wounded cowboys spent the day resting, and Jed took food and coffee to them as Monty prepared it, taking the dirty dishes down to the creek to wash them afterwards. As she worked, she kept glancing toward Chuck's grave, in a peaceful spot under the trees, and her breath hitched. She still felt guilty.

"Don't feel bad," Monty told her later that afternoon, as she leaned against the chuck wagon, staring at the grave. "Men die on cattle drives all the time; it's the risk they take, being drovers. Doesn't take a gunfight, either." He reached out and patted her shoulder. "Out here, death is part of life."

She gave him a weak smile. She knew all about death—she still mourned her parents every so often. Life had certainly been much easier when they had been around, but she took great comfort from the fact that they had died together. Her parents had shared a fairytale kind of love, the kind of love she wanted for herself. Cal would never have given her that, that's why she'd refused to marry him. And now she'd found Mr. Jordan, and she knew he would make her happy, despite his rough cowboy ways and his strong, hard hand that found its way to spanking her far too regularly for her liking.

She was jolted out of her musings by the return of the drovers and the strays. A quick glance told her they'd managed to find nearly all of them, and she breathed a sigh of relief. She knew Mr. Jordan's reputation was built on his ability to get nearly all the cattle to market in Sedalia; she didn't want to be responsible for ruining that.

She ran to greet him. "Did you find them all?" she asked.

"All but twenty-two." He smiled down at her, sweeping her into an embrace.

"That's good, right?"

Mr. Jordan kissed her, his rough lips bruising hers as he devoured her hungrily. "It'll do," he replied as he broke off the kiss. With his arm around her, they walked into camp.

• • • • • • •

"We're going to sleep in the supply wagon tonight," he told her. "I want us to have some privacy." He winked rakishly at her and her heart melted at the sight of her handsome cowboy. Her breath quickened and she felt a moistness growing between her thighs. How did he manage to have such an effect on her with just a wink?

There was a bed already made up in there, so she kicked her boots off under the wagon and climbed in, waiting for Mr. Jordan to join her.

"I want to marry you, Jed," he told her as he shed his shirt.

"I know." She smiled. "I want to marry you too."

"I've got some money saved up; after this drive is over

I'll have enough to buy us a ranch somewhere and we can settle down. I'm done with trail drives; I'm too old for it. I might do one more, with our own herd, but that will be it." He pulled her shirt off, running his hands over her breasts softly.

"That sounds good. I don't know that I'm cut out to be a drover, but I know ranching. Even when ma and pa were still alive I helped a lot; after they died and it was just me and Neil, then the hands left… it was mostly just me. Neil was too busy drinking."

"So you'll be happy married to a rancher, then?"

"I'll be happy anywhere with you, Wes." And as she spoke those words, she knew them to be true. It didn't matter to her where they lived; as long as she was with her cowboy, she would be happy.

She sighed in contentment as Wes ran his hands all over her naked body, trailing kisses up her shoulder and neck. She was lying on her side with her back against his hard body, and she could feel his erection pressing into her bottom. He was propped up on an elbow, and her head lay on his outstretched forearm. She reached forward and kissed his wrist, tickling it with her tongue. It felt strangely erotic to taste his musky, sweat-stained flesh, and she licked her lips, brushing her wetness over his wrist again. She heard him moan softly and grind his pelvis against her.

"You're mine," he whispered huskily. "I'm going to claim you again tonight."

He nibbled her earlobe gently and she responded in kind, kissing and nibbling her way up the side of his hand to the end of his thumb where she bit his knuckle softly. Then she arched her back and sucked in her breath with a hiss as his erection pressed urgently against her, trying to find entrance. Reaching back a hand, she guided him into her, pressing herself back against him, moving her hips slowly in a circular motion as he filled her completely. His large hand enclosed firmly around her breast and squeezed, and he bent forward and kissed her nipple, nipping it, teasing it with his tongue, grinding his pelvis against her, sending the most exquisite sensations pulsing through her body.

"Mmmmmmmmm," she murmured, arching her neck so he could kiss her throat, reaching back over him to squeeze his buttocks.

Their bodies fit together so perfectly, and as their hips rocked together in perfect harmony, those exquisite sensations built up within her, getting deeper and deeper.

Thrusting harder, faster, Wes pounded against her, and she moved with him, bringing them both right to the brink of orgasm at exactly the same time.

"Oh, Jed," he murmured softly in her ear as he exploded within her and she felt his warm seed spill out of him, filling her to overflowing.

She shuddered in his arms as she came with him, tipping over the edge into perfect oblivion.

They lay there, sated, for a long time, before Wes sat up. "We've got a wedding to attend tomorrow," he announced. "Better get some sleep."

The End

STORMY NIGHT PUBLICATIONS WOULD LIKE TO THANK YOU FOR YOUR INTEREST IN OUR BOOKS.

If you liked this book (or even if you didn't), we would really appreciate you leaving a review on the site where you purchased it. Reviews provide useful feedback for us and for our authors, and this feedback (both positive comments and constructive criticism) allows us to work even harder to make sure we provide the content our customers want to read.

If you would like to check out more books from Stormy Night Publications, if you want to learn more about our company, or if you would like to join our mailing list, please visit our website at:

www.stormynightpublications.com

Printed in Great Britain
by Amazon